THREAD
OF
DREAMS

Emily Barnett

OWL'S NEST PUBLISHERS
Cross Plains, WI

OWL'S NEST
PUBLISHERS

Est. 2021
Owl's Nest Publishers
P. O. Box 63
Cross Plains, WI 53528
owlsnestpublishers.com

Thread of Dreams Copyright © 2024 by Emily Barnett

The moral right of the author has been asserted.

Cover Design & Images: Ash Schlax, Katie Stewart, Karin Hoyle, @Vintage
Illustrations via Canva, @Katerina_Tyshkovskaya via Canva
Chapter Images: Katie Stewart
Title Font: Supa Mega Fantastic
Text Font: Cochin

ISBN: 978-1-957362-21-2 (hardcover)

Thread of Dreams / by Emily Barnett
Summary: Nova harvests threads from human dreams to help fight a
malicious parasite invading her planet. But when she visits a boy who is
already dreaming of her, the threat to her world also becomes a threat to her
heart.

Printed in the United States of America

THREAD
OF
DREAMS

Emily Barnett

Praise for

THREAD OF DREAMS

Thread of Dreams beautifully explores themes of perseverance, sacrificial love, and the truest good that can only be found amid the fires of hardship. With her lyrical prose and masterful world building, Barnett has achieved that perfect tension between our own human failings and the belief in something *greater* that gives us hope. This is exactly the kind of book every teenager should read—starting with my own. —**Andrea Renae, author of** *Where Darkness Dwells*

Barnett creates a beautifully lush landscape that engages the imagination with characters you'll carry with you long after reading. Filled with joyful whimsy and aching wonder in equal measure, *Thread of Dreams* captures the heart in this story of self-discovery, friendship, grief, and redemption. —**Katee Stein, author of** *Glass Helix*

Dedication

To my boys, Kiah and Ru, for giving me the spark of this story.
May you always be brave enough to dream of a better world.

PROLOGUE

"**T**he forest is a dangerous place, little flame." Her father's voice held a slight tremor. "Here, the Void is strong."

"If it's so dangerous, why did they put the Harvesting Center all the way out here?" Nova asked.

They were walking the path through the woods toward Dream Glade. Giant mushroom caps glowed brilliantly above and crocuses lining the path looked as if they had dipped their heads in a pail of purple light.

"The Harvesting Center is nestled in the forest because outside the city there are fewer people to interfere with the dream connections between Earth and Lyra. Fewer buildings and less technology. Less *noise*. The glade gives us a clear view of the stars. And it's peaceful."

Nova took her father's hand and they walked on in comfortable silence until she saw a dark shape off the path. She paused, squinting past a spindle tree's bare, spiral branches. "What's that?"

"That's why we're here," Atlas said, pulling Nova off the trail. "Come."

Nova resisted, eyes widening. "We aren't allowed to leave the path!"

Atlas slowed, releasing his grip and looking back at Nova. "I would not lead you into danger, little flame. But if you do not wish to come, I will not force you. Wait here if you must."

Nova hugged herself as she watched her father's steady, sure steps toward the mysterious object on the ground. The wind shifted and wafted a scent of rotting animal toward her, and . . . something else. Something indescribable. She couldn't let her father face that alone, nor did she *want* to be alone.

When she caught up, he placed an arm around her shoulders. Closer to the black mound, the scent worsened, and Nova plugged her nose. A sudden terror overtook her, and she buried her face in her father's robes.

Atlas crouched until he was even with Nova's gaze, placing his hands on either side of her face. "Our leaders — the Ancients — would have you believe our world is healing. That we have the Void under control. But the Void is a plague that will continue to destroy Lyra until someone finds a way to fight it."

Nova straightened and Atlas dropped his hands.

Then she looked. And screamed.

Atlas covered her mouth. "It's alright, little flame."

Nova nodded, eyes watering. Atlas dropped his hand and she immediately wished it was back over her face to block the smell of decay.

Ahead of Nova was a creature resembling a moon bear — larger than a full-grown man, with flecks of glowing white against its black fur on one side. But the side that faced them was mutilated. Its insides spilled out onto the moss as if it had been ripped open, giving space to the creeping entity that seemed to be growing out of it — shiny black vines attached to the bear and leached back into the ground like roots. Infected flesh bubbled around the vines with yellow and white pus. Nova gagged into her hand.

"W-what is it?" she whispered.

"The Void," Atlas said. "In the flesh."

"But I thought the Void lived in the sky!" Nova shivered and looked up.

"The Void lives everywhere now," her father said. "There" — he pointed up—"here"—he gestured around the forest. "And that means sometimes, also, here." He tapped his chest, then hers, right above her thundering heart.

"But . . . I don't want it in me!" Nova backed away in horror. "How can it be *here*?"

Atlas frowned, his eyes misty as if he were far away in thought. Nova knew that look. She loved that look. It meant her father was on the brink of something brilliant. But right now, she was terrified to hear what he was thinking.

"It found a way," was all he said.

"Why did you bring me here? I want to go. *I want to go.*"

"Oh, little flame." He took her face in his hands again. "The weight of this world can be heavy, can't it? But I promise you, Nova. If it's the last thing I do, I'll take on this burden so that the load will be lessened for you."

Chapter One

Have I ever really fit
Into this house, school,
This freckled skin?
In this life?
I'm like the dirty laundry
On my floor.
Messy and inside out.
Wanting to fit neatly. Pushed out of sight.
But I can't fold myself perfectly enough.

I grab onto things.
The things Dad wants of me—
Basketball, honors.
Sights on the far future
That feel way too close.
Suffocating me
Like I'm breathing fumes,
Exhaust pipe pouring
Under my bedroom door.

I hate these expectations.
But what else should I expect?
I'm gasping for a breath,
For a life I fit into.

And then, *it* happened—
Mom.
And I forget how to breathe.
Again.
And all I want is to fold myself up
and fit the way she needs me to.

But I'm flailing
Without anything solid
To grab onto.
I'm just a rumpled mess
On my bedroom floor.

I close my eyes and pretend
That I'm somewhere else.
Where I'm light enough to float.
Where I laugh at disappointments
because they hold no gravity
over me. Over my life.
There — Mom is well, Dad smiles more.
I'm neither a mess nor folded perfectly.
I'm just *me*.
And I can breathe.

CHAPTER TWO

Nova stirred from her bed after a fitful Darknight of sleep. It was moonrise. Sweat coated her forehead and she was on edge, the way she always was when escaping a nightmare. Lying awake, Nova tried to remember something, *anything*, from her dream. It was an exercise she liked to run through, and one she always failed at.

Hands shaking, Nova threw back her covers and pulled on her trousers and blouse. Her shawl, woven of Threads she'd plucked from human dreams over the years, squirmed on the end of her bed. It barely covered the top half of her torso, but she never left the pod without it. She placed it over her head, smoothing her black hair over her shoulders and onto the colorful weaves.

She spied a silver-white Thread—one she'd unraveled from a snowy dream—hovering near her rounded window ceiling. "It's time to go," she said. The Thread turned and shook its fiber head. A light pink Thread then curled out of the shawl. Nova snorted in exasperation, patting it until it lay still once more.

The Threads were especially unruly during moonrise and moonset. It was too close to Darknight when her magic could no longer command them. When the moon, Selene, hid on the other side of the world.

"*Now*," Nova said to the snow Thread, letting the moon's magic rise in her and fill her with power.

With a flurry of flakes the Thread flew back into her shawl, tying itself around the others. Nova touched where it was squirming and she received a shock of playfulness.

She'd taken the Thread from an elderly woman's subconscious last week. The gleaming snow in the dream world had been so breathtaking that Nova had wanted to bottle it up, take it home to Lyra, and keep it forever. Lyra didn't have such cold winters, and the woman would never notice the absence of one dream Thread. Nor had she noticed Nova at all.

Dreamers never did.

Nova tied up her hair in a loose bun, grabbed her satchel, and made her way to the kitchen. Calypso was eating an algae cake at the table. She ran a scrutinizing gaze over Nova.

"You look pale."

Nova sat down and slid a honey-soaked cake onto her plate. "*I* look pale?" She eyed her big sister's arm with a teasing smile.

Cally was not just Nova's legal guardian now that their mother and father were gone, but she looked like their mother too. Light skin, white-silver eyes, and bright red curls. Nova, on the other hand, looked like their father. Tan with silver eyes flecked with gold.

Cally swallowed her bite and dabbed carefully around her mouth before speaking. "Did you have another nightmare?"

"Um, no I'm fine." Nova shoveled in a mouthful of algae, loamy and sweet, nearly melting on her tongue. She didn't want to talk to her sister about the nightmares that always slipped away, leaving all the feelings and none of the visions; it was too depressing. "How was *your* night? Talk to anyone interesting?"

"The usual," Cally said, brushing cake from her fingers. "Scouted a few concert venues. Attended a wedding. Interviewed a politician. Went to a funeral."

Nova dropped her fork, pulse quickening. "A concert? What

7

kind of music?"

"The loud kind."

"Rock? Or . . . pops?"

Cally snorted. "There's no s on the end. And yes, I think it was a *pop* concert."

"You get to have all the fun." Nova sighed and gazed out of the domed window that covered the top half of their pod. She had seen bands in the dreams of humans, but she was never in control in those instances.

"Nova," Cally said. "Stop looking so wistful. It's just a job."

Nova scoffed. "Just a *job*?"

"A *dangerous* job. Do we need to go over this again?" Cally folded her arms and leveled her gaze on Nova.

"No. I *know*." Nova stabbed her breakfast.

Cally was a Walker, a mage who teleported to Earth to monitor and talk with humans. Being a Walker was relatively safe—as safe as visiting that old planet far across the Cosmos could be—as a human mind forgot a Walker as soon as they looked away from one. And Walkers were necessary to the survival of Lyra, as they located the targets for the dream Harvesters—Harvesters like Nova.

Nova envied her sister's magic. She got to walk among the humans in their dreams, but she never got to interact with them the way Cally did. She never got to *visit Earth*—that marvelous world that filled her dreamers' heads with such a variety of images. Nova touched her shawl.

A place with Threads capable of beating back the darkness in her own world.

Cally drummed her fingers on the table and then said, "Hurry up. I'll take you to the Center before my shift."

"You don't have to—"

"I know I don't have to." Cally stood and ruffled Nova's hair. "You may be the youngest Harvester at the Center, which probably means you're some sort of genius. But you'll always be my baby sister."

~

When Nova entered the sleep chamber at the Harvesting Center a few hours later, she looked around for Eris, then remembered he had the night off. Her shoulders tightened.

There would be no one to stand between her and the hostile glances of the other, older, Harvesters. No best friend to distract her. She tried ignoring them as she sat on the white silk bed at her station, but she could practically feel their gazes boring into her.

Nova lay back, massaging her forehead. *Breathe in. Hold it. Out. Again.* As her emotions cooled, she checked her assignment card.

Harvesting Director Archer had assigned Nova to a boy named Arlo James. Age thirteen—*Like me*, Nova thought. She darted her eyes at Archer, wondering if he'd done it on purpose. Harvesting from adolescents was more challenging than harvesting from adults, but Nova was up to the challenge. *Thirteen, sick mother, only child—*

"Harvesters, to your places," Archer said from his station against the wall.

Nova pressed the dream circlet over her head. *Breathe in. Breathe out. Focus on the target . . .*

Archer counted down.

The circlet tingled and pulled her under, under—

"See you on the other side," Nova whispered.

She entered the space between worlds like a sigh. Subconscious floating in an inky abyss, her thoughts were somewhere between dazed and hyper-vigilant. She was lost one moment; found the next.

The galaxy rushed by. Stars, planets, and secrets hidden in the creases of the universe. Her skin tingled as if she were being unfolded, her hair drifting around her shoulders in a celestial wind. Even so, Nova knew her body was still back in the sleeping chamber, while only her mind skimmed the heavens.

She was never ready for her trip through the Inbetween to end. Those seconds when her mind split open felt as if she were one breath away from discovering some truth teetering on the edge of the stars.

Her worries turned to nothing but stardust as her subconscious fell and rose. The Inbetween sharpened her senses. It opened her mind to a universe bigger than herself—even if she couldn't quite grasp its true expanse.

But her fingers always scraped air. Her mind, redirected.

And then, Nova arrived in a desert, the sky streaked with rich purples and solemn blues, the air ripe with the sharpness of far-off rain.

Nova took a step forward, staggered back. Forward again.

She'd never seen this setting, exactly. Deserts were fairly common in dreams, but . . . it felt as if she should know *those* distant barren trees by name. She shielded her eyes. Or *that* bird calling near the horizon.

The hair rose on her arms.

"Where are you, Arlo James?" she said with a shiver, looking for the dreamer whose name was written on her card.

Apart from the distant trees, there was no green dotting the landscape. Nothing growing. The wind was bitterly dusty and wild with misery. But . . . there! A rivulet running through the desert like a silver trail. Nova walked toward it, shoulders prickling with anticipation. Over a rise the stream broadened into a river, and she spotted two children sitting alongside it. A girl and a boy.

Nova crept closer, her unease rising to a new level. The boy was sobbing, his shoulders shaking, head bent. But her eyes were drawn to the girl whose arm was draped around his shoulders.

A girl with distinctive blue-black hair like hers.

Nova stumbled, kicking a rock with her foot. The boy startled and turned, his red and puffy gaze narrowing on her. *Her.* Nova froze. Why was this dreamer acknowledging her? She shouldn't be able to make any noise or interact or—

"Hello?" the boy said. He wiped his eyes on his sweater and stood.

Nova got a whiff of the boy's curiosity as it spiced the air, and the clouds became lighter, fluffier. A few flowers bloomed near the riverbed. Nova took a step back, her eyes flitting between the changes and *him*.

She looked around, desperate and confused, before her sight landed back on the boy. "Are you . . . are you Arlo?" she said.

He nodded. Nova pressed her lips together and closed her eyes, disoriented. She'd never talked to a dreamer before. *It shouldn't be possible.*

"Who are you?" Arlo asked, a strum of familiarity hidden in his voice.

Nova's eyes snapped open. The boy was closer and now looked older than before, as if he'd merely been perceiving himself as a younger child—the same age as the girl still sitting by the river. The girl with blue-black hair who did not acknowledge them. The girl who looked like her.

Nova looked over her shoulder, searching for a person, an animal, anything behind her. But there was only an expansive desert—*endless grief*. He really *was* talking to her.

Spores and rot!

"I'm—I'm Nova."

"Are you *my* Nova?"

Nova gave him a sideways smile, trying to hide her unease. "What do you mean, am I *your* Nova?" Her eyes darted to the girl. "Last I checked, I belonged to myself."

He grinned and the clouds broke.

"I always dream of us as kids." He glanced at the riverbank. The girl took no notice of them and reached out a hand to touch the water. Nova's stomach flipped. The girl's left arm was decorated with silver markings. Nova recognized the design. It was the same pattern that marked her own arm.

She had received the glowing marks when she was a toddler— Four bubbles in a line starting at her shoulder and trickling down to her elbow; the symbol of Callisto, her home. If the girl turned, Nova knew she would see her family crest as well: a soleil owl.

Nova touched her collarbone, where the owl's wings opened wide on both sides. That Nova had been young enough to have her home and family magically inscribed upon her body, but not yet her mage mark.

"She's . . . part of your dream?"

Arlo cocked his head, a piece of russet hair falling over an eye. "I always dream of you, Nova. Well, not *every* night. But on the harder nights, you seem to find your way here. You help me sleep." He pushed his hands into his jeans pockets, glancing at the ground as if he were embarrassed. "But you've never been so grown up before."

"I'm not grown up! I'm only thirteen!"

"Well, so am I!"

They eyed each other for a long moment, and then Nova tossed her hands into the air and said, "I—I don't understand. It isn't supposed to happen this way." Stepping around Arlo she made her way to her younger self. The girl didn't even flinch when Nova crouched beside her.

Nova stared, trying to work out the problem. She pushed out a huff of air. "This is hard to explain, but *she* is part of your dream." Nova pointed to her past self. "And I am real."

Arlo raised a brow. "You're real, but part of my dream?"

"I'm *visiting* your dream."

"Right."

It was clear by Arlo's expression that he didn't understand. Frustration tightened her chest.

"So you're saying you don't remember me?" Arlo said. "Not from when you first visited?"

"I—I'm not sure." Her cheeks grew hot in confusion. "There *is* something familiar about your mind, but . . ." She lifted her arms in a pitiful shrug. Human dreams were second nature to Nova, but right now, all she felt was lost.

Arlo seemed to read her restlessness because he softened. "So why are you here now?"

"I'm a Harvester." Nova's racing mind slowed as they entered back into something she *knew*. "Lyrans use human dreams to survive."

Arlo's brows flew up into his hairline, revealing the splotchy areas around his eyes. But her own curiosity cut off his next words.

"You were crying," she blurted.

Arlo swallowed hard. The landscape shifted, growing jagged trees from its rocky bed. The sky shattered slowly, like ice breaking. Nova's breath grew unsteady. If his dream turned deadly, would she be harmed?

"*Hey* . . . Hey, it's okay," she said. She couldn't believe she was talking to a human. Like she'd always wanted to! Like Cally did. But the dangers of her sister's interactions jumped to mind, and Nova eyed the landscape nervously.

I need to calm him down.

"So . . ." She grabbed for her shawl, only to remember it didn't follow her into dreams. She fumbled and played instead with a piece of hair that had fallen from her bun. Arlo watched her movements with darting eyes, and the harsh branches on the trees blossomed with leaves. "Do you know where I'm from?"

He glanced toward the river. Nova's younger self was gone. In her place was an ivy-covered bench. "*You*—the other you—told me you were from someplace called Lyra. Is that right?"

"Yes." She gnawed her lip. What else had she told him? She couldn't remember ever speaking with him before. "So you know about Lyra and our magic . . ."

His eyes lit up. "You didn't mention magic." Humans didn't have magic, so he probably didn't actually believe her, not really. It was the power of a dream: acceptance and denial were woven within the same tapestry. But maybe that could work in her favor.

"Our moon, Selene, doesn't reflect a sun like in your world, it makes its own blue light and magic."

The air crackled with interest. "What kind of magic?"

"Well . . ." Nova scratched her head then sat on the ivy bench. Arlo followed her lead and angled his body toward hers, his green eyes wide. A dark blue flower bloomed from the ivy and inside were question marks. Nova took a deep breath. "There are five different kinds—or branches—of moon mages."

He nodded for her to continue.

"There are Walkers, like my sister, who gather information on humans. Harvesters, like me, unravel human dream Threads and bring them back to Lyra." She touched her right arm where her Harvester mark was: a circlet with an abstract star. He didn't even glance at it.

"What?" Arlo yelped. "You unravel *what*?"

"Pieces of your dreams. It doesn't hurt. And you don't miss them."

Arlo arched a brow and leaned forward. "How do you know we don't miss them?"

"I—well . . ." She crossed her arms. "That's what we're told. Do you want to know about the other branches or not?"

Arlo nodded tersely. "Go on."

"There are mages called Processors—they turn Threads into resources for our land. Messengers read and speak into minds. And then Healers—like what my mother was—well, heal."

"And your father?"

Nova's chest puffed out. "A Harvester. Like me."

He squinted. "Show me."

"Show you what?"

"You're a Harvester. Prove it."

Nova's lips tightened, but she reached up and grabbed the end of a cloud that seemed far off at first but was easily stolen from the sky. It unraveled and she spun the Thread around her hand.

"*This* is part of your dream," she said. "It's what we harvest."

Arlo gaped. "Can I hold it?"

"I suppose so."

Arlo took the thread from Nova, and it crawled up his arm. He choked out a strangled yelp. When the Thread tried escaping, Nova snatched it back. Arlo's intrigue was embedded deep within its fibers. The feeling was somehow familiar, like the curve of Cally's smile, or the sound of her father's laugh.

Her smile dipped.

"Are you alright?" Arlo asked.

She tugged at the end of her shirt, surprised he had noticed her subtle shift in mood.

The sun was setting now, and she stared at it until her eyes watered. It was one of her favorite things about dream harvesting—getting to see the Earthen sun, if only in the minds of the dreamers. What would Lyra look like if their sun had never been destroyed? What would her father have given to see such a thing?

"I was just thinking about my father," she said, looking back at Arlo. "He would've loved meeting you." Her heart squeezed. "He always talked about how great humans were."

"Talked?" Arlo shifted closer to her. "Does he not anymore?"

"He . . . he died." She swallowed, her throat as dry as the ground in Arlo's dream. "He and my mother were in an accident."

Arlo's head hung. "Nova, I'm so sorry."

Tears teased the corners of Nova's eyes, but she blinked them away.

"How did it happen?" Arlo asked, then added in a rush, "If you want to talk about it, that is."

Nova glanced warily at Arlo. Cally never wanted to delve into the past and would change the subject when Nova brought up their parents. But Nova's emotions beat painfully inside of her chest the longer she held them in. Still, she hesitated. As familiar as he seemed, Arlo was still a stranger.

Who would he tell? He was worlds away from her. Likely, she'd never see him again.

"I believe they died trying to make my world—Lyra—a better place," she said. "Maybe even bridge the gap between your world and mine. We have this darkness, a plague in Lyra that's trying to consume everything, but we know there's a power on Earth—or in your dreams, at least—that hinders it for a time. My father was interested in finding out more." Nova's pulse quickened, her grief tempered as she remembered all the possibilities Atlas used to talk about. "Like, what if it isn't just the dreams?"

"What if what isn't just the dreams?"

"The power—the magic—that can save us from the darkness."

"The darkness is the Void, right?"

Nova shivered. "How do you know that name?"

"*You* told me!" He snorted. "Well, younger you."

Nova looked around for her younger self, but it was just the two of them on the bench.

"The girl from earlier was a projection of my past self." She shook her head. "I was just coming into my powers then and must have accidentally slipped into your dream before they could teach me to control it. Harvesting came early for me. I didn't know what I was doing." Nova chewed on her lip. "I must have imprinted myself in your brain somehow. Broken through." She frowned. "It was also around the time my parents died." She turned her knees until they touched his. "What else did I say?"

His brow wrinkled and cracks began to appear in the arid land. He lifted his shoulders to his ears. "You mostly had questions about *my* world."

Nova slumped. That time was a haze in her mind. It would've been nice to glean something from her earlier visit.

"Why me?" Arlo asked, jarring Nova from her thoughts.

Vulnerability was weaving around them. She looked at Arlo questioningly.

"Why do *I* get a special visit from an alien-girl?"

"To—to harvest your dreams."

"Yeah, but you said yourself that this time is different. And I just—" Arlo's face hardened, then crumpled. Their surroundings shifted. The bench beneath them dissolved, and they scrambled to their feet. They now stood in a building with white, glossy floors.

Nova peered down a hall leading to thousands of bleak rooms. Something sterile and depressing strung through the air.

Arlo tripped back a few paces even as white walls pressed closer. His chin quivered, chest rising and falling too rapidly as he looked at the rooms where wheeled beds peeked out.

Nova reminded herself that the fear rising in her throat was not hers, but Arlo's. She had to keep him calm, otherwise his dream might shift to nightmare.

Arlo entered the third room as if in a trance. Something astringent, like healing tonics, flooded Nova's senses as she followed him through the door.

"Arlo?" Nova collided with him where he stood facing three

people. His pale skin looked sickly under the yellow ceiling lights and he held himself at rigid attention.

They were in an office, and a woman—a human doctor in a white coat—sat with folded hands at her desk. The doctor's expression was kind but sad, and her eyes rested on the russet-haired woman across from her.

"I'm sorry I don't have better news for you, Claire," the doctor said.

The man cleared his throat. "How . . . how long?"

Nova frowned, glancing between Arlo and the people.

The doctor sighed and leaned back in her chair with a creak. "I don't want to give you false hope, but I *do* want to encourage you to try treatment. Even so, this cancer is aggressive. It might only lengthen your life a few years, but—"

Her words cut out as she glanced at the doorway. Nova gasped and gripped her shirt, but the doctor was looking *past* her and Arlo to a boy who stood beyond them. Another Arlo who looked the same as the one who stood by her side.

She recalled the card Archer had given her in the sleep chamber. *Sick mother.*

This was a dream of real events.

The red-headed woman, Claire, turned and locked eyes with the other Arlo. Claire's bottom lip shook, but her watery gaze was fierce, as if fear would not have a hold over her. Nova's throat tightened.

Claire nodded, still looking at Arlo. "I'll take all the time you can give me, Doctor."

The dream dissolved until it was just Arlo and Nova again, standing in a patch of Earthen moonlight. No longer a hospital. No longer a barren desert. Just an unending field of night.

Nova touched his arm. "That was your mother?"

Arlo nodded. "We just found out a week ago." His voice wavered and when he turned to Nova, tears glimmered on his cheeks from the starlight. "I—I can't lose her. She's all I have."

His shoulders shook. Nova could feel every ounce of sadness and pain spilling off him. Her breath caught, and before she could second-guess herself, she wrapped her arms around Arlo, squeezing tightly. He sniffed and hiccupped, the tension in his shoulders slackening at Nova's embrace.

When Nova pulled away, Arlo breathed deeply and wiped at his cheeks. "Thanks for that."

A tear slid from his chin and Nova caught it before it hit the ground. The tear unraveled into a blue Thread and curled around her wrist.

Arlo stared at her wrist, brow furrowed. "Did you take a Thread?"

"Sorry—" Nova stepped back. *Why did I do that?* It felt wrong taking Threads from someone who understood what was happening. And at such a vulnerable time. Shame filled her, and she wished she could give it back to him.

The dark field shimmered in and out of focus and Nova recognized the signs of Arlo's waking. If she didn't leave soon, she might end up trapped in his mind until the next time he slept.

"I have to go," she said.

"Will you be back?" Arlo's voice cracked.

"I'll try. I promise." She looked down at Arlo's grief Thread and an idea struck her. She unwound the Thread and looped it around Arlo's arm—then tied off the blue ends.

"What are you doing?"

"Trying to prove I'm real so when you wake up, you don't forget me."

"By tying one of those dream Threads on me? But I'm not like you. I won't . . ."

The field grew blurry and Arlo faded from her grasp, his questions echoing and faint.

Nova closed her eyes and thought of home.

Chapter Three

Waking feels like closing a door.
I shut my eyes
Wishing to go back
To see *her* —
The girl with the midnight hair
Eyes like shiny steel
Silver crawling up her shoulder,
Like a snake in desert sands
She took my dream —
A strand of clouds.

Something bites my arm
A snake on arid lands?
A strand — no, a Thread.
I can hardly breathe
Again.
Was this more than a dream?
Was *she* more than a dream?

Nova. Nova of Lyra.
What does that even mean?

My loneliness says *yes,*
But reality screams *no.*
Before I can decide,
The Thread disintegrates
And I wonder if it was ever there
To begin with.
I close my eyes, ignore reality
Because sleep feels like opening a door…

CHAPTER FOUR

"**N**ot the first to finish today, Nova," Archer said. But when his gaze landed on Nova's empty hands his eyes bulged. "What—no Threads?"

Nova folded her arms, hoping he wouldn't see her trembling, or spot Arlo's cloud Thread she'd hurriedly shoved into her pocket. It felt wrong giving his dreams to Archer now. She didn't know if her nerves were from the thrill of making contact with a human, or from anxiety that Archer would read it in her face.

When she said nothing, his disbelief grew stale and was replaced with a shrewd smile.

"I suppose no one is perfect. Extra next time, or it will come out of your coin."

Nova nodded stiffly, then edged out of the sleep chamber. Most of the others had gone for the night, and it was strange seeing the room so bare.

Once Nova exited the building, she broke into a run. Adrenaline pumped through her limbs so forcefully she barely acknowledged the spongey ground under her feet. Waist-high pulse plants crowded the glade, and she brushed through them, causing waves of violet bioluminescent light to ripple, leading her toward the dark trees and vibrant blue of the towering mushroom caps. She plunged in amongst them, keeping to the path. Only a little farther now.

Nova felt as if her skin would rip open if she didn't tell someone about her encounter with Arlo. And there was only one person she trusted enough for that.

Eris's home was nestled near the center of Callisto. As she ran from the forest and through the city gate, then flew down the side streets, she prayed he was home. And that he'd believe her. And that he wouldn't lecture her too badly.

When she reached his house, she edged her way around the side of the pod until she came to his room, and then she tapped on his glass door. She bent over, struggling to catch her breath, and waited. After a long moment, Eris opened the door, and Nova barreled inside.

Eris looked as if he'd been napping as he blinked slowly at her. His Zyne family crest, a horned beetle, seemed to be creeping out of his wrinkled shirt collar.

"Are your parents home?" she asked.

"Um, hello? No, they aren't." He darted his eyes over her appearance. "Why are you so *sweaty*?"

"I ran here . . . from . . . Dream Glade." Her words came out in loud gasps.

"On purpose?"

"Of course." She collapsed on a pouf. "Would I run here on accident?"

"Were you being hunted?"

She scowled at her friend's smirk. "Eris, be quiet and listen! Something *happened*."

Eris sobered and sat down across from her. "Tell me." He leaned forward, his bright silver eyes intensified, glowing against his dark brown skin.

She cleared her throat. "I met a boy in his dream."

Eris laughed and leaned back. "Yes, Nova. That's our job."

She shook her head. "You don't understand. *I met him.* We talked. He . . . saw me, Eris. And he's met me in a dream before, somehow, when we were children." She told him about the younger version of herself.

Eris listened intently, eyebrows drawing together. "How is that possible?" He seemed bemused.

"I don't know."

"It *shouldn't* be possible."

"I know!" Nova fidgeted. "But you believe me, right?"

"Of course I believe you. Why would you lie?"

Relief washed through Nova. "Thank you, Eris."

"Why did you tell me about this — aside from wanting to tell me?"

Nova bit her lip. "Because I'm going to visit him again."

Eris eyed her darkly.

She grinned, hoping to charm the worry from him. But she could practically see it billowing out from under his cool facade.

"Nova . . ."

She stood, wanting to have a height advantage over him. "I have to find him again."

Eris got to his feet, towering a head over her. "The human."

"Arlo."

Eris shook his head, eyes widening. "What if Archer finds out what you're doing?"

"He wouldn't *know*, Eris. It's all in my head. How can he monitor that?"

"It's literally his job!" Eris mopped a large hand over his face. "*Nova,*" he said, sounding more like Cally than like her fourteen-year-old best friend. "Why?"

"Because I think my dad would have wanted me to."

Eris's gaze snapped to hers.

Nova burrowed her chin into her shawl, and it squeezed her gently. "I know you don't agree, but finding Arlo is worth whatever risks there may be. Father would have given anything to converse with a human. And Arlo knew things about Lyra he only could have gotten from, well, *me*. But I don't remember visiting him before. I have to know what it all means!"

Eris went to stand by the window, crossing his arms tightly. "What do you need from me?" His words were slow, as though dragging something heavy from his throat.

Nova looked at him in surprise. "You're going to help?"

"Since you'll do something stupid with *or* without me, yes, I'm going to help."

Nova grinned, but then her smile faded. "I don't know how to find him," she said. "Not without . . ." She twisted her fingers lightly in the edge of her shawl.

"You need a circlet."

"Yeah," she said with quiet resolve.

Eris fell silent, most likely thinking through every scenario, or any possibility that could change her mind. "When?" he finally asked, resignation thick in his voice.

"Well, tonight there is a predicted dust storm."

"Everyone will be in lockdown!"

"Exactly." Nova bounced on the balls of her feet. "*Everyone* will be in lockdown. Which means it's the perfect time to break into the Harvesting Center."

Eris snorted. "Or a perfect time to lose our minds or be killed by the Void."

Nova pulled a gray Thread from her shawl. She gave it a shake and a gleaming shield manifested in her hands. Her whole body sagged under its weight, but its heaviness was masked by the thrill of victory from the dreamer's emotion when she'd unraveled the Thread. Now, that emotion pumped through her veins until she grew dizzy with power. She wanted to charge into battle. To fight her way to a castle she'd never been to.

Eris stared at the shield. "What use is a shield going to be against moon dust?"

"Perhaps it will shelter us enough to keep us from going mad."

"Okay, but there's no way you can carry that over your head the entire way. It's bigger than you."

Nova wriggled her eyebrows and hefted it toward Eris. "But you should have no problem."

~

Nova waited for Eris near the trailhead to Dream Glade. She had gone home to change into darker clothes. Thankfully Cally hadn't been around to argue with her, or stop her—probably off with *Ceres*. She adjusted her bulging satchel, which was stuffed with her colorful shawl, over her shoulder.

Eris walked up to her with a huff and a surly look. "I don't like this." He'd been saying this repeatedly since they'd formed their plan. "And I had to lie to my parents. I hate lying to them."

The storm was predicted to begin at moon fall, which meant the end of Nova and Eris's mission would be during Darknight. No moon. No light. No magic. She didn't love the timing, but there wasn't much she could do about it. They would just have to be swift and hope for the best.

"Nova? Eris?"

Nova jumped. "Ceres," she said with a strangled voice. Her skin tingled, her moon mage magic telling her the dust storm would be starting within minutes. "I thought—I thought you might be with my sister tonight."

"I'm on duty." Ceres's brown hair was pulled back in a low ponytail, accenting his sharp jawline. Heavy brows contrasted his silver eyes and olive skin.

"Didn't you hear the alarm for the dust storm?" Ceres glanced at Nova's satchel. "What are you doing out on the street? Do your parents know you're out here, Eris?"

"Of course they do," Eris said, not skipping a beat. "Nova was over, and my parents said we should get a little fresh air before being stuck inside."

Nova tried to keep her expression neutral.

"I see." Ceres's gaze darted again to Nova's bag.

"Where are *you* headed?" Nova asked.

"Making the rounds."

"Oh, right."

Her gaze slipped to his right arm and the glowing ink of two intersecting circles with starbursts emanating from them. Ceres was a Messenger, which was useful as a Sentry. He could use his thoughts to communicate with other Messengers across far distances. Though Ceres couldn't break into Nova's mind without her knowing, she still didn't trust Sentries in general. They took orders from the Ancients. The same Ancients who'd told the city her parents had died as traitors.

But Ceres was her sister's bond which meant Cally would be united with him one day. Ceres was going to become *family*. And if anyone was ever a stickler for the rules, it was *Captain* Ceres of the Callisto Sentries.

"Are you okay, Nova?" Ceres asked. "You seem . . . jumpy."

His concern caught her off guard, and she stammered for a moment. "Uh. Yes."

Nova's stomach twisted as Ceres opened his mouth again. She said, in a rush, "Eris, can I have a minute with Ceres?"

"Sure, but remember—the *storm*," he said with such meaning she was sure Ceres would glean their entire plan.

"It'll be quick," she said.

Eris marched toward the trailhead that began at the forest. When he was out of earshot, Nova tipped up her chin and fixed Ceres with a determined look.

"Ceres, I'm okay. You don't have to follow me around. I'm not an infant."

"I told you I was on rounds," Ceres said, even and unreadable, as always. "Maybe . . . we should talk sometime, Nova. You know, about our future? Just to see if we're okay with each other."

Nova swallowed. She crossed her arms over her chest and darted her eyes to the mouth of the trail where Eris stood waiting. *Another time. Any other time.*

"I understand if it's difficult for you, with Cally and me—but I promise I'm not trying to be your father or anything."

The word "father" struck something sensitive in her, but she didn't have time to wade through that right now. "Okay, but . . . can we talk about this later?" Nova's insides felt as if they were tied in knots and the storm beat closer and closer in her senses.

Ceres leaned in and placed a hand on Nova's shoulder just as the wind picked up. The scent of spiced oil that kept Sentry uniforms waterproof swirled around her. "The storm will be here soon. You should get to safety. Cally will never forgive me if she found out I saw you outside and didn't at least warn you."

"Alright," Nova said. "I've been warned."

Ceres lifted a brow, waiting.

Ceres *could* invade her mind to find the truth, but it was against the law to break into another Lyran's thoughts unless they were under trial. For once, she was grateful for Ceres the Stickler.

"I will go inside. Promise," Nova said. *Eventually.* She jerked her thumb at Eris, lurking almost out of sight. "Do you think he would let anything happen to me?"

Ceres nodded, then stepped back. The captain once more.

"May Selene keep you," he said.

"And light your way home."

Nova watched him fold into the shadows, stomach churning, remembering the *other* Sentries—the ones who had come when their dead parents were labeled criminals. Nova and Cally's lives had then been turned upside down. Frankly, Nova was surprised Ceres hadn't broken the bond with her sister when that had happened, but he'd stayed—for some reason. When Ceres married Cally, he would be attaching himself to her family's unsavory history.

The wind whooshed again, stirring loose a few strands of her hair. She shook herself and hurried toward the path Eris had taken. She wondered if anyone saw her passing. The streets were quiet, the homes lit with blue foxfire orbs to keep back the beasts of Darknight. Nova pressed on, into the looming darkness.

CHAPTER FIVE

The forest stirred with tension as Eris and Nova jogged down the cap forest trail. Gloom bats with silver bodies and a wingspan the size of Nova fluttered nervously around the bending, rubbery trees, while primates with glowing eyes and spots scrambled along the branches. Her dad told her once that the primates used to be called "Aye-Ayes," when Lyrans' ancestors brought them over from Earth long ago. Then Selene changed them, like she changed everything on Lyra.

Ahead of her, Eris ducked under a fungus cap, scattering an eclipse of moon moths that had gathered under its bioluminescent dome. Nova paused and stared for a moment, mesmerized by the white crescent designs on their wings, before catching up to her friend.

The pulse plants scattered through the forest burned with burgundy: *danger, danger, danger*. Nova's skin tingled with foreboding; they only had a few seconds before the dust storm arrived.

The magic inside their moon was continually trying to get out, causing a layer of outer crust to break and crumble. As pieces of the moon's crust were incinerated by the atmosphere, they turned to dust that drifted over the surface of Lyra.

The mushroom caps gave them some coverage, but they couldn't run through the glade like this.

The Threads in her shawl quivered, and Nova slowed, drawing out the gray Thread. Taking a calming breath, she tried to prepare herself for the emotion that would flood her. As soon as the Thread morphed into the gleaming shield, her soul blazed with victory. Her head swam with vengeance.

Side by side, Eris and Nova lifted the shield over their heads, though Eris had to keep his arms bent so Nova could reach. "You good?" he said.

Nova closed her eyes, breathing in the blood of her enemies.

No. Not enemies. She needed to steal a circlet. That was all.

"Yes," she said, shakily. "Just don't let me slay anyone, will you?"

"*What?*"

Nova pulled them along. A shiver of sound like falling sand reverberated against the shield and Nova exchanged a wild look with Eris.

"I wish I had a sword," she said.

"What good would a sword do us?"

They entered the glade of blood-red pulse plants swirling madly in the storm. Nova smiled widely, hair whipping about, eyes flashing.

I will wear the bones of the slain! All will fear my name!

Nova let out a hoot of victory, pumping a fist in the air and causing the shield to dip. Nothing could touch them!

"Shhh!" Eris said through gritted teeth. "What are you doing?"

Nova lifted the sagging shield. Right. Covert mission.

Covert.

The glass domed Harvesting Center sat in the dream glade before them, surrounded by rubbery pulse plants that blazed red. Shimmering dust rained around the bulbous structure like exploded starlight. Nova hoped the storm would keep all personnel and Sentries safe within Callisto's walls. And far away from the center.

They raced across the meadow, shield overhead. Nova scanned

her palm on the building's entrance pad and they slipped inside. She unraveled the shield, and with it, the heady emotion. Nova sagged against the wall, rubbing her head at the sudden drop of adrenaline. The Thread weaved itself back into her shawl, and she blushed, remembering her *glorious* charge through the field.

"Ready?" Eris asked.

She nodded, some of her strength returning. The quicker they got the circlet, the better.

Once in the sleep chamber they crept to Archer's tidy office. A blue foxfire orb hanging in the center of the ceiling illuminated a wall of circlets, each on an individual moon-rock shelf, polished and gleaming. She took one from the far-left corner, hoping Archer wouldn't notice. At least not for a while. Eris picked up Archer's tablet, his hands slightly trembling.

"His name was Arlo?"

"Arlo James."

"This is going to take a while." He glanced at the circlet. "What if you put that on and thought of him? Maybe I could do a backward search."

Nova frowned. "Is that possible?"

"No idea."

"*Great*." But Nova pressed the circlet on her head and closed her eyes. *Arlo. Arlo. Arlo.* Her mouth formed his name. It didn't take her long to gather up his image. There he was: russet hair, smattering of freckles, a sad smile.

"Got him!"

Nova jumped, opening her eyes. "Really?"

"I think so. Is this him?"

She looked down at Archer's tablet which displayed an image of Arlo. She smiled at Eris. "You did it."

"*You* did it. The tablet locked on as soon as you began thinking of him."

"So can we tell if Archer knew I was talking to Arlo in that dream?"

"Uh . . ." Eris said, his fingers working swiftly over the tablet. "Here's his report. Let's see if he flagged anything." His eyes roamed across the screen while Nova's stomach fluttered like moon moths.

"Well?" she said.

"I . . . don't see anything here . . . The only thing he flagged is that you didn't bring back any Threads last night." Eris paused and looked at her. "Really? No Threads at all?"

Nova shrugged. "I kept one, but Archer doesn't know. And the other, well, I left it with Arlo."

"You *left* your Thread with a *human*?"

"Yeah, so?"

Eris gaped.

"*Eris*. Snap out of it, for Selene's sake."

Eris shook his head, glancing back at the screen. "I don't think Archer could tell that anything out of the ordinary happened in that dream."

Nova's body slackened and she leaned on the desk. "Thank the Heavens."

There was a soft sound, a door shutting down the hall.

Nova looked at Eris in panic. "Someone's here!"

Eyes wide, Eris fumbled with the tablet before it fell—*Smack!*—on the desk. Nova's mouth dropped open at his badly timed clumsiness. "Seriously?" she whispered. Eris grabbed her sleeve before tugging her and the tablet under the desk with him.

They barely fit in the space, and they huddled closer so as not to be seen.

The slap of boots grew louder, and Nova's heart pounded along with them. The footsteps entered the office and paused.

Had Ceres sent someone to look for them after seeing through their lies? *No*, Nova thought. Ceres was a stick in the moss, but he wouldn't risk his Sentries like that. She chewed her lip. There must have been a Sentry stationed in the Center to guard it while no one was there. She groaned inwardly.

Had an alarm been triggered when they entered the Center? Would the Sentry check who had accessed the door? Nova's palms sweated onto the bag she gripped in her lap.

If only it was darker in here! The foxfire globe was practically lighting the way for the Sentry to find them.

Nova and Eris needed to blend in with the shadows. Her gaze dipped to the bag.

She slid her fingers inside and tugged out her shawl. The colorful Threads glowed but were much dimmer than the office. She ran her palm over the weaves. There was one particular Thread she needed . . . *There.* She pinched a black strand. It seemed to suck the light from the other colors. She hesitated.

Eris's eyes bulged and he shook his head.

But the footsteps were rounding the desk now and Nova had no other choice. She tugged out the Thread and threw it over them both. It expanded into a sheet of shadow.

Instantly, Nova broke out in a cold sweat, and fear crawled up her throat until she was sure she'd vomit. Her whole body shook. The dark would conceal them if the dreamer's terror didn't consume her first.

The Sentry—Nova could now see the crisp gray pants of the uniform—stopped just before their feet. But the Thread had concealed Eris and Nova with shadows, though Nova was the only one to feel the horror that accompanied it.

We're going to die. She fought the gut-wrenching panic. She *knew* it wasn't real, just an echo of the dream she'd taken it from, but in the moment it didn't matter. The emotion was too much. The formidable dread tricked her into thinking it was the only thing that mattered.

Eris placed an arm around her trembling shoulders. It brought little relief.

After a few terrible moments, the footsteps left. When they clacked across the sleep chamber Nova tugged off the Thread with a gasp. She toppled out of the tight space and breathed in the cool stone floor.

"*Spores,* Nova!" Eris said, gripping her shoulder. "Why do you have that awful Thread?"

She glanced at Eris's upper arm where a sleeve of woven Threads lay dormant over his Callisto tattoo. He only had ten or so Threads, unlike the hundreds Nova refused to sell. There was safety in having a Thread for any circumstance.

"Without it," Nova said, sitting up and slick with sweat. "We would've just been caught."

Eris frowned. "Just—you have to be more careful. You were shaking so bad."

Nova nodded and put her shawl back in her bag before getting to her feet. "We should go before the Sentry comes back." She swayed and Eris steadied her.

"Are you okay?" Eris said.

"I feel sort of . . ." Her gut roiled and her knees shook as she stood. This was something more than the effects of the Thread. The back of her arm tingled and she twisted it around, lifting her sleeve. Moon dust from the storm clung to the back of her elbow from when she had exposed herself in a fit of *glorious victory*. "Rot," she said. "We really need to go."

They crept out of the building, but Nova shrunk back from the blue swirling eddies of dust whipping around the glade and clouding over the stars above. There was no way they could get back to the city without being exposed to the moon's pure elements even more. Already her head was pounding and magic seemed to be pressing outward, as if it wanted to tear through her skin. She took a deep breath, trying to stay calm.

Raw dust didn't normally *kill* a person, but it made them very sick. It also made people see things that weren't there for days and weeks, and sometimes—depending on the level of exposure—for a lifetime.

"Shield?" Eris said.

Nova reached for the gray Thread but her hand shook too badly. "I c-can't. And what's the point?" She gestured bleakly at the blanketed world.

Eris followed her gesture, then he said, "I may have something that will help."

He tugged on a gray Thread and it hovered for a moment before it transformed. A gust of wind took Nova's breath away.

"What *is* that?" Nova yelled over the noise.

"A gale." His fingers gripped something invisible to Nova, like he held the tail of the wind. His face contorted as he fought the Thread's emotion—perhaps, sadness? "It might be able to blow the dust away from us."

Nova nodded, her head spinning. It would have to do.

Eris wrapped his arm around Nova's shoulder and held the gale Thread before them as they charged into the storm. The Thread created a funnel of wind that Eris directed wherever they needed to run. Even so, Nova felt bits of dust fly into her mouth and nose as she gasped for breath. It was a storm within a storm. The Thread was trying its best to protect Eris, but it couldn't care less about the girl clinging to his side.

Finally, they reached the cover of the mushrooms and trees and collapsed on a bare patch of moss. Dizzy, Nova felt the outline of the circlet in her bag. Their mission would be in vain without it. She bent over and braced her knees, wishing for clarity to return. But the world refused to right itself. Even the flora was dimming. The blue foxfire that flickered inside the mushroom cap was sinking down its stalk and into its roots.

"Eris," Nova said. "The dust—my eyes—everything is fading."

"That's not the dust," he said. "Darknight is coming." He hoisted her up beside him. "We need to get back before Selene fully sets. Ready?"

"Just another minute. Please. I—"

A shrill howl pierced the air as if it were pouring through a keyhole. Chills scattered up Nova's back and she dug her nails into Eris's arm.

They ran, dodging trees—Eris pulling Nova's sluggish body.

She had only heard the faint call of the miedo beastias once before as a child, shortly after her parents' deaths. It had been Darknight, and she'd stolen outside and wandered near the city gates. A Sentry who'd been on watch had found her and ushered her home.

There was something in the beastia's cry that had filled her with both fear and longing. A longing to understand what had happened to her parents. She had a sense, even as a young girl, that the darkness knew their true fate.

Now, Nova teetered on the brink of madness, suffused with more magic than she'd ever experienced. The moon would soon be gone, and with the onset of Darknight the foxfire would sink into the mushroom's roots, and the rest of the forest's light would blink out. Even the forest creatures would dim themselves.

They'd be lost in pitch black. Where nightmares ruled.

Nova tripped and Eris cursed. With a grunt, he hoisted her over his shoulder and kept running. She was too muddled to resist—pictures of hunting beastias filled her mind.

The miedo beastias were birthed from the Void itself: creatures that could rip out throats or infect living things. Nova had heard stories of Lyrans who'd strayed from the path and became lost during Darknight. Those who survived the attacks from the miedos claimed the beasts were like shadows—dark, shifting smoke—but when they stood still, had four legs and a wolfish build. One bite was enough to infect a person with the Void's disease.

Another howl jolted Nova—they sounded closer.

But the caps and spindle trees were becoming sparse, and Nova cried out in relief when they burst from the forest. Selene's glow gripped the horizon, like she was clinging to the edge long enough for Nova and Eris to survive. But Nova knew that wasn't true.

She was thankful for the moon's power, and though she spoke to Selene, Nova knew she was nothing more than a silent, magical rock. A rock that could drive her to madness.

"Eris," she gasped, his shoulder jamming into her stomach with each step. "We're s-safe." The howls had quieted. The dust storm was over.

The moon disappeared completely, draining the forest behind them of every drop of luminance.

Eris slung Nova off his back and they hobbled to the city gates.

She glanced at the walls of Callisto, impenetrable to any but Lyrans. The foxfire lanterns around the stone walls flickered desperately in their orbs, even the flames seemed to cower before the looming Void in the sky. The firelight kept the monsters at bay, just as processed Threads helped strengthen the land against the lack of sunlight and growing blight.

Their only defenses against the Void.

Blue dust coated everything, but it no longer swirled in the air. City workers would douse the streets and homes in water, so the remnants would trickle down the sloping hills of Callisto.

Nova's neck prickled and she looked up. No stars. No moon. It would have looked like nothing if it weren't for the *something* she felt pressing in. Watching.

"Nova!"

Nova blinked wearily at the two blurry figures running through the gates. Someone tackled Nova in a hug and she got a whiff of jasminum oil. "C-Cally?"

"What were you *thinking*?" Cally said, her voice catching. She pulled back and looked Nova over. "Are you hurt?"

Nova shook her head and her thoughts sloshed. "Tired."

"What happened?" the other person said. Ceres.

"Uh," Eris said. "We were taking a walk on the path and lost track of time."

"After I warned you to get home?" Ceres's voice grew louder.

Cally's arms tightened around Nova, and Nova rested her head on her sister's shoulder as she was led into the city gates and up the blue streets. No doubt Nova would have to explain her actions tomorrow, but she could barely form a word, let alone defend herself.

"An alarm was set off tonight," Cally said, her voice a distant echo. "In the Center." Cally sighed. She sounded much older than her twenty-four years. When she spoke again it was a tight whisper to Nova. "I hope whatever you were doing in there was worth it. Who knows what will happen now."

Panic fluttered in Nova's chest. If they knew it was Nova who had broken in, what *would* they do? Would she be allowed to continue as a Harvester? What would she do without the beauty of human dreams? And Arlo . . .

Nova's arm grazed the side of her bag, and she pressed her hand into the fabric. All she felt was her shawl. Nothing hard met her palm. Tears threatened her already bleary gaze.

The circlet. She didn't have it.

Bile rose in her stomach.

Arlo. The boy from Earth who could see her; the boy who understood the grief she'd barely talked about with anyone else. They may punish her, but it would've been worth it if she still had the circlet—she would give it all up if it meant visiting Arlo's dreams whenever she wanted. Nova grasped for hope, searching again for the circlet in her bag, but it was empty. Arlo was lost to her.

She slumped further into Cally.

What if Arlo remembered her but she had no way of getting back to him?

No, Nova thought miserably. *It hadn't been worth it at all.*

Chapter Six

The Thread shone like a star,
Then crumbled.
Dust to dust.
I buried the ashy remains
In Mom's flower bed,
Hoping it would grow again.

The sun shifts.
Shadows are all that grow now.

I bury my hopes deep
As Mom lays bedridden
And Dad lays into me with harsh words.
Helplessness consumes me
like *cancer.*
What can I grow in soil
That is so dry and deadly?

Not even dreams carry me away.
Nova — where are you?
All I want is to forget,
To write it all down,
To leave,
To stay.
My thoughts ping
Back and forth between
What I want to do
And what I have to do.

I am left frazzled. Tired,
Confused.
Left with dead dirt

And long shadows.

CHAPTER SEVEN

Nova hadn't experienced a duller six months in her life.
She knew her punishment for breaking into the Harvesting Center could have lasted two years. She knew this because her sister reminded her of it every day. Since Nova was underage, and Archer hadn't detected anything stolen, and Captain Ceres was "on her side," she'd escaped with only a six-month sentence. She wondered if her ease at gathering Threads shortened the suspension, too. Callisto needed all the Harvesters they could get.

Her fourteenth birthday came and went, spent mostly confined to her room, staring up at Selene's blue glow and the smattering of constellations that reminded her of freckles. She wondered if any of the stars were planets, and if any of those planets were Earth. She wished she'd paid better attention in astronomy. But, like every other Lyran child, her schooling had ended when she was twelve. Once a citizen's magic was cultivated, they were sent out to help their community.

Unless they were suspended, of course.

There was a knock on Nova's door and she jumped up, eager for any outside news. Cally had grounded Nova, and not even Eris could come for visits. She wished her best friend was a Messenger so they could've at least communicated—though Eris probably would've been just as strict as Ceres was. But it no longer mattered. Today was her last day in captivity.

She jogged to the door and saw Eris grinning through the domed glass. Nova squealed and burst through, throwing herself into his arms. He let out a startled *oof*. She squeezed him until he awkwardly patted her shoulder.

"I've missed you!" Nova said, stepping back. "Let's go to the market! Or the star fields? Or maybe the—"

Eris laughed. "I've missed you too. But we need to talk." He rubbed the back of his neck, and his eyes darted around the room. Was he *nervous*?

"Can we at least leave my pod? I'm sick of this place."

Eris ignored her plea. "Is Calypso home?"

"No. She's at work. What's going on?"

Eris sat at the table and placed his bag in front of him. He stared hard at it as if a gloom bat was about to burst from its seams. Nova sat across from him, her smile falling.

"What is it, Eris?"

Her voice seemed to jar him from his thoughts, and he sighed, opening the flap. The gray-blue edge of a circlet peeked out from the bag.

"You stole another . . ."

Eris looked side-eyed at her.

Nova gasped. "Is this the one *we* took?"

Eris closed his eyes and nodded. "I grabbed it from your bag outside of the gates. Cally and Ceres were running up and . . ." His shoulders fell. "You scanned your hand to gain entrance at the Center. If Archer knew that much, they'd search your pod for anything out of the ordinary. So I took it."

Her chest squeezed. "You did that for me?"

"Of course. What are best friends for?" He smiled lightly, but she knew how heavily dishonesty sat with him.

Nova's eyes watered. "But they could've suspected you just as easily. Ceres knew you were with me."

"I went off a wild hope that he wouldn't turn me in."

Nova snorted. "You got lucky there. Your parents would've—"
She grimaced thinking of Eris's parents. They were under a lot of
pressure as two of Callisto's Processors, even more than
Harvesters. Without processing dream Threads into rejuvenating
resources for their sunless planet, the Void would completely take
over.

They didn't need the stress of their son being suspended. Yet he
had still helped her.

"Thank you, Eris."

He nodded.

Nova focused again on the circlet and her stomach flipped. Arlo
was just a dream away. What more did the human know? What
else could she explore in his mind? She reached trembling fingers
toward the bag, but Eris placed his hand there first.

"You have to promise me something, Nova."

She curled her fingers into a ball. "What?"

"That you won't be reckless. No Harvester has spoken to
someone in their dreams before. If he remembers you, he could
grow an attachment. And if he grows curious about Lyra, who
knows what he could do? Human emotion is volatile—you've felt
it in the Threads."

Nova laughed and sat back. "He isn't dangerous. He's just . . .
sad."

Eris sighed then slid the bag to Nova, his mouth in a thin, tight
line.

~

Nova tried to enjoy her time outside, but she had barely left their
street of pods before turning back. She owed it to Arlo to visit him
first. He needed an explanation for why she'd never returned. And
also, she was dying to know if he *did* remember her.

Back home, she curled into her bed, circlet in hand.

"No one will know," she assured herself.

But she stared at the circlet as if it would brand her. Claim her.
Eris's words had planted seeds of doubt and now her excitement

was dimmed under the shade of growing anxiety. Her fingers trailed the edge of the cool rock hoping it would grant her sure direction. Though the stone circlet contained flecks of moon rock, there was just the right amount to guide her magic, rather than overwhelm it. Even so, a shiver ran down Nova's spine when she remembered the dust storm and the shrill howls.

Nova rubbed her head and stared at Selene's reassuring glow. Darknight was far away, and she was safe within her pod. She had to focus. On Arlo.

Her stomach did that weird flip again. Speaking with Arlo was so unlike speaking to Lyrans. Their connection was a mystery to be solved. A question to be answered. Another world to be explored.

Hands shaking, Nova slid the circlet over her brow. Her shawl tugged playfully, energized by her own pounding heart. "Sorry, you can't come. Behave while I'm gone." She was unable to keep the grin off her face.

Nova closed her eyes and repeated, *Arlo James*, in her mind, just in case the circlet needed some extra guidance. But the coordinates were already there. It should work.

Sleep tugged her under.

Stars swirled and shifted as she was turned inside out. Painless, yet disorienting. After gliding past spiraling stellar remnants, Nova entered an uncomfortable tunneling—a claustrophobic squeezing around her body, as if the rushing lights had grown arms to embrace her.

She emerged inside a house in an empty hallway with photos of an even younger Arlo than she'd already met, standing in between the man and the red-headed woman she'd seen in his last dream. His mother. Claire, was it?

Nova's excitement at finding Arlo evaporated as she was led by the dream into a room off the hallway, its white doorframe chipped in places. Nova paused, but Arlo's presence within the room called to her, his grip tightened. She let him pull her inside.

Claire lay sleeping in a large bed, her skin sallow, head bald. Nova's throat constricted. Beside the bed, Arlo sat slumped like a rag doll in an overstuffed chair. He looked stretched since Nova had last seen him. Not just because of his longer legs and arms, but also because of his posture and features. There was something "older" about him that had nothing to do with age, and, she imagined, had everything to do with the grief she felt now, pressing on her skin.

Her eyes stung. The weight was suffocating.

And familiar.

"Arlo—?"

He blinked, looking at Nova in surprise. "Is it really you?"

"Yes." Nova took a step closer, unsure whether she should invade such a vulnerable place. "I'm so sorry I didn't come back sooner."

Arlo stood, scratching at his arm. He was a few inches taller than her now. His shoulders a bit wider. He smiled sadly and the sorrow enveloping the room lessened a touch, the sun shone stronger through the window. "I'm glad you're here." He cocked his head, studying her. "Why *did* it take you so long?" Arlo's insecurity curled a few sheets of wallpaper at the edges.

"I had to steal something so I could find you again—and I got caught." She felt her cheeks flush.

"Oh. I'm sorry you got caught, but thanks for doing that." He flashed Nova a lopsided grin, but it was still sad. "No one has risked prison for me."

Nova didn't correct his assumptions, only laughed lightly. Though it felt strange to show any kind of happiness in the room. Her eyes slid to the bed again. "How long has she been like that?"

"A few months now. Chemo is a—well, it's bad. Sometimes I wonder if the cancer wouldn't have been better."

"Chemo?"

Arlo hesitated. "It's a drug that's supposed to kill the cancer." His gaze darkened and the sun completely disappeared. "But it's making her suffer too. She'll probably die either way."

Nova took his hand. He didn't pull away. The seconds ticked by until she didn't think her chest could take the pressure. She pressed her lips together to keep her jaw from trembling.

"We should go," he finally said. He led her out of the room and into a living space with flowers printed on a matching couch and chairs.

"I'm alone a lot these days," Arlo said. "And my dad is no help." His words fell out of him, clattering to the ground hollow and heavy. "My parents were already at odds, but this was the last straw for him, apparently. As if she could help getting cancer."

"Did he leave?"

"He still lives here, just works all the time. Mom has a nurse that comes in while I'm at school. Otherwise, I'm all she has."

Arlo released Nova's hand, flexing his fingers. "So"—he caught her gaze—"how does one get to Lyra? I could use a vacation."

Nova forced a light chuckle and glanced out the window. At the sea. The house creaked under her. Arlo's mind had placed this house on the edge of a cliff. Unbalanced, teetering. "Well, you'd need a rift for that. And they aren't created anymore. Something, or someone, made them once to let our people pass between Earth and Lyra. But they were all destroyed."

"But . . . you're here now."

"Not *really*. This is different."

"Because I'm dreaming."

"Right."

"Are you dreaming, too?"

"Yes."

"That's too bad." He leaned against the wall near the window. He took a shuddering breath and the whole house shuddered with him. "I think I'd like to meet you for real."

Nova braced her hands against the window. "Me too."

"But you said your dad was working on a way to bridge our worlds. He thought it was possible, right?"

"He did, yeah. But it also got him and my mom killed." She nudged a chair with her toe. "By the Void. The one thing we can't seem to beat."

Arlo glanced back at Claire's rooms down the hall. "I see."

Nova pinched the corner of the windowsill, giving it a tug. The entire frame and glass came with it, forming into a deep brown

Thread that pulsed in her palm. It felt like safety tinged with frailty. Home.

Arlo watched her. "Is that why we don't always remember our dreams? Because they're stolen?"

Nova eyed the Thread. His words caught in her chest. She took pieces of dreams. She took the circlet. *Was* she a thief? "Would taking a cup from the ocean deplete its waters?" she said.

Arlo snorted. "No. But my brain is not an ocean."

"You're right. It's bigger."

Arlo laughed. "Oh, okay. Now you're just trying to make me feel better."

Nova shook the Thread in front of his face. "I mean it! Your brain is enormous, and your dreams are constantly being made. Your mind can only remember so much. Would you have missed this window upon waking?"

"I don't know. I guess not."

Nova offered him a tentative smile. "It is true that what I take, you forget—but I never take anything important. I promise."

"It still feels *invasive*." He flaked a chip of paint from the wall. "If you're even real, that is," he said, as quiet as the wind.

He still didn't fully believe her. But Nova would've felt the same in his position. She glanced out of the window. The ocean air drifted in and lightly ruffled Arlo's deep red hair. Red, like the muscaria mushrooms that grew on the edge of the forest back home.

"Have you been to the ocean?" Nova asked, enjoying the salty air on her tongue. "Is that why we're"—she gestured—"here?"

Arlo nodded. "Yeah. It's one of my favorite places. Swimming in it is tricky, though. You have to be a really strong swimmer and keep your eye on land, or you'll drift."

"And the beasts in your waters? Do they not harm you?"

He shrugged and wobbled his head. "They *can*. But they really just want to be left alone." His eyes found hers. "Do you have oceans?"

"We call them brines, and the one nearest is the Black Sea. No one has attempted to cross it in years."

"Why not?"

"It's deadly. The beasts in our brines are Void beastias. It's impossible to cross the brine all in one night. When Selene is out to protect us we are safe in the waters, but once Darknight falls, the beastias will hunt the ships. No expedition has ever survived."

Arlo gave her a wide-eyed stare. "I didn't understand any of that, but it sounds horrible."

"Now you *sea* where I'm coming from?"

Arlo hesitated, then smiled. "Was that a joke? Do Lyrans *joke*?"

Nova grinned and plucked at the top of a lamp. A Thread wavered at its edge, but she let it remain. "Only the Lyrans who spend half their time in the brains of humans."

"Well, your humor needs some work, but we'll get there." He winked good-naturedly, and Nova laughed.

They fell into a few moments of silence. Nova's mind was whirring with questions, but one jumped out of her mouth before she'd had a chance to consider if it should be asked.

"When you feel angry or sad, how do you deal with it?" Nova twisted her fingers together. "I've sensed about twenty different emotions from you since I've been here, and though you feel deeply, it never consumes you. When my parents died, I was overwhel —"

"Wait. What do you mean, you've *sensed* my emotions?"

Nova realized her mistake as soon as she felt suspicion crawling through the rafters of the house. "I-I should have told you, but I can sense what you feel inside your dreams."

Arlo's brows rose. "That is *not cool*." He pushed away from the wall and stormed to the center of the room.

Nova flapped her hands helplessly. "I don't try! It just happens."

"Did you ever consider that stealing things from people's heads while they were sleeping was bad enough without also invading their feelings?" Arlo was shouting, but he didn't sound angry. He was afraid. His fear shook the walls of the house.

"I don't invade, Arlo. I just feel what you do. I can't shut it off."

Arlo put his hands on his head, closing his eyes tight. When he opened them again he dropped his arms. "It doesn't matter, Nova. I doubt this is real, and if it is, this is so beyond my reality."

Nova bit the inside of her lip. "I *am* sorry, it's just . . ." She held out her arms. "Every day I feel as if I'm about to explode."

Arlo shrugged. "So do it, then. Explode."

Nova gaped. "*What*?"

"Scream. Yell. Throw a lamp." He shrugged. "It's a dream—you can't hurt anything in here. Right?"

"Right." She folded her arms across her stomach. "How do you do it? What do you yell?"

"Whatever you need to let out. Why are you angry?"

Nova frowned. "I'm not angry. Well, not really. I'm—" She blew out a long breath. "I guess maybe I *am* angry at my sister for shutting me out when I want to talk about our parents. And I'm angry their reputations are now lower than loam. Father was just trying to help, I know it. And my mother—" Her voice hitched.

Arlo took Nova's hands in his. They were cool and strong and Nova gripped them back.

"Ready to yell?" he said.

"No."

"Good." Arlo threw back his head and let out a guttural cry that sent a spike of shock through her body. Nova tried to tug away, but he held her hands. All she could do was stare slack-jawed at his obvious madness.

Lyrans believed that humans were too emotional and those abrupt and volatile feelings often led to horrible acts. Lyra's bloody past with Earth didn't help their outlook, either.

Watching Arlo let loose, Nova could see the validity of those concerns now. He looked as if he were about to crack. And the walls *were* cracking. She whipped her head around, taking in the crumbling structure while Arlo took another deep breath and yelled again.

Then, something in Nova's chest burned. Her veins felt as if they pumped with foxfire. If she didn't do something, she felt she really *might* combust. Thinking of the anger swirling in her heart, she opened her mouth, and let out a scream that was weak at first but grew in strength. Soon, she could barely even hear Arlo.

It was very un-Lyran of her.

And it felt wonderful.

Off balance, she gripped Arlo's hands tighter. But it wasn't her that had grown dizzy. The entire house was tipping.

Nova's scream turned into one of terror as the structure tumbled over the edge of the cliff. Arlo gasped, and they clung to one another as they spun around, mid-air, while the house turned over and over. *It's only a dream. Only a dream*, Nova told herself, eyes closed and gripping the back of Arlo's shirt as if it could save her.

The house landed with a *crack!* and exploded. Nova and Arlo tumbled onto the floral couch, debris and broken ceiling swirling around them in a nonsensical way. Rainbow sea spray burst from the ocean just feet from the battered walls. It tasted sweet, not at all like the brines from her own world.

Nova's chest heaved, and she sucked in gulps of air. Her body felt sore, but the dream—Arlo's mind—had kept them safe. She'd been in many near-death or should-have-been-dead dreams and had woken in the Harvesting Center quite safe. But the fear always lingered.

"Are you okay?" Arlo said. He sat beside her, still holding her hand. She pulled it from his grasp and patted her cheeks. Dust from the explosion clung to Arlo's long lashes and coated his upper lip.

"I'm okay."

Arlo turned to the hallway.

"She isn't there. Not really," Nova said.

He nodded.

"Um," Nova said, "Sorry for breaking your house."

Arlo shook his head, but he was smiling. "Did it help?"

Nova turned her sights on the ocean, listening to its waves pounding the shore. Over and over again. Relentless and bold. She listened to her own heart. It wasn't as bold, but she imagined it beating stronger than before. Her shoulders and chest felt looser—releasing her anger had freed up more room for other things.

"Yeah," she said quietly. "I think it did."

Talking with Arlo felt safe. She didn't have to hide.

It was easy, like it had been with her father.

The ground rumbled and she felt a tug in her belly.

"You're waking up."

"Already?" He scrambled to his feet, pulling Nova up with him.

"I wish I could control when you wake up."

"I wish we had weeks."

She blushed.

Her hand slipped from his. "I'll come back," she said.

"Promise?"

"Promise."

Chapter Eight

Sun rays paint rainbows
On my dingy walls,
Through oddly-cut glass.

The bend of light,
Throwing tiny miracles
Where there should be none.

If I were to bend —
Angle myself just right
Could I create anything good?
Would that chipped paint,
Those scuffed corners
Be made right again?

It feels like I'm on the brink
Of something.
Something beyond these walls.
I extend my fingers
Palm catching motes of dust.

Light is warm,
But sometimes sharp,
When it bounces off my flesh.
Do I glow or does it cut
Across me?

CHAPTER NINE

Nova appeared in a dim cafe that smelled of coffee and something sweet. She glided through the people, keeping her sights on the stage—where Arlo's subconscious was focused.

She pushed past a group of people, eager to see what this dream was about.

Arlo was on stage. He wore a sweater as usual, this one forest green. The light directly above him made his hair brassy orange and his pale skin white as the paper on which he recited his poetry. Nova stepped closer.

It was intimately crowded, but Arlo's deep voice cut through the room like it was a cavern, echoing and bouncing off the walls. Everyone leaned in, drawn forward.

Sometimes people dreamt of true things or embellished truths. Sometimes, they dreamt lies. For two years Nova had been slipping into Arlo's dreams between her regular assignments in the Harvesting Center. She and Arlo had gotten to know each other well during that time. This performance, Nova sensed, was a true thing. An event that had happened recently.

He had been wanting to do this very thing for months now, but anxiety had always held him back.

Arlo stared at the paper, tiny specks of sweat lining his brow. Nova's gut roiled as Arlo's nerves penetrated the room. She blew out a sharp breath, trying to expel the stress. But it didn't budge. Nova flitted her eyes over Arlo's face and focused on his words, the room lightened, and Nova found she could breathe again.

"We've touched the skies.
Scraped away moons and
studied the vast, speckled dark.

What are we looking for?

We press into outer space
into our hidden spaces.
Into the trenches of sea,
and into what we can't see.

What are we hoping for?

A discovery.
To prove
we are not alone.
That we create
our own destiny.

Or maybe,
proof we don't?
Perhaps there's something else,
Somewhere else, calling
In the song of the stars
for us.

Can we reach far enough to find it?
Do we dare?

Nova's chest fluttered. Arlo's words settled in the cracked parts of her heart. She smiled. There was magic in humans too, it was just quieter.

Arlo looked up from his paper.

"Hey," he said. "You're here."

She tipped her head to the side, feeling Arlo's uncertainty that she was indeed real. But mingling with his uncertainty was hope that she was not just a recurring dream.

The room faded away. They were in a meadow near an ocean cliff. His ocean—their ocean. Nova held up her palms to collect the sun's rays.

Arlo watched her; the last words of his poem still hummed in the air around them.

"You did it," Nova said. "You read some of your work!"

Arlo laughed. "In front of people too. Can you believe it?"

Nova touched a petal of a strange red flower that was parchment thin. "I knew you could." She looked up. "Art and music and poetry isn't as appreciated on Lyra."

"Why not?"

Nova shrugged. "Its use is more practical—songs to memorize our history, art to remember where we came from and who we are." She touched her collarbone and the silver soleil owl tattooed on her skin. "Even in its beauty, it has purpose. Making is never just for inspiration or enjoyment."

Arlo nodded and she sensed his pondering. Nova wondered if she was making any sense at all. She shifted awkwardly.

"How is Claire?" she asked.

Arlo laced his fingers behind his head in his tangled hair and looked out to sea. His hair was a bit longer than the last time she'd seen him, curling just at the edge of his shirt collar. At sixteen, he was wiry and tall.

"Mom's still in remission, thankfully. But now that she's better, Dad saw it as his way out."

Arlo's emotions were jumbled and layered together—Nova could not grasp what he was feeling, besides, *a lot*. "He moved out?" she asked.

"Abandoned us, yep."

There came a crack and a shiver through the meadow. Far-off lightning danced on the sea cliffs. Nova spotted a lone boat bobbing on the waves. The ocean fluctuated between the color of Arlo's green eyes and a silvery-blue.

"I'm so sorry, Arlo. Do you want to talk about it?"

Arlo's eyes dropped to the meadow. "Maybe someday. But not right now." He swept his gaze over Nova. "It's been about a week since I've seen you. What's going on with you? Tell me of your strange, glowing planet, alien-girl."

"Yeah, sorry. I've been busier at the Center, and sometimes I can't get back to sleep when I get home. And when I do, I've missed *your* sleep window."

"Time zones are hard enough on Earth."

"Huh?"

Arlo chuckled. "Never mind." He motioned to a forest at the edge of a meadow, and they wandered into its shaded covering. Not many things glowed in the woods of Earth, but when the sun shone through the green leaves, it glowed in its own way. It was like a dance between sun, trees, and wind. Nova yearned to know what Lyra had been like before the Void. She loved the bioluminescence of her world, but this light had a power that took her breath away.

"Cally giving you any more freedom?" Arlo said, nudging Nova's shoulder with his. "Or are you marked a thief for life?"

Nova laughed. "She's more lenient since I haven't broken into any buildings for years." Her smile faded. "I wish you could see Callisto. It's so unlike any of your cities."

"Me too. If only we could swap places. Then I could Harvest *your* head."

"Gross, Arlo." She giggled as they passed a prickly pine. "Don't say it like *that*."

"Whatever, alien-girl. I've seen enough movies to know what you guys do." His eyes sparkled with amusement.

Nova grinned. She felt as light as moon dust.

"Do you . . . do you ever dream of my younger self anymore?" Nova asked. "The young-young me. The me I can't remember."

"No. I stopped seeing her as soon as you showed up." Arlo ruffled his hair. "That sounds strange." He laughed lightly, cheeks turning pink. "Not that *you're* strange, or anything."

"Just a head-harvester."

"Right." Arlo glanced at Nova from the corner of his eye, and she sensed apprehension.

"What is it?" she said.

Arlo scowled, clearly annoyed by her reading his emotions. "Have you found out anything else about the Void? Are you okay on Lyra? Just hearing you talk about it gives me chills."

Nova chewed her lip. She'd been so preoccupied with her secret meetings with Arlo—and proving her responsibility to Cally and Archer—that her burning curiosity about the Void had been reduced to a simmer.

"The Void is just . . . there, you know? It's always been there. I don't know how to stop it and no one will talk to me about my parents' deaths or my father's research." She shook her head. "It's not like I could do anything about it, anyway. I'm not my parents. The Void is consuming our entire world and I'm just one person. A child, in the eyes of my people."

Arlo stopped walking and turned Nova until she faced him. "You're not *just* anyone, Nova Celeste. You're a traveler of space. An invader of dreams!" He threw his hands up as if he were exclaiming it to the entire forest. "You help your planet with *magic!*" Arlo's voice quieted and then he blushed, his neck and cheeks nearly matching his hair. "And most importantly, you're an amazing friend."

Nova stilled, though her thudding heart betrayed her calm. A spark in her chest flared to life.

"Don't give up, Nova," Arlo said. The pines around them drooped, caressing her shoulders as Arlo's determined expression shifted. "There is too much bad in *any* world for you to give up fighting now."

The back of Nova's eyes pricked with heat and she swallowed hard.

"And you," Nova said. "You can't give up either."

The corner of Arlo's lips quirked. "I'll try not to."

Then the forest bent and swayed. The Inbetween beckoned Nova home.

Chapter Ten

Don't give up, I say.
Nova tells me the same.
But running away—giving up
It's what we do.
Dad's bag was packed before
I could take a breath to ask
Why?
So, I didn't ask.
I didn't want to know the reason he left.
But I wonder now—
Did he go because of something out *there*
Or because of something in *here:*
In our house, in our family,
In me?
So, I smile and do homework
Play video games and make friends—
All the time wondering
Why Darren's dad is in the baseball stands
And mine can't stand to see my face?

My pillow knows the hate
That swirls in my chest.
I yell
Quiet enough so Mom doesn't hear
Loud enough that someone else might.

He abandoned us.
But as much as I wish he never comes back
I cling to my anger.
Without it, he disappears forever.

CHAPTER ELEVEN

The plaza's market hummed with life as Nova and Cally made their way to work an hour later. Nova's shawl jittered excitedly, and she placed a hand over the Threads to settle them. And to settle her own racing heart. She couldn't quite wipe the grin off her face every time she thought of Arlo's dream.

"What are you smiling about?" Cally said, lifting a brow.

"Nothing." She cleared her throat. "Can we get some echin on the way?"

Cally wrinkled her nose. "I don't know how you can stand eating those spiky creatures." She shuddered.

Nova laughed and let her eyes roam up Callisto's gentle ascent.

Their city held a hundred thousand within its towering walls. Enormous glass orbed buildings, similar to the Harvesting Center, were surrounded by the smaller pods that housed its citizens. Between were bioluminescent fungi growing tall as trees, their caps fanning out like white umbrellas, just like in the forest.

Nova thought her city looked like bubbles tumbling out of an ink-stained sky.

The citizens wore practical clothing, an array of robes or tunics made of moon moth silks or even more rare, the wool from eridanus ewedens—descendants of sheep that came from Earth, long ago.

Nova paused at a stall where the scent of musky portobellions clashed with the tang of berrios. One of the bins held bright yellow tubers, another was ripe with striped roots. But Cally steered Nova away from the brine booth before she could snag an echin or any other water creature Cally found disturbing.

The market's din grew quieter as they walked down the main road that would lead them to a branch in their destinations. Nova's hands suddenly grew clammy. Arlo's words and concerns were still caught in her mind.

"Cally?" She glanced at her sister. Her red hair was not like Arlo's—it was paler, but Nova wondered if Cally's hair would take on a different vibrance under the Earth's sun.

"Hmm?"

Nova twisted her fingers in her shawl and it gripped her back. "How did Father and Mother think they were going to do it?"

"Do what?"

"Defeat the Void."

Cally stumbled and then whipped her head around. A bright blue mushroom cap backlit her shocked expression. She gripped Nova's arm and pulled her close. "Be careful, Nova." Her words were slow, hushed. She glanced down the streets then up at the sky as if the Void were watching them.

Maybe it was.

Nova leaned in. "Be careful about what? What did Father know?"

"They were playing with things they didn't understand."

"What do you mean?"

Cally hesitated, glancing furtively at the pods' windows, which took up most of the structures.

"Cally . . ." Nova followed her sister's glance. She'd never seen her sister act this way before. "What are you afraid of?"

The tension grew thick, then Cally smiled and it snapped. "No one. Nothing. Don't be silly." Her gaze caught on a figure approaching them, and she straightened. "Oh, Eris!"

Nova glanced at her best friend and then back at Cally. "But—"

"I've got to run. See you two later."

Cally waved and hurried down the stone road that would lead to the Walker Facility.

"What was that about?" Eris asked when they began their own trek toward the gates that led to the Harvesting Center. They stepped aside as a spark trolley rolled down the street, letting off rainbow smoke. The tall, open vehicle was powered by processed dream Threads and held around ten passengers, but it took coin to ride a trolley, and Nova and Cally had little money to spare.

"I don't know," Nova said, as they resumed walking. *But she's definitely hiding something.*

"So . . . have you visited *him* lately?" Eris said.

Nova was brought back to the surface of her thoughts. "Um. Yeah. I just left his dream, actually." She said it quietly, embarrassed in a way she'd never felt before. But why should she be? Arlo and Eris were both her friends, they just didn't know each other. *Yet.* Maybe one day Eris would finally relent to taking the circlet and sharing her experience. So far, he'd been resistant to meeting Arlo, and Nova couldn't get the true reason from him.

"He's doing good, then?" Eris asked, but his voice sounded strained.

"Yeah, he's alright. Listen"—Nova nudged his shoulder—"We don't have to talk about Arlo. How's your father?"

Eris blew out a long breath. "He's better. Back at the Processing Center. Though my parents will keep getting sick with the hours they put in. They're always exhausted."

Nova frowned. A mage could grow stronger with practice, but like anything else, going overboard with magic was taxing. Though Processors didn't feel the emotions of the dreamers like Harvesters, they often felt the physical effects of processing so many Threads a day. Recently, the Processors had complained of becoming depleted, lethargic.

"Why are they working so much?"

"Research takes time. One Thread used to be able to fertilize an entire crop. Now, they need four of the same variety to do half a field."

Nova's stomach tightened. "And they haven't figured out why the Threads aren't as powerful."

"Not yet. I wish I could do more. I know we're already putting in extra work to collect more Threads, but maybe Archer would let me take on even more hours."

"You already take on two shifts a night! I barely see you anymore."

He scratched his chin and she gaped at the tiny black stubble. "Eris!"

He startled. "*What?*"

"You have facial hair!"

He laughed but averted his eyes. "Well, yes. That's what happens when boys grow up."

Nova's smile tightened. She hadn't noticed it before. As they turned a corner of pods, the gates came into view.

"We *are* growing up, aren't we?" she said, unsure how she felt about it.

Eris grunted, and Nova studied her friend. There was a tightness in his shoulders. A darkening in his silver eyes. A heaviness that shouldn't be on the shoulders of a seventeen-year-old. "Soon, our parents' worries will become our own," he said.

Nova looked away. Her father's words from long ago, so like Eris's, washed over her:

The weight of this world can be heavy, can't it? But I promise you, Nova. If it's the last thing I do, I'll take on this burden so that the load will be lessened for you.

Nova shivered and glanced at Selene, letting the moon's magic reassure her.

She squeezed her friend's shoulder and his neck muscles tensed at her touch. "It will be alright, Eris. They'll figure out what's going on with the Threads. We'll be okay." Eris smiled, but it looked as if he were appeasing her rather than agreeing. Nova dropped her hand and played with the ends of her shawl.

As she and Eris passed through the gate and followed the crocus path in silence, Nova tried to believe her own words, but they felt as flimsy as fungus. If she pressed just so, they'd rip apart.

They slipped beneath the caps and Nova's shawl glowed steadily. Nova wished she had some hope to offer Eris, but she knew her words would not be enough. When Arlo's cloud Thread grazed her arm and she felt a zing of curiosity, she turned to Eris.

"Wait."

Eris stopped and faced her. *Spores* — he really was growing up. He stood nearly as tall as a moon bear now. "What is it? We can't be late."

"You have time for this." Nova tugged at the cuff of threads on Eris's bicep and plucked out the bright green one. She knew his Threads almost as well as she knew her own. She held out its squirming body — the Thread was clearly perturbed someone was handling it other than its master.

"Take it, Eris."

He exhaled, hands on his hips, trying his best to look stern. But his stringency never could last with her. "Really, Nova. We don't have time for playing around."

"*Take it,* Eris Hyperion Zyne."

He snorted, shook his head, but grabbed the Thread from Nova.

It instantly unwound into a baseball bat, gleaming silver in the dark. Eris's shoulders loosened; his mouth slackened, and an easy smile lit up his face. Nova knew he was feeling the effects of childhood — joy, fun, ease. He'd told her of the dreamer he'd harvested it from years ago.

After a few moments, he shook the bat and it turned back to a strand, wrapping around his arm again. He studied Nova with a strange smile that had only slightly dimmed when the magic's emotion left. "Thank you."

"I thought that might help," Nova said, grinning widely. She looped her arm through his and tugged him down the path. "*Now,* I think we're ready."

CHAPTER TWELVE

"**T**en seconds!" Archer said.

Nova concentrated on her assignment and the cool circlet around her head.

Elaine Shebert. 2045 Founders Lane. Elaine Shebert.

"Eight, seven, six . . ." Archer counted down.

Seeing Arlo was her favorite part of her magic, but Nova still loved entering the minds of others. Encountering the places, the sights and sounds, the feelings of each dreamer. Even if it was not quite reality. Dreams were like starlight on a lake. Her fingers would only ever meet water, never the star itself. Still, it was something only Harvesters got to experience, and Nova wouldn't trade it for all the universe.

It had been one year since Eris had told her about the issues plaguing his Processor parents—one year since they had tried not to let adult concerns weigh on their young shoulders.

But now rumors had begun to circulate beyond the Processing plants into the main population of Callisto. The Ancients were confident the Threads would be enough to hold back the Void. But the darkness was growing closer to their cities' borders, and it was killing more crops and animals than they could grow or hunt. More and more stress rode on the citizen's shoulders. Remnants of nightmares—slipping into their minds during Darknight—haunted the stoutest of people. A fog of hopelessness filtered through streets and homes, minds and hearts. The howls of miedo beastias were heard more frequently. Could they breach the border of Callisto?

Following Eris's early example, Nova and the other Harvesters had taken on more shifts, while the other Callistians did all they could. Even so, Nova visited Arlo when she had time, though their visits had become short. More sporadic. She saw him so infrequently, she feared their bleak situation would consume her.

"Three, two, one—"

Nova's worries diminished as her subconscious slipped through the spinning cosmos. She breathed easy. The Inbetween gave Nova perspective. She should have felt *lesser* in such an endless space, but it was always the opposite. It made her feel as if she were connected to something bigger than anyone could imagine. Like what she did mattered, but in the same breath, it wasn't all on her shoulders.

The vibrant tunneling began, and Nova squeezed into Elaine's mind.

She was instantly accosted by the overwhelming emotion of . . . love? But not the kind she felt for Cally, Eris, or her parents. This was a longing that made her stomach flip-flop and her heart squeeze. Nova gripped her chest. Was this romantic love?

"*Spores.*" Why in the worlds was it so *painful*?

Elaine's fiancé drifted into a pink wallpapered room, his arms filled with flowers and . . . kites.

Kites? Nova laughed, tucking herself into the corner, though there was no reason to hide. The couple took no notice of her—just like every other dreamer but Arlo.

With a flourish of bright white, the kites were let loose, swarming the room like doves. Nova ducked but one grazed her shoulder, and she was washed in bubbling joy.

The fiancé set down the bouquet and Elaine rushed into his arms just as the setting shifted to a gazebo surrounded by a forest sparkling in a diamond rainfall. It was their wedding day. Though Nova sensed happy anticipation inside the gazebo, the rain itself held a melancholy—a change in Elaine's life that seemed to haunt her, even as she sped toward it.

Nova reached out to catch the rain. Bringing her arm back inside, she inspected the droplet in her hand and found the frayed edge. Nova pulled the water until it lengthened into a blue Thread. Its sadness sunk into Nova's chest even as she tucked it inside her satchel.

She then stepped toward the couple reciting their vows and pinched the hem of the groom's jacket. A black, shimmering Thread peeled off. Pulling harder, it un-wound and the man's very essence came with it. Elaine looked shocked as her fiancé came undone, and Nova felt sick at what she'd done. Was Arlo right? Did she steal from people?

No, she reminded herself, shoving the Thread in beside the other one. This was for her city. This was her job. It didn't *hurt* the dreamers.

The vision shifted.

Elaine sat in the middle of a barren room, surrounded by flat snakes. Nova bent to examine them and realized they were lists. *Thousands* of lists. Elaine's brow grew concerned and Nova felt her joy unraveling as quickly as her fiancé had. Anxiety crowded Nova's lungs as she watched the lists slither up Elaine, drowning her in ink and paper cuts, trying to pour into her open mouth.

Elaine screamed.

"It's alright," Nova said, instinctively. But Elaine only heard fear. The worry in Nova's own chest rose as the ground shook under her feet.

Elaine's dream was shifting to nightmare.

Not wanting to face Elaine's fears—or worse, be stuck in her mind when she woke, because *nothing* wakes a person quicker than fear—Nova grabbed one of the paper snakes, its body transforming into a white Thread, and closed her eyes.

Harvesting Center, Callisto, Lyra.

She felt the tug behind her belly button and was rushed through the stars once more. A space where light and dark collided. Where time held no meaning. She relaxed into the bigness of the Inbetween, squinting into its depths. Why did everything feel so *right* here, when her world was so wrong?

Then, a slight pressure on her back, around her forehead. Her own heartbeat thrummed in her ears. Nova smelled the damp moss of Lyra. The sheets were silky under her fingertips.

Sitting up, Nova checked the clock on the back wall by Archer's desk. It had only been an hour since she'd entered the dream, but the Threads buzzed with power. She glanced at Eris in the bed next to hers. His eyelids trembled.

She hesitated, torn between taking another shift or leaving. Maybe Cally would be home early and she could have a real conversation with her sister about what she was always so afraid of. Nova wondered whether it had anything to do with the Threads, Processing, the Void getting stronger. But Cally was probably out with Ceres. Every time Nova saw the captain, he seemed weighed down. The Sentries now dealt with more disputes amongst the citizens as resources began to run thin. Not even the Ancients' warnings to control their emotions could appease Callistians any longer. Fear ate away at everyone. Ceres and Cally had delayed becoming united until things settled down. Nova wondered now if that would ever happen.

Nova walked up to Archer's desk and handed him the three Threads she'd gathered from Elaine.

"Good. Good," he said, weighing them in his hands and documenting their worth for the Processors. He took her circlet next and wiped it clean of Elaine's location with his tablet. "Are you staying for another?"

Nova looked again at Eris. "Yes."

"Very well." He inputted the next assignment and handed the circlet back, along with a new card. She noticed how ragged Archer looked but didn't say anything. He would take it as an offense. A few of the other Harvesters had woken and, bleary-eyed, made their way to the desk for another shift.

Nova hoped Archer would give them happy dreamers, but she

knew grief produced just as strong Threads as joy. Nova sighed and settled back onto her bed.

She could hear Archer counting down once more and Nova glanced at the assignment: *Cecily Reynolds*. She closed her eyes, wishing it was Arlo's name on the card.

~

A week later, she found her way to Arlo's dream.

She plopped down on the floor where he sat, scribbling furiously in a notebook. He jumped in surprise, tearing a hole in his paper with his pen. They were in a small dwelling, and when she moved to the window to get her bearings, she laughed. "Are we in a *tree*?"

"Tree house." He smiled, freckles stretching. "I always wanted one as a kid."

She sat on a stack of paper and looked around. It was crowded with books, notebooks, and canvas. She reached out a hand to touch the bright red walls—they smelled sweet. "Are the walls—?"

"Candy, yeah." He shrugged, and pulled off a long piece, popping it in his mouth. "Mmmm. Cherry."

She grinned but didn't try it.

Arlo set down his pen and leaned forward. "You look tired."

Nova wiped a hand over her face and ran it through her hair. "Why thank you."

"I didn't mean you looked bad. Because you don't. You never look bad. I just meant . . ." His neck turned splotchy and the treehouse grew warmer. Arlo's embarrassment and hers mingled into one. "I need some air."

He stood, and to Nova's surprise, jumped out of the window.

Nova gasped and shot to her feet, her instincts overriding the logic that they were in a *dream* and Arlo couldn't be harmed. Peering from the window, she saw tall mushrooms that looked like the caps on Lyra. Though their bioluminescence was white instead of blue, and they were slightly wider. Arlo steadied himself on the top of a mushroom, arms wide, the king of his dream.

"What is this?" Never had she seen Earth mushrooms that

mimicked Lyra's.

Arlo motioned around with a hand. "I think a lot about the stories you tell me. Write about them too. About Lyra and Selene and Callisto. About you and Cally and your people." He tucked his hands in his pockets. "I daydream about some of the details, though I doubt I get much right."

Nova stepped over the windowsill, her sandal finding the spongey fungus. Arlo took her hand, steadied her. "Our caps glow blue," she said. "Other than that, they're perfect, Arlo."

He traced her knuckle once before releasing her hand.

Arlo looked away, squinting through the trees and caps as if he could see what lay past them. "Mom's cancer came back," he said, voice low and rough. The wind shifted, cutting across them.

"*What*? I thought it was gone?"

"They were never certain they got it all."

"*Spores*, Arlo. I'm so sorry. How bad is she?"

"It's even more aggressive this time. They gave her a year. If she chooses to undergo another round of chemo, maybe a bit longer." He shrugged, but his quivering bottom lip and the emotions swirling in the air told Nova he was far from fine.

She pulled him into a hug. Arlo's breaths shuddered and Nova squeezed her eyes shut, wishing more than anything she could take away his pain as easily as she harvested Threads.

After a few moments, Arlo pulled back and wiped his red-rimmed eyes. "Thanks. I needed that."

"I wish . . ." Nova huffed, frustrated. "I wish Earth had magic. Then you could process Threads and maybe they could be turned into some kind of medicine. Or, or a Healer could fix your mother's ailment."

"What do you mean? Do your Processors make medicine?"

"Well—no, not really. Not directly for people at least. They change harvested Threads into something other than what they were in dreams."

Arlo cocked a brow.

"So, for example," Nova continued, "in a dream recently, I harvested a Thread that had been a paper snake. I can only turn that Thread back into a paper snake. But a Processor can transform it into an element or mineral that nourishes our sunless planet."

Arlo nodded. "That's trippy. Glad I never asked for details when we were kids." He laughed, eyes sparkling with leftover tears. "I never would've believed you then."

"But you believe me now? I'm not just a figment of your imagination?"

"I have a pretty vivid imagination, but I don't think even I could've dreamt up you and Lyra. Besides"—he smiled, lopsided—"you won't leave me alone. So, you're either real or I'm delusional or something." He brushed her arm where her Harvester mark gleamed, his gaze softening.

Nova's lungs constricted and she crossed her arms, forcing out a chuckle. "Oh, *really*? Well, I'll just go then." She turned and jumped to another cap.

"Hey! I'm joking!" Arlo called.

Nova jumped to the next cap, righted her off-kilter balance, and then smirked back at him. "Come on!" She leapt to the next, then the next, gaining speed with her long legs. Every step was a step further from her worries.

Arlo laughed and giddiness sparked the sky with flashes of light that looked like tiny explosions.

As they ran over the mushrooms, the caps flared brighter. Nova's eyes stung with gladness. This reminded her of long ago, playing chase with her sister under the mushroom caps on Lyra. The fond memories of her childhood washed over her. Things had felt lighter then. Not even the Void had seemed so dark.

They were out of breath by the time they reached the end of the Earth-Lyra forest. Before them was a mountain range, rimmed with snow peaks.

"Why"—Arlo said, collapsing on the cap—"am I out—of shape—in my dreams? It's not—not fair."

Nova tried to steady her own breathing as she sat beside him. They remained quiet for a while, letting the sunset spill over them. As the great star slid behind the peaks and the sky sunk deep into violet, cold reality settled back on their skin.

"If a rift was found," Arlo said his unsure voice blending hope and fear, "I wonder . . . could I bring my mom through? Maybe your Healers could help her?"

Nova bit the inside of her lip. She wanted to be honest; Lyrans would more likely capture and interrogate a human who stepped into Lyra, rather than help them. If they ever found out Nova was *talking* to a human, and spilling their planet's secrets, she would be punished. The Ancients would not want anyone from Earth to find out about Lyra. And the odds that they would *find* a rift was even more far-fetched. But Arlo didn't need more bad news tonight.

"Yeah, maybe." Nova shrugged. "Though Lyran bodies don't suffer from cancer, so our Healers would have no idea how to treat it." Arlo stiffened and she knocked her shoulder gently into his. "But you never know. Stranger things have happened. I'm talking to *you*, for one."

"Did you just call me strange?"

"Hmm." She twisted her lips in thought. "Yes, I guess I did."

Arlo stretched his legs, crossing them at the ankles. "I know it's a long shot. Anyway . . ."

He turned to study Nova and she realized how close they were sitting. She could count the freckles littering his cheeks and forehead.

"What's going on in your life, Nova? Tell me everything."

She stilled, glad Arlo couldn't sense her fears on the wind like she could his. She glanced away from him. "The Void is more problematic. Though—according to Cally and Ceres—the Ancients ignore it. Everyone's on edge. I barely see Eris these days unless it's at work." She blinked slowly, looking at Arlo. "It's why I'm tired. When I sleep during Darknight I'm hounded by nightmares I can't remember. And when I sleep at the Harvesting Center it isn't restful *because* I'm working." She shrugged. "The only time I can truly relax is when I'm . . ." She flitted her eyes again over his freckles. She couldn't just count them; she knew them as if they were constellations she had named, and the feeling flip-flopped in her gut. It reminded her of Elaine Shebert's dream. The *longing* she'd thought was so silly at the time. *Had that only been a week ago?*

"When you're what?"

"Well," she said, chest tight as if she were tunneling into a dream. "When I'm with you."

CHAPTER THIRTEEN

Nova woke from Arlo's dream and blinked at the fading moonlight above her bedroom window. She shivered. Darknight was almost upon her.

A Harvester's magic was null during Darknight, but if they were already *in* a dream when the Void took over the skies, strange things happened. Nova had heard stories of past Harvesters who had glimpsed horrific visions and harmed human brains when they were caught in a dream. One of Archer's jobs was to make sure Harvesters were safe and pulled out of dreams before Darknight.

Tonight, in her bed, without Archer to watch over her, she'd nearly woken too late.

Rubbing away the shiver bumps forming down her arms, Nova walked dazedly into the living area of their pod. She stopped short when she saw Ceres and Cally conversing at the table, voices low, heads bent over some documents.

Nova flushed, first assuming they were whispering of romantic things, but their tone sounded urgent, and their posture was too tense.

"What's going on?" Nova said.

Cally jumped, and Ceres lifted his eyes like a predator caught with a kill. Cally scowled and gathered the paperwork. "Nothing, Nova." She rubbed her temple and stood with the papers. "I thought you were out?"

"No. Just been sleeping." Nova stepped closer to the table. "What are you guys doing?"

Ceres's strong shoulders sagged, his family crest, a leo ray, glowed just above his robe's collar. He and Cally glanced nervously at one another, and seemed to be holding a silent argument. Finally, Ceres leaned back, crossing his arms.

"I think it's time to tell her."

Nova's breath quickened. Ceres was on her side?

Cally mimicked his posture. "She's too young."

"She's of age now. The truth—"

"The truth is *dangerous*, Ceres."

Nova stepped forward. "Please, Cally." Her throat felt swollen. She hadn't expected her emotions to be so close to the surface. "I need to understand. Our parents' deaths—what *really* happened? I know I haven't been told everything." Her voice caught, and she placed a palm over her chest.

Cally took a slow breath, but when she finally met Nova's eyes, she nodded in resignation. "Alright, Nova. I'll tell you everything."

~

"You can't repeat this to anyone. Do you understand?" Cally said.

Nova, Ceres, and Cally sat around the table, hot mintle tea drifting from the clay mugs in their hands. Nova gripped her drink so tightly she barely felt its heat stinging her palms.

"I understand," Nova said, legs jittering under the table.

Cally's voice was low and quick. "A few days before they died, I heard our parents arguing in their bedroom. Father told Mother he'd found *it*. A rift."

"Wait—what?" Nova's ears rang. "But . . . how? Where did he

find it? Do the Ancients know?"

Cally shook her head. "He didn't say where. Mother wanted to tell the Ancients, but Father was hesitant. He said it was important—a matter of life and death—that they *not* know. Mother was furious and said he had an obligation to inform them. Father said he couldn't trust them."

"*Spores!*" Nova stood, her heart racing as quickly as her thoughts. She dragged her fingers over her scalp. "Is that how they died? *Do the Ancients know?*" Her voice pinched high and loud. "I-I don't understand!"

Ceres winced and glanced at the window. "Let's just remain calm."

"*Calm?*" Nova gaped at him.

Cally reached inside her sleeveless robe to a sewn-in pocket. When she pulled out her hand, she was holding a letter. "First, read this."

Nova snatched the letter and opened it.

Was it from her father? Had he confessed something?

But the clean scrawl was unmistakably her mother Ascella's handwriting.

Calypso,

If you are reading this letter, then your father and I have returned to the stars. I am sorry to leave you with the burden of not only losing your parents, but also becoming one at the same time. Protect your sister. Nova is much like Atlas, and she dreams of things that may not be attainable. Lean on those you can trust. Hold fast to the truth.

Your mother,

Ascella

The letter fluttered to the table.

"I found it in her belongings," Cally said. "Check the date."

Nova swallowed down her rising bile. The letter was dated a week before their death.

"This is why we must be careful, Nova. It seems Mother knew whatever they were meddling with was dangerous."

74

"Mother didn't like *any* research Father did. She was strict on us, on him—even by Lyran standards. Of *course* she thought his meddling was dangerous." Nova's jaw tightened. "She never believed in him."

Cally folded the letter carefully, sliding it back inside her robe. "She just had a different way to show her love, a quiet and careful way."

Nova swallowed back tears.

Cally met Nova's eyes with a gaze that could pierce moon rock. Hard and unyielding. "I can't do anything about what happened to our parents, Nova. My job now is to protect *you*. I can't lose you. That's why I've kept things from you."

"What *things*, Cally?" Nova said, voice rising.

Ceres placed his hand on Cally's arm, giving it a gentle squeeze. She hesitated, shaking her head at him. "Once we tell her, she's no longer innocent. No longer safe."

"She was never safe, Cally," Ceres said.

Nova sat back in the chair and gripped her sister's arm. "Just talk to me! Tell me what's going on, please!"

Cally held her breath before letting it rush out. She stood, her red hair flickering around her shoulders like the flames in the globe behind her. "Okay. Okay. You're right."

Cally sat back down.

"There is a group of people who do not agree with how the Ancients have handled things. A"—she glanced at Ceres then sat up straighter—"a rebellion. Ceres and I are part of the Movement to overthrow the Ancients."

Nova felt her eyes grow as wide as moons. "Are you *serious*?" She released a shocked and strangled laugh. "You're the biggest pair of rule-followers I've ever known!" Nova looked between the two of them. "It can't be—you can't—"

"Why do you think we follow the rules?" Cally said with the hint of a smirk. "If they don't suspect us, we can move more freely."

"How many are in the rebellion?"

"Hundreds—thousands maybe. It's been hard to gather as a whole, so we meet in small groups and send correspondences, sharing intel and plans. Sometimes in letter form. Sometimes Ceres and any other Messengers on our side communicate back and forth."

Nova glanced at Ceres—Captain of the Sentries. "It must be exhausting, pretending to be loyal to the Ancients and working against them." She cocked her head, studying her sister's bond.

"It is." Ceres nodded. "But my position grants me more information than most."

Nova leaned her elbows on the table, face nestled in her hands. "Alright. So, there's a secret rebellion against the Ancients. Why? What is it you're so against?"

"We believe the Ancients do know of the rift to the Inbetween—the one your father found—but they are refusing to close it," Ceres said.

A rift. "Why wouldn't they want to close it?"

"Because it's somehow connected to the Void," Cally said. "And the Ancients do not want to take drastic action against the parasite claiming our world."

"But—it's the *Void.* Everything we *do* is to fight it! The Threads." Nova touched her shawl. They were dormant now that Darknight had settled over their side of the world. "We process them to *fight back the Void.* Everyone knows that!"

"It isn't enough," Cally said. "It's a bandage on a seeping wound."

"Right, I know it's not enough. I've been working double shifts—we all have. I'm so tired. And . . ." Nova's eyes burned and she looked away. "And nothing seems to make a difference." Hopelessness flooded through Nova. She'd never trusted the Ancients after the lies they spread about their parents, but this was far worse than she'd even considered. "How do you know they don't want to get rid of the Void?"

Ceres shook his head. "That is what we've been trying to ascertain. Perhaps control? It is easier to manipulate people when they are afraid for their lives."

"No—not *why.* How? How do you know this? Have they said anything?"

Cally's fingers clenched into fists on the table. Her eyes and mouth screwed up, as if she'd tasted something sour. "Because we believe they killed Mother and Father. To silence their findings on the rift."

Nova's lungs emptied of air as if she'd been punched in the gut. Ceres tenderly touched her shoulder, and she sucked in a shuddering breath. Then many more. Her head spun and she rested it on her palms.

"Nova, look at me," Cally said, grabbing Nova's wrists. There was venom in her tone, but also something hard and weathered. "We haven't lost yet. We won't give in to fear." She softened as a tear slipped down Nova's cheek. "I need you to be strong for me. I know it's a lot, but we are not alone in this fight."

A fight. Not only against the parasite, but the rulers who were meant to keep them safe. Nova almost wished she hadn't learned any of it.

"What do you mean—we aren't alone?"

Cally stood and went to her room. She heard her sister moving her bed, then something like stone moving. "What is she doing?" Nova asked.

"Some things are too precious to destroy," Ceres said.

Cally came back in with a packet of papers, then spread them on the table.

"What is this?" Nova asked, but she recognized her father's handwriting. She had a few cards and notes from him in her own room. She cherished them more than her Threads. "Father's research?"

Cally pushed the stack closer to Nova.

"Doors between our worlds," Nova said, eyes skimming over the top page. She placed trembling hands on either side of the paper and read aloud:

"Rifts cannot be detected by non-magic humans. Only those who feel the pull to Lyra can detect them."

Nova's eyes flew over the words, eating up every sentence scribbled frantically in her father's slanted cursive. It looked to have been written in a rush, as though he'd been afraid of being discovered.

"A rift is like a magnet," Nova mumbled. "On Earth, the rift becomes an insatiable itch to magic-oriented humans—a need to enter through a gateway, to dive into a dangerous whirlpool, shimmy through a crack in a mountain, enter a door that wasn't there before. Humans may feel the pull of Lyra's magic because their DNA is the same as ours. Selene calls to those who can develop a gift, and their cells respond, urging the human through so the dormant magic can awaken in them."

Nova remembered to blink, rubbing her dry eyes.

"For a Lyran, the pull is different. Not every moon mage is affected. Our bodies do not desire Earth and are content to stay in a world where we've evolved into something more powerful.

"The pull of the rift—from what I have surmised—lies within Harvesters. They are the key. A Harvester's ability to visit a human mind gives us an edge of curiosity, a draw to emotion, and an ability to find the bridges to Earth. However, rifts are not meant to be created. Or kept opened.

"They open and close at the Inbetween's bidding, and no one else's. If we forced a tear in our reality to remain open, our planet would be compromised. Who is to know the catastrophe such an act would bring?"

Heart racing, Nova flipped through the rest of the pages. There were theories on crop rotations, moon dust, when the best time of night to plant was, what type of Threads were more powerful once processed, foxfire's unique qualities, and so on. But nothing was as chilling as her father's warnings about the rifts.

Nova's arms had grown numb. "So, he faced this horrible thing to help us. To help everybody. And was killed for it."

Cally looked at her fingers. "I remember the night they left. It was moonrise. I was barely older than you, Nova. Mother looked frightened, but Father . . ." She laughed sadly. "He looked like a man possessed by some great need. Like he could save the world."

Nova's chest squeezed. Memories of her parents' faces were so foggy, being seven when they died. But, her father's voice and words were still imprinted in her mind.

"They didn't return," Cally said. "A Sentry and Ancient showed up at our door a few nights later. Ancient Belinda said our parents had been consumed by the Void. But worse, that they'd been experimenting on it." Cally's hands curled into fists. "She claimed that the Void spread more quickly after their deaths, implying that their meddling had made it stronger."

"And they were labeled as traitors," Nova said. "I remember that part. But I never believed it, and neither did you—right?"

Cally frowned. "Of course not. It's what led that same Sentry back to our door the next night." She placed her hand on Ceres's hand and smiled. "He was the newest member of the Sentries—and particularly handsome—and he told me his suspicions of our parents' deaths." Cally fell quiet and Ceres cleared his throat.

"The Ancients caught a whiff of your father's intention to find and close this rift," Ceres said. "They sent a squad after them to Polaris. To stop them." His eyes crinkled in silent misery.

Polaris. Nova had never been to the fishing village at the base of the mountains before. Was that where the rift was? Was that where they died?

Nova swallowed down her rising grief. She had to get through this—to hear everything.

"Were they part of the rebellion? Or did—did they start it?" she asked. *Why had no one come to their aid?*

Cally surprised her with a watery-eyed smile. "Their death was the spark that lit the fire. There *would be no* rebellion without them."

"We owe everything to them," Ceres said.

Heat gathered in Nova's chest and behind her eyes. The betrayal of the Ancients was gut-wrenching, but she couldn't help feeling pride in her father. Even her mother. She hadn't been close with Mother, but she'd stood by Father's side in the end.

Before Nova's throat could close completely, she said, "Father's life work was about finding answers to the Void's reach and to stop it. To close a rift that isn't meant to be open." She paused, her pulse quickening. "We're meant to finish what he started, aren't we?"

Cally's smile wavered. "Yes, Nova. I believe we are."

Chapter Fourteen

Dread haunts each morning.
As I slip out of bed
Finding Mom in hers
Barely moving
But also moving too fast—
Slipping
To where I can't follow.

What lies on the other side
Of our beating hearts?
Our paper lungs?
Of failing bodies and
Broken homes?

My dreams whisper of other worlds.
A planet aglow, with power in its roots,
And magic in its people.

But what of a deeper magic?
Are there places untouched by suffering?
By death?

I long to see blue fire
Reflected in ink-black hair.
To feel the hum of Lyra's moon,
The possibilities of anywhere else.

How can I be Mom's constant
When I'm constantly wanting out?

I'm on a treadmill, full speed

Exhausted and going nowhere.
I'm here now—needed.
But when Mom slips away
What will I have left?

CHAPTER FIFTEEN

A few hours later, when Nova appeared in Arlo's dream, he was in an unfamiliar office, arguing with a man.

Arlo's father.

He had strict posture and an even stricter tone. The atmosphere was so thick with Arlo's tense emotions Nova could have sliced through it.

"It's the same old thing with you, Arlo," he said, throwing his hands in the air. "What are you going to *do* with your life?" His dream father didn't notice Nova, but Arlo hesitated, glancing between them both. Shame clouded the room in a thin smoke.

Nova strode up beside Arlo, facing the man. Arlo stood a bit taller in her presence.

"Well?" his father shouted.

"I'm seventeen, Dad. Do I need to figure out my entire life right *now*?"

"If you don't want to screw it up."

Arlo ground his teeth, and prickly thorns grew from the wallpaper, like what Earthen roses wore on their stems. Other than the thorns, the walls looked fragile enough to shatter.

"Fine. I want to—to—" He hesitated. Arlo's indecision made Nova's mind grow hazy.

His dad stared down his long nose at Arlo. "Just like your mother. Head in the clouds. That's why she never amounted to anything either."

Arlo's eyes, which had been planted on the floor, snapped up. The room's lights flashed a deep red, reminding Nova of the pulse plants outside of the Harvesting Center: *Warning. Danger.*

"*You*—" Arlo lurched toward his father, but before he could reach the desk, the man vanished. Nova released a tight, angry breath, but the room was still hot and prickly. Arlo's hands trembled at his sides.

"Arlo?" she said, tentative.

Arlo shook out his shoulders and arms and then turned toward Nova. His face was blotchy, but he offered her a stiff smile. "I'm sorry you had to see that. *Him.*"

"I've seen him once before." That dream hadn't been pleasant either.

"Should've had you unravel him."

Nova nodded, wishing she had. Though, even if she had unraveled Arlo's dream father, the truth of who he was wouldn't be forgotten. That, she couldn't help Arlo with.

Arlo folded his arms. "This was my dad's old office in the house we lived in when I was a kid. He was at his worst here. All business."

"But you find comfort here, too." She touched the arm of a leather chair. A brown Thread hovered at the edge of her sight, but she left it.

Arlo's gaze skipped to the window. "I loved it as a kid, before I really understood his ways—before his expectations weighed on me." He pointed to the large folds of the curtains. "I'd hide in there, listening to his voice. He had a way with words, my dad. Concise and . . . direct. He made everyone he talked to feel special. But his words could also pierce like a dagger." A river of regret swam through the room. Arlo heaved a breath. "At some point I realized what a waste of time it was trying to prove myself to someone who abandoned us. To prove myself to someone who never came back, not even after she got sick. And some days I'm afraid . . ."

"Yes?" Nova said.

Arlo looked back at her. "I'm afraid of how much of him is in me."

"Oh, Arlo, no—"

Arlo shrugged, as if it didn't matter. "I'm glad you came back tonight. But, enough about me. How are you? I can't read you like you read me, but it looks like something's up."

Nova hesitated. She wanted to dig deeper, to assure Arlo he wasn't anything like his father. His words had been like a balm to her over the years. But she felt his urgency to move past his painful memories.

"I found out some things about my father. About the leaders of our world." She hesitated. "Even about the rifts."

Arlo sat on the desk beside her. "What kinds of things?"

Taking a deep breath, Nova relayed everything Cally and Ceres had told her the night before. It felt good to loosen her tangled thoughts—to sort through them as she spoke.

When she finished, Arlo looked stunned. "That's *a lot* to hear in one night. Are you okay?"

"Not really. But if there's one open rift, maybe there are others. Maybe we can meet for real one day!" It was the one spark of hope that had come to her after her conversation with Cally and Ceres.

Arlo scratched his head. "Sounds like open rifts are a problem this Movement wants fixed."

"The rift connected to the Void is definitely a problem, but . . ." Nova stood and paced the room. "Father said the Inbetween opens tears in reality for humans if they are ready to pass through. Who knows—"

Arlo's brow furrowed in thought. "Mom probably would've felt the pull to Lyra, if she was meant to go, then."

Nova lifted a shoulder. "I don't know how it works, Arlo. But that's what I want to find out. Think of the possibilities!"

He grinned and it lit up his entire face. The room suddenly felt less oppressive. "It would be awesome to meet you. For real, I mean." His eyes glazed over. "To see Lyra."

"Even now? After you've learned about the Ancients and the Void?"

"Maybe a quick visit." He winked and they laughed, the sound getting caught in the heavy curtains.

"Do you have any ideas why the Ancients would want a rift to stay open? Seems like it's harming them too."

Nova chewed on a nail. "I can't come up with any reasons."

"Maybe the Void planted bugs in their heads or something."

Nova winced. "Bugs?"

"You know—brainwashed them. You have people who read each other's minds. Don't tell me it isn't possible!"

"It's—" Nova shook her head. "The Void doesn't work like that."

"Not that *you* know of. Maybe your planet needs a human to save you all." He opened his arms wide, as if accepting applause. "You're welcome, Lyra. You're welcome."

Nova giggled and swatted his arms down.

"Hey!" Arlo grabbed at her hand to keep her from hitting him again. "I was living my *moment,* alien-girl!" They locked eyes and Nova's stomach flipped again, then they both looked down at their hands.

"I like talking with you," Arlo said. "It isn't fair, really. Reality pales when compared to these moments."

Nova bit back a smile.

"Sorry. That was so cheesy." He chuckled and let go of her hand. "It definitely sounds better in writing."

"No—it's okay. I like talking with you too." She frowned. "But I am sorry your days are not as enjoyable." She wondered if he had any close friendships on Earth like she had with Eris and even her sister, despite their age difference. Arlo had mentioned a few names in passing over the years, but no one who seemed to stick.

"Yeah. It's just weird. Most of my friends are making college plans, but that isn't even an option for me. I'm stuck here taking care of Mom." The room grew hot again. "I shouldn't talk like that. She needs me and I'm being a jerk." His face grew red.

"It makes sense to feel stuck," Nova said. She swallowed,

stepping away from him. She couldn't go far, but she needed some space. Some air. It was too hard rifling through the heavy feelings and wondering which were Arlo's and which were hers.

"Could we change scenery?" she said, fanning herself.

"Oh." Arlo shoved off from the desk. "Um, let's see . . ." He screwed up his face.

The walls began closing in.

"Not what I was thinking," Nova said, inching toward the center of the room.

"This isn't me. Is this you?"

"I can't manipulate your mind, remember?"

The walls kept pressing in. Arlo's emotions were more of curiosity and confusion than fear over the claustrophobic heat continuing to choke her. Maybe he was waking up? Nova closed her eyes, thinking of home, waiting for the Inbetween to pull her through. The walls kept coming.

She felt no pull.

"Arlo . . ." Her voice shook. "Something's wrong. I can't leave." Nova breathed in staccato beats. Arlo's face was warped in concentration, veins bulging from the side of his forehead.

He took a deep breath and said, "I don't know what to do! What will happen to you if you can't get out of my dream?"

Nova leapt closer to him with a squeak as the leather chair and desk were absorbed into the wall. "I'll, uh, I don't know exactly! Get sucked into your subconscious? Get lost in an onslaught of your thoughts and feelings until you sleep again?"

Arlo cursed and yanked her to his side. "That's not great."

"Not really, no!"

The walls crept closer still, and Arlo said, his voice quiet and steady, "I've got you, Nova. I won't let you get lost."

As if a chord tugged to unravel her limbs, all the tension went out of her, and Nova threw her arms around Arlo, pressing her face into the spot between his jaw and neck. He smelled like dewy sheets and something sharply sweet, like baked honeycomb. His sweater was scratchy against her bare arms, but she didn't let go. He didn't either.

The walls were so close she could feel them press against her back. She clenched her eyes closed.

Arlo vanished like a flame spluttering out. Nova stumbled but caught herself before she fell over.

There were no walls. Only wide-open space. At first, Nova thought she'd made it to the Inbetween, but the gleaming wood floor was still beneath her feet, stretching into infinity. Above were stars and planets and deep night.

Nova? Arlo—distant and weak.

She whirled around, but he was nowhere to be seen.

Nova's stomach lurched. *Was* she lost in his mind? She summoned up images of Lyra—*glowing flora, Cally, Eris, Ceres, Callisto, the Dream Glade*—but the vision before her was set. She wasn't going home.

Nova!

"Arlo? Where are you?" Her voice didn't echo how she thought it would. It sounded too close, like it was inside her head.

A ripping sound stopped Nova cold. She flinched, bringing up her arms. The distant stars were falling, bending. The sky, tearing away. A dark, writhing mass was slipping through the wretched emptiness.

Horror held her silent as she watched its inky tendrils snaking toward her.

The Void.

How was it *here*? Arlo couldn't dream it so perfectly. But there it was, breaking into his subconscious.

It loomed closer. Watching her. Waiting. Nova took a shaky step back, acid rising in her throat.

Nova!

She didn't answer Arlo this time. She couldn't speak.

A single tendril drifted near her. It looked smoky—like what made up the miedo beastias. It writhed and lurched, and that's when Nova realized it was trying to squeeze itself all the way through the tear it had created. But would it pull itself into Nova's mind, or Arlo's?

"The Void lives everywhere now," her father said. *"There"*—he pointed up

to the sky—"here"—he gestured around the forest. "And that means sometimes, also, here." He tapped his chest, then hers, right above her thundering heart.

The tendril curled around like a ribbon, pulsing with energy and otherworldliness. A sentient parasite, radiating intelligence.

It was intoxicating.

It gently tugged at Nova's mind, beckoning her even as she inwardly screamed at herself to run.

Run? Run where?

Who could outrun this?

They were doomed.

Nova took a shuddering breath and bent over her knees.

The smoky tendril fluttered nearer; a whisper of euphoria rolled over her like waves in a stormy sea. Dizzy with desire, Nova lifted her hand. She reached out, drew back her fingers with a gasp.

What was the harm in a single touch?

The long-ago night with her father and the moon bear swam before her eyes.

A single touch was lethal.

"*What are you?*" she screamed.

More confusion. More noise and hunger. Fear paralyzed Nova and she realized this thing, this entity, was bigger than anyone knew. They couldn't defeat it with processed *Threads*.

It was toying with them. They couldn't defeat it at all.

Hopelessness found its claws and sank them into her.

All she could think of was Cally and Eris. *Home. Take me home. Please.*

Her stomach tugged.

She was in darkness once more, but not that of the Void's. This was something much sweeter. Something reassuring. The Void had *withdrawn*? How? Why?

Nova had been delivered to the Inbetween. She was going home.

Relief spread through her aching chest.

But she was not alone.

She felt someone gripping her hand—gentle at first, then tighter.

It was a boy with russet red hair and a sea of constellations written on his cheeks. A boy who'd promised she would not be lost.

CHAPTER SIXTEEN

Nova's eyes flew open. A dark figure hovered over her bed and she shrieked, throwing out her arms. The Void's presence clung to her every nerve and for a wild second she assumed it had taken residence in her pod.

"Nova! It's me!"

Blinking, Nova sat up, her eyes adjusting to the soft blue light of the orb hanging from a hook on her wall. The person in front of the light was coated in darkness. But she knew that voice, knew his tall outline, knew that wavy hair.

"A-Arlo?"

He stepped back and looked around the room. "Are we. Did we—" A piece of hair stuck up on the side of his head and his clothes were odd—shorts and a baggy shirt. "Nova, where are we?" By his incredulous tone, Nova already assumed he knew.

And she knew, too, even though it was impossible. If it hadn't been for the lack of Arlo's emotions pushing in on her, or the perfect details of her room, she might've assumed they were still dreaming.

She got out of bed, trying to read his expression. "We're on Lyra, Arlo."

"This—*what*? How? I don't understand!"

Neither did Nova. Had she brought him through?

The door opened and Cally's silhouette paused in the arched doorway.

"What's going on?" Her eyes widened when she saw Arlo. "What in the *worlds*?"

"It's—it's not what it looks like!" Arlo said, scuttling away from Nova's unmade bed. He tripped over a small table and crashed onto the floor.

Nova gasped. Her face felt like it had been baked under Earth's sun. She helped Arlo to his feet and they both stared dumbly at her sister.

Cally's gaze fell on the circlet still dangling from Nova's hand. She snatched it away, then took in Arlo's clothes and lack of silver eyes and tattoos.

"It *isn't* what it looks like? Because what it looks like is that my sister has used a circlet—illegally, I might add—to visit a human. And then, *somehow*, brought him to Lyra."

"Oh." Arlo deflated, glancing at Nova. "Well, then it's exactly what it looks like, yes."

"Cally, I can explain," Nova said.

"Can you?"

"I—" She lifted a hand, then waved it around helplessly. "No not really. Not about how he was pulled through, at least."

"How long have you been using this?" She lifted the circlet.

Nova lowered her head. "Three years."

Cally scowled at them. The silence rang in Nova's burning ears.

"*Why?*" Cally glanced at Arlo who had retreated from their argument. "And why aren't *you* more scared? You're on a different planet with two strangers!"

"*One* stranger, actually," Nova said, trying not to shrink from her sister's wrath. "Arlo can see and speak with me in his dreams—which is why I went back." With a shaky breath, Nova revealed everything to her sister, including the reason she'd broken into the

Harvesting Center all those years ago.

Cally cursed, sinking onto Nova's bed. She still gripped the circlet in her pale hands. "And you don't know how he came through, or how to send him back?"

Arlo shifted. He was leaning against the wall with arms firmly crossed, clearly not wanting to get between the sisters. But now, he pinned Nova with a torn—even pained—expression. "I was wondering that myself. I want to explore Lyra with you. To see the glowing caps and the Dream Glade, but," he hesitated, "there *is* a way to get back, right?"

Nova's throat felt raw as if her screams in Arlo's dream had really happened. She shivered, remembering how the Void's smoky tentacles had grasped for her. Its intelligence. An ancient mind of destruction—

"Nova?" Cally said.

Nova rubbed her arms. "I don't know. I've never heard of a Harvester bringing a human into Lyra. It shouldn't be possible." But, she reminded herself, neither was speaking to a dreamer.

"Do you remember anything?" Cally asked Arlo. "How you might have been brought here?"

Arlo's brows lowered, jaw tightening. "I remember something whispering to me. Something dangerous. Something . . . powerful."

The Void. Nova bit her tongue.

"But you saw nothing?" she said.

"I just saw you. You were scared. And you were talking to something." He scrunched up his eyes as if the nightmare was slipping away from him. "But I couldn't get to you, like some invisible wall was in front of me. A force field, or something." He pressed his hands out, fingers shaking. "And then, it gave way and I fell toward you. You were fading and I . . . ." He looked down.

"You grabbed my hand," Nova finished. "Right when I was called back to the Inbetween."

"Yeah." He curled his fingers into a fist and dropped it to his side.

"You didn't know what would happen, Arlo," Nova said, walking to him. She touched his shoulder and marveled at how much more real he felt.

Dreams heightened a human's emotions while other sensations shifted like sand. But this was Arlo. Truly him. *Here!* Not just his mind's projection. He had more freckles in real life, and a scar over his left eyebrow, and as he studied her, she noticed his eyes were more turquoise than mossy green—most likely because of the foxfire—but otherwise, he looked the same.

"Maybe not," he said, blowing out a breath. "But I can't stay here forever."

Nova's stomach sank, but she knew *why* he couldn't stay—and why he needed to return sooner rather than later. "Your mom."

He nodded tightly.

"What about his mom?" Cally said.

"She's sick," Arlo said. "And I abandoned her."

"No you didn't," Nova said firmly. "We'll find a way to get you home before she even realizes you've left. Alright?"

"How?" Arlo said.

Nova turned to Cally. "The rift the Ancients are hiding—how do we find it?"

Cally shook her head and stood, dropping the circlet back on Nova's bed. "We aren't finding anything right now, Nova. It's too dangerous and we aren't ready. Ceres and I were going to search for it in a couple months. The plans were to—"

"Hang the plans, Cally!" Nova said. "What do you think the Ancients will do if they find a human hiding in Callisto? They will lock him up or—or worse." Until last night Nova wouldn't have thought their cities' leaders capable of such actions. But if they'd killed her parents—*Lyrans*—for trying to defeat the Void, what might they do to a human who came through from Earth? At the very least, they wouldn't let him return with the knowledge of Lyra. But Arlo already looked scared enough, so she just said, "They'll assume we used a rift. And you know Arlo will be linked back to me. To *us*."

Cally groaned. "Then the Movement would be compromised." She buried her face in her hands. "*Spores.*"

Nova held her tongue, waiting for Cally to sift through the probabilities. Rushing her sister never helped. She did not act on impulse; facts and a clear objective was where she thrived.

"Alright." Cally nodded and walked to the door. "I need to speak with Ceres. You two—don't leave the pod." Her eyes scanned Arlo's hair and face. "He's the most human Human I've ever seen. He'll be a *rotting* target once he steps outside."

Arlo frowned after Cally's retreating form, and then he looked at Nova. "I don't think that was a compliment."

~

Ceres entered the pod behind Cally, and to Nova's surprise, so did Eris. When the two of them saw Arlo sitting at the table with Nova, they stopped short. Ceres seemed more curious than anything, but Eris's eyes flashed to Nova.

"Is that—?" He pointed to Arlo as if he were a specimen in a lab.

Nova nodded. "Arlo meet Eris."

Arlo jumped up, hand extended, grin wide as the moon. "I've heard a lot about you from Nova."

Eris looked down at Arlo's hand with distrust.

Nova laughed nervously and got to her feet. She stood between them. "Actually, Arlo. We don't shake hands on Lyra, we do this." She touched two fingers to the top of her sternum—on the soleil owl's forehead—then flipped her hand over, palm up, with the two fingers now pointing at Arlo. "It is a way of saying *our family honors your family.*"

"Um," Eris said. "Could the lessons maybe wait? I really need to know what's going on."

"Same," Ceres said.

While Cally brewed a strong batch of mintle tea, Nova explained how Arlo came to be there. Ceres's attention danced between them, but Eris folded his arms, his intense gaze fixed on Nova alone. She began to sweat under his scrutiny.

When she was finished, Eris nodded toward Arlo. "So we have a plan to return him then?"

"That's another complicated story," Cally said. She slid the steaming clay pot to Eris so he could fill his cup. Her eyes landed on Ceres. "We have to move up our timeline."

Ceres rubbed his smooth chin. "I thought that might be the case."

Eris looked at Ceres. "What are you talking about?"

"The plan was to bring you and Nova in on the Movement around the same time—when she was seventeen."

"*Movement*?"

Cally nodded at Ceres, and he revealed what they'd told Nova the night prior. She was glad they were telling Eris, because she was certain she couldn't have kept something so big from him. When Ceres had finished, Eris sat back, looking more surprised than when he'd first spotted Arlo. Nova didn't blame him. A human coming to Lyra shifted how they viewed dreamers. But a simmering rebellion shifted the way they viewed their city, their world. Their way of life.

"I—I don't know what to say," Eris finally managed. He raked his hands over his short hair and let them rest at the back of his head. "Why are you telling me this?"

"We want you to be part of it, Eris." Cally leaned forward. "You work tirelessly to help Callisto, and so do your parents, but it isn't enough. Not with the Ancients withholding information. Possibly even withholding a way to fight back with more force."

"If they knew how to fight back, why wouldn't they?" Eris asked.

Cally sighed, leaning back in the chair. "Fear, probably. If they battled the Void head on and failed, what would become of us?"

"But you want us to take that chance?" Eris asked. He frowned at Nova. "And you? You're on board with this?"

Panic rose in Nova as all eyes turned on her. The ancient voice of the Void still rattled around in her mind, and she thought she might never be rid of it. Her earlier confidence in helping Arlo back through a rift seemed less certain now. Adrenaline had worn off and reality was crawling back into her mind.

Going up against the Void would be like flinging a pebble at a boulder. Could they even make a single dent?

She twisted her fingers in her shawl, but her Threads were willful during Darknight and didn't soothe her with any happy feelings.

"Our parents died believing that it could be defeated," Nova said, raising her chin. Her father had stepped off the path to show her the infected moon bear. He'd faced it. He had looked into the Void's decay and had not cowered. "And I want to believe that too."

"That's the problem," Eris said, dropping his arms to the table. "If you're right about what the Ancients are capable of and I'm caught, my parents would suffer too. The Ancients would assume they're part of the Movement as well." He shook his head, looking more lost than Nova had ever seen him. "I want to believe there's a way to fix this," he said, "but I have too much to lose."

Nova's heart squeezed.

"If we do nothing, we might lose everything anyway," Ceres said and put his hand on Eris's shoulder. His tone was not cruel, only quiet and sure.

Eris froze, brows pressed together.

"I do appreciate you asking me. For believing I could help." He looked at Ceres. "Can I have time to think on it?"

Ceres tensed, as if suddenly unsure where Eris's loyalty might lie. But Nova knew Eris. He would never spill their secrets.

"Of course, Eris," Cally said. "It's a lot." She hesitated. "But we will leave at first moon light to find the rift—and try to get this human back where he belongs."

Eris nodded and rose. Nova tried not to feel betrayed as her best friend walked to the door. He was right—he had his family to think about. The people Nova was closest to were already in on the rebellion. Though she wanted him to help, she didn't want her words to sway him. It had to be his decision.

"And Eris?" Ceres called. "This information is highly sensitive."

Eris nodded. "I'll be as silent as the stars." He slipped from the pod.

"Alright," Cally said, jumping up and rifling through the cabinets. "Here's the plan: we go to Polaris. Mother and Father's trail led there before they were . . . stopped. There's also a safe house there."

"Then what?" Nova asked.

Cally pulled down glass containers of dried fruits and fungus, dumped them out, and began wrapping them in sheets of paper. "Then we use your magic—and Eris's, hopefully—to try and locate the rift. Father said Harvesters could sense them."

"Me?" Nova stood and helped her sister. "Wouldn't I have been drawn there before if that were true?"

Ceres joined them at the counter. "Not if the rift was far enough away. You've never been to Polaris, so perhaps you can only sense one when you're near."

Cally left the room, returning a moment later with five leather bags. Nova was glad to see they had two straps, so the weight would be dispersed. Hauling a load of clothes and essentials would be extremely taxing in her satchel. "That should feed us for a couple days. Enough to reach Polaris."

"Wait—what about the Void?" Nova asked. They would be traveling during Darknight. In the forest. "What of the beastias? And—and the other creatures?" The miedo beastias were the only land Void creatures, but there were other dangers apart from them. "Are we taking a transport?"

"Not with a human in tow," Cally said, glancing at Arlo. He was standing now, staring up at the Darknight sky through the window with a slight frown. "And even without Arlo, it would be risky. There would be too many questions. We have to operate with stealth."

Nova ground her teeth. Her sister was right. The Sentries were very strict about who could leave and where they could go. A spark tram on the moon rock road was the only safe way to travel between towns, but it was heavily monitored. And no one was allowed to travel off path into the woods, nor did many attempt such a foolish thing. If someone became infected by the Void, they could bring it back to Callisto. It wasn't worth the risk.

Until it was.

"How will we survive out there, Cally?" She dared not look up through the window at the pressing black that smothered their world. Could it hear their plans? Was it watching them now? "What if we're walking right into its arms?"

Cally stopped packing the bag and cast a wary glance at Ceres. "Whose arms, Nova?"

Chill bumps spread up Nova's neck and she shook her head. "No one's. It's just—miles of forest stands between here and Polaris. There is *one* safe road, but we can't use it without being spotted."

"I know." Cally squeezed Nova's chin and tipped her face up to the globe of foxfire flames above their head. "When Selene falls and our magic dims, we will not be left to things that lurk in the dark."

"But, I don't think—"

Cally cupped Nova's face. "We will not be on our own."

Nova's eyes stung. Her chest grew so tight she thought she might rip open. Stepping out of her sister's reach, she sucked in a quivering breath. Did they not understand the horror of what awaited them in the darkness? Besides that, they expected Nova to be able to *sense* a rift?

What if she failed them?

"Nova?" Arlo's voice was soft but piercing. She turned to him. He looked paler. It seemed shock had finally settled and leached all the color from his skin. No matter what she was feeling, Arlo had to be feeling it more. He was cut off from his whole world. His dying mother. His entire reality.

Arlo's calm voice, the smooth tenor she'd rested in during his dreams—it was here. *He* was here. And he needed her.

Nova's breaths slowed and she gave him a firm nod. There was a reason they were linked, she felt it deep in her gut. And if she had somehow brought him here, she could see him safely home.

Nova couldn't save Lyra, no matter what her father's notes said, but maybe she could save the Dreamer.

Chapter Seventeen

Stars carried me to a world
I barely believed was real.
But between worlds—
In that ocean of space—
With Nova's hand in mine
I was shaken, undone.

A single sentence in a story
But read all the same.
Laid bare and *seen*.
All my faults and fears,
Shame.

Spit out into a world
So alien and *blue*.
Like I'm in a dusk-lit pool.
Something calls to my mind,
A voice deep and ancient and . . .
And dark.
But something else sings
Through my veins.
I feel
As if I'm flying.

But have I flown too far?
Leaving behind every responsibility—
A mom who gave me everything.
My joy corrodes,
Wonder is tainted.

I'm no better than Dad.

What family crest would brand my chest?
A door. A suitcase. A road.
Abandonment written on my
Skin and in my blood.

Forgive me, Mom,
I'll find my way home soon.

CHAPTER EIGHTEEN

Worries crowded Nova's mind and tightened her limbs as she sat on her bed. The circlet was on her pillow and she touched its cool surface. Would it even work now that Arlo was here? Did she need it if she could just speak to him in person?

After Ceres left and Cally had made Arlo a mat in the living room and retired to her room, Arlo and Nova had whispered under the Darknight sky. His voice had held both wonder at being there—with her—and sorrow at leaving his home behind.

Nova felt unsettled when she finally left him to rest. Though Arlo had been the one to reach out and take her hand, Nova knew none of it would have happened if she'd been more careful. If she hadn't gone back to him all those years ago.

She slid the circlet under her bed and laid down.

The black mass above seemed to pierce her. She rolled onto her side and hid her face in her pillow. But she *felt* the Void. A cold chill ran down her spine and prickled her flesh. Heat pressed at the back of her eyelids, and she folded her arms around her body, trying to shrink.

It took several long minutes to control her erratic heartbeat and quick breaths, but finally the events of the night caught up with her, and weariness lulled her to sleep.

Like a riptide, Nova was pulled into a nightmare.

She scrambled against it.

But then she was blinking at the far-off Eridanus mountains— she'd seen the mountains in drawings of Polaris, but never in real life. There was a section jutting up like rows of crooked teeth. She spied the largest constellations above the cliffs: Juniper Lark's seven-point wings, and Orpheus Marrow's star bones.

Selene's glow trilled inside her. The forest leading from the ridge she stood on to the base of the mountains was lit with colorful flora like any other Lyran night.

With one step, she'd left the ledge and was surrounded by gnarled trees. The crocuses were too large—big enough to swallow her whole with their purple-petaled lips.

The path curved around a pond, its ground changing from squishy moss to something feathery. She looked down. Earthen grass? Nova marveled at how each blade moved with her fingertips.

Further in, said a soundless voice, a thought, but not her own. She ran.

Breathless, Nova burst into a clearing. Blue moonlight assailed her again, and it was brighter than before. When she took a step forward, her feet wouldn't move. The grass had grown into ropes, swallowing her ankles. Nova wrenched at her legs.

"Just a dream," she said between gasps. "It will be over soon. Just a dream. Just a—"

The moon dimmed, turning a dark, sickly gray. Dying. Dread crawled down Nova's body, planting her further.

The forest changed. Grass—except that which held her—was sucked into the ground like food into a hungry mouth. Cracks formed in the barren soil. Plants wilted, falling with incredible speed. Caps toppled over and released violent foxfire. Nova ducked as a blast of heat rolled over her head like a storm cloud, then clawed its way through the bent trees. Nova swore she heard the trees screaming.

A crash echoed through the burned forest, and Nova looked up to see a moon bear slamming into the ground and sliding across the blackened soil. Toward her. Nova yanked at her grassy chains to no avail. It stopped, its whiskers grazing her shins. The bear's shimmering black fur was growing duller as its life ebbed away. Its once glowing blue eyes, now pitch black.

She covered her mouth and nose. The bear's fur was rotting away, its stench engulfing her. She couldn't tear her eyes from it. It was like being back in the woods with her father, seeing the Void's work up close.

"Wake up," she said. *Just a dream. Just a dream.*

A howl interrupted her thoughts.

The miedo beastias swept in like a gale, white ribs and teeth gleaming under a storm of black fog that rolled over the entire clearing. Barks and cackles surrounded Nova and she plugged up her ears with a cry. She wanted to close her eyes, but fear pried them open with sharp fingers.

The stormy pack circled Nova and the bear, and she fell to her knees against the slashing wind and claws. Pain sliced her arms and legs and the beastias laughed in their husky way, their breath smelling like stale caves—rotten and musty. Nova tried taking in air but it was sucked from her lungs. They had stolen every small shimmer of light.

She reached down to feel the grass, the bear's fur, anything but the madness around her, but a sharp bark held her back. Gripping her throat, she pulled in the smallest amount of breath. The beastias' high-pitched, deafening howl pierced through her and she doubled over.

The wind lessened and she gasped with relief into her knees.

Were they retreating?

Looking up she could see the shapes around her. She swallowed down bile when her eyes fell on the bear. Its fur and flesh was stripped clean, not a single piece clung to its bones. Only that archaic scent of decay.

But the beastias had not left. They were watching her.

One billowed forward, its wolf shape transforming. Its back legs elongated until it stood upright, front arms dragging on the ground. Its snout stretched into a point, and the fur around its neck and face writhed like worms. It wore a dark cloak now, or rather, the cloak wore the beastia. Nova shuddered when its eyes beheld her — intelligent and endless, like the Void itself.

Let us taste your nightmares.

The voice was quiet but as deep as buried graves. Nova screamed.

She tore the grass at her ankles with aching fingers. The beastia stalked forward. Darknight was its cloak, and it seemed larger than it looked, as if it could swallow the stars.

Let us drink your dreams.

"No! Get back!" Nova reached for her Threads and cursed.

Wait. No. This was just a nightmare. Just a dream. The Void couldn't touch her here.

Could it?

The miedo stepped forward and its legs were bone and black tendrils, its feet mostly claws. The ground shook with its steps — enough power to rattle the world. To tear down galaxies.

It reached out a smoky hand, bone-fingers dripping with blackened roots, cloak skimming Nova's legs.

She went numb. What if she never woke up? What if —

Crack!

A splintering shot rang through the mountains. The beastia, mere inches from her, yelped and drew its tendril of an arm back. Its pointed snout stared up at the sky and Nova saw past its writhing fur and cloak. Another crack. Nova's gaze snagged on the heavens and she let out a strangled shriek.

The moon was shattering.

Nova couldn't look away, even as the grass cuffs shriveled and released her ankles. She stood, staring up at Selene. Lyra's source of life — crumbling. Nowhere would be safe if Selene was gone. The pack of miedos seemed to sense the same and they grew larger, their harsh barks and cackles consuming the air.

They were the Void. The Darknight. And their victory was complete.

Nova took a step back.

The glowing flora dimmed and the night grew darker.

Where could she hide?

Another crack, and the ground opened beneath Nova.

She fell into a pit that seemed endless.

When she finally landed, it was onto something soft.

Close walls caged her in.

Nova burst from her nightmare with a scream. She shook her head, but the haunting visions stayed. All her life she'd been curious to know what her own muddled dreams entailed, but now—now she wanted to forget. But for some reason, it remained. Just like in Arlo's dream. Heart hammering, lungs burning, Nova gripped her blouse which was soaked through with sweat.

Were the forgotten nightmares of every Lyran similar to her own?

If so, forgetting was a gift.

Looking up, Nova whimpered with relief. The stars and a deep blue were sweeping back the Void's presence as if it were nothing but an ink-soaked scroll.

Selene was rising.

"Our moon is strong," Nova reminded herself.

Not even the Void could cause such a horrific event.

A whooshing sound whispered from across the room, and Nova bolted from her bed as though she were hearing Selene break apart all over again.

"Nova?" Cally entered, looking around as if expecting someone else. "I heard you scream. Are you alright?"

"Just—just a nightmare."

Cally's shoulders relaxed. "I was worried you'd pulled another human through."

Nova laughed nervously. "Just the one."

"You're soaked with sweat." Cally crossed the room and felt

Nova's head. "Are you sick?"

"I told you. A nightmare." Her limbs shook and she closed her eyes for a moment, but it made the memory stronger. Her sister's familiar smell steadied her. "I'm fine."

Cally studied her. "You remember it—the nightmare." She cocked her head to the side. "I can see it in your eyes."

Nova glanced away but nodded. "It was the Void, Cally. It was in Arlo's dream first, and again in my nightmare—but this time it took the form of miedo beastias."

Cally's face drained of color. "What . . . what did it look like?"

Lyrans kept no drawings of beastias in any old scrolls or modern text. But even so, the stories had passed through generations.

"Like giant decaying wolves at first," Nova said. "And they were horrible enough. But then as one came toward me it changed. It grew and shifted and walked more like a person, as if it were reading my fears, as if it knew what would scare me the most."

"Father wrote how the miedo might be shapeshifters." Cally touched Nova's shoulder and squeezed. "But it was only a dream, Nova. Your mind formed them that way because you read Father's research just yesternight. Nothing more."

Nova's hope rose. "You think so?"

Cally nodded.

"There was something else," Nova said, gaining courage. "Selene broke apart. Darkness was everywhere."

Cally smiled lightly. "That isn't possible, Nova. If anything, it proves I'm right. None of this will happen."

"It felt like a warning."

Cally's silver-white eyes roamed her sister's tight expression. She took Nova's hands and then pulled her into a hug. Cally's Walker mark, an arrow shaft with three arrow heads in a row, gleamed at Nova from the corner of her eye.

"If we *are* being warned," Cally said into Nova's hair, "then finding the rift is even more important. Now, it's time to leave. Get ready." Cally released her and left the room.

Nova sponged off her sweat in the bathroom before dressing in a comfortable outfit, boots, and her shawl. She glanced up at the deep violet sky before taking a bracing breath and stepping out of her room.

~

The city was quiet when Nova, Arlo, and Calypso slipped out of the pod, but they still took the side roads toward the gate to meet Ceres, and hopefully, Eris. Cally insisted on silence and speed, but neither happened. Arlo couldn't help but remarking on everything he saw.

"So the foxfire is from giant mushrooms?" he said, pausing at the globes they passed under. "And what do you use to power your houses and vehicles? Do you have electricity?"

"Pods and transports," Cally said with impatience. She tugged on his elbow to get him moving again. Arlo wore one of Cally's robes to hide his human clothes, and though there wasn't much difference between female and male robes, Nova had to keep biting her lip when he adjusted the curved collar. Hopefully Ceres would deliver on bringing better suited clothing.

They turned another corner before Cally answered Arlo's question. "We get our light and some protection from foxfire, but the Processors create energy out of Threads for our other needs — but creating enough energy is difficult. So we use them sparingly."

He pressed his hand on the base of a fungus that was situated between a little storefront and another pod. The foxfire inside flickered and gathered at its white skin, as if investigating the stranger. He chuckled at the swirling light. "Incredible. How does it stay inside? It seems like it could burst right—" Arlo hissed and drew back his arm.

"What's wrong?" Nova said.

"It burned me!"

Nova took his hand to look at the damage.

"That's odd," Cally said. "Foxfire has a mind of its own outside of the caps, but contained, it's relatively safe." Her brows furrowed. "What did you do?"

"*Nothing,*" Arlo said, taking a step away from the fire and pulling his hand from Nova's. The flames flickered more frantically than she'd seen under Selene's calm glow. She almost felt sorry for the fire but had heard accounts of the havoc it could wreak if let loose without proper care.

"Maybe it's because you're human," Nova said.

Arlo rubbed his palms together. "Yeah, maybe."

"We need to keep moving," Cally said. "Ceres is waiting."

They zigzagged down seven more streets before they came to the edge of the city. Two forms crept from the shadows and Nova backed into Cally, heart thundering. But then she broke into a smile when she recognized Ceres and Eris.

"Eris—you came!" She threw her arms around him and squeezed until he grunted with discomfort. She knew how much he hated to be touched, but in that moment she didn't care. Finally drawing back she looked up at him. "What about your parents?"

He shrugged a shoulder. "Father is the one who inspired me to come, actually." Ceres looked at him sharply, but Eris waved a hand. "I didn't tell him anything. I just said to him, 'if there was something you could do that would turn our world around, would you do it? Even if it risked everything you cared about.'" Eris met Nova's gaze. "He said that if he didn't use his gifts and knowledge to help our people, then what was the point?" He looked around at the group, his gaze hesitating on Arlo. "If there is a way to turn the tide, I want in. Not just for my family and friends, but because it's the right thing to do. And it's what my parents do every day in the Processing Center."

Nova's eyes stung. Eris had always been the noblest and kindest person she knew, but the fact that he would risk everything . . .

"Thank you for coming with us," she said, her throat tight.

"Yes," said Ceres. "Welcome to the Movement. Now, to the fun part." His tone sounded anything *but* fun. "Eris and Nova, we need a small distraction so we can get out of the gate undetected. We are relying on stealth so they don't detain us for any reason."

Cally nodded. "But first, I'll walk the bags to the forest, so in case someone spies us, we can say we're going for a quick hike down the path. But with a distraction hopefully no one will see us leave at all."

"Wait," said Arlo. "You're a Messenger, right, Ceres? Can't you convince the guards to leave?"

Ceres looked surprised by Arlo's knowledge of him but cleared his throat and nodded. "I could. Unfortunately, Lyrans are not mindless while I direct them. Once they are fully back in control of their bodies, they remember what has been done to them. As soon as I released the guards, they'd report what happened and the entire fleet of Sentries would be upon us. Which we want to avoid."

"Oh." Arlo blushed and folded his arms.

"It was a good suggestion, Arlo," Ceres said. "Keep using that brain of yours. As an outsider, you will have fresh ideas we might not have considered."

Arlo seemed to grow three inches.

Ceres turned to Cally. "Be safe. And don't tire yourself."

"Stop worrying." She winked at him, and then put a bag on her back and grabbed two more. "See you soon." With a breath of wind and a spark, she was gone.

"Whoaaaa." Arlo stumbled to where Cally had been moments ago. "Okay. Who do I talk to to get *that* power?"

Nova laughed. And then, with another gust of wind, Cally was back. Her entire body vibrated in a blur, as if she were caught between two places. She took the last two bags without a single word, and on her return, she slouched. Ceres moved behind her and let her rest against his chest as he handed her a bag of morellen crisps. "Eat."

Nova handed her water.

Though a Walker's power was helpful for being quick, her sister hardly used it. It physically took so much out of her. After a few more moments, Cally's jittering stopped and color crept back to her cheeks.

"Alright. Now for the distraction." Ceres looked at Eris and Nova. "We need something loud and bright a few spheres down the main street. The Sentries should rush in to investigate and that's when we slip out." He looked at Arlo. "I have clothes for you." He pulled out a pair of baggy pants and a long-sleeve shirt to cover his tattoo-less arms. "Put these on."

Arlo ducked into a dark corner to dress while Nova and Eris skirted along the pods. "What should we use?" Nova asked.

"I have an explosion Thread," Eris said, pulling a red strand from his arm band. "The dreamer was a real fan of blowing things up. And a fan of anger."

"Great. I'm looking forward to Raging Eris. But please don't hurt me."

He frowned. "Never."

Nova ran her palm down her shawl, thinking through her options. Sparks and flashes of emotions tingled under her fingers. She paused on a listless Thread. "How about a thunderstorm?"

"That would work. Alright, we've gone far enough." He turned to her. "Ready?"

Nova's stomach tightened. She'd never used her Threads in such a way. It was kind of exhilarating. And terrifying. *Mostly* terrifying.

"One, two, three—"

They flung out their Threads and sent them into the center of the street. Eris's explosive dream filled the air with flashing light and a *boom!* Nova yelped as they were both thrown back. She gripped her friend's arm who looked as stunned as she did. Thankfully, none of the pods had been harmed in the process, but a storefront had. That was *not* the stealth Ceres had wanted.

"*Spores!* That was too big." Eris scanned the area. "We need to go!"

Nova's Thread was forming into a storm cloud just above the orange flames. "Wait." She watched the Earthen fire in wonder. It changed the colors of the surrounding pods and street. Eris's dark skin took on a warm hue. She looked at her own arms, admiring the light browns and amber tones she'd only seen in dreams. "Eris, look how beautiful—"

"Come on. *Now.*" He grabbed her roughly under the arms and hauled her to her feet and into a side street. She pawed at the ash clinging to her loose hair and shoulders, choking on the suffocating smoke. But her thunderstorm would help douse the fire. "Hurry up!" he said. Nova frowned at his brusque tone. She didn't like Rage Eris.

Nova couldn't quite remember what her dreamer's emotion had been. And she was starting not to care at all.

"Why are we running?" she said as Eris tugged her along. "Everything will be *fine*, my friend." She giggled. "Friend is a funny word. Like frond . . . Are we fronds, Eris?"

"Nova, stop acting like a fungcake and hurry up!"

Nova laughed lazily. "Fungcake. *Fung.*"

They arrived at the meeting point where three frantic gazes peered around an abandoned pod. Nova could hear distant thunder and shouts. But it was fine. Everything was *fine*.

"A little overkill!" Cally snapped.

"Overkill? You told us to do it!" Eris said. His chest heaved.

"*Easy*," Ceres said, a sharp edge to his voice. "We have to go and take our chances."

Nova slapped Eris's back. "You were perfect, my frond."

"Oh, Selene. I hate those Threads." Cally looked down the street. "Let's go."

Just as Ceres said, two Sentries on post outside of the gate rushed inside the city, responding to the explosions. When they passed, their group bolted from the gate, cutting through a field. Pulse plants flashed a deep purple as they swept past in a rush. Nova had to be dragged by her sister. She didn't understand why everyone was so hasty. If they just *explained* their predicament to the Ancients, they'd surely just give the group a ride to Polaris.

"What's wrong with her?" Arlo said, as he ran alongside Nova.

"Arlo!" Nova burst out. "I'm glad you're here. Did you know your hair looks like a mushroom?"

"The Threads make them take on the emotions of the dreamer," Cally said. "It isn't always helpful in dire situations." She yanked Nova, who had stopped to speak with a glowing caterpillar. "Apparently the storm Thread my sister used has made her feel at peace, or unbothered, or something."

When they reached the tree line, the group stopped to rest behind a tangle of yellow tubular plants with hairy strands on the tops.

Arlo squinted at their swaying branches. "These look like *coral*. Or something from our oceans."

Nova thought coral sounded delicious.

Ceres, who was gripping Eris by the collar to keep him in check, nodded. "It's possible they are related. When humans first found Lyra, scientists brought all sorts of plants, animals, and organisms through to test them in the environment. The magic killed off some, but others flourished. When the sun was destroyed, the dark-dwelling creatures continued to thrive and even evolve." He motioned to the plant. "Cally has told me the similarities of our worlds. Though it all must look very strange to you."

Arlo laughed, looking around the forest. "It's as similar as night and day." He grimaced. "But I guess day might be a bizarre concept to *you*."

"Indeed. Night and Darknight are all that we have."

Nova giggled. "Bizarre." *What a funny word!*

Arlo laughed and she thought it sounded like ringing bells.

"Nova, Eris, you need to call back your Threads," Cally said sternly. "The job is done and we need to keep moving."

"Oh, Cal, you worry so much," Nova said, slinging her arm around her sister's shoulders. She got a mouthful of red curls and spit them out. "If only you could feel so free. Do you think the stars speak to one another?"

"Heavens help us."

"Fine," Eris said with a grumble. A thin streak of light shot toward them, barely perceptible, before wrapping itself around Eris's bicep with his other Threads. He shuddered and stretched his neck from side to side. "That was a rush."

"Your turn, Nova," Cally said.

"But—"

"*Now.*"

"Alright, alright. Calm down." Nova blinked lazily and then sent her thoughts to the Thread, calling it home, just like the Inbetween brought her back to Lyra. A tiny blur of deep gray shot toward her and then twisted into her shawl.

Nova fell to her knees as all her worries returned. "Oh." She gripped her shawl. "I think I might be sick."

Arlo crouched beside her, hand on her back.

"*Rotting* Threads," Cally said.

"They got us out," Ceres said. "I don't think we were seen."

Nova gripped Arlo's hand as he helped her to her feet. "He's right. It was worth it."

Arlo studied Nova with concern.

"If you're feeling alright, we need to get further in." Cally pulled on one of the packs piled behind the yellow plant.

Nova grew cold at the phrase *further in* but shrugged it off. She had to stay focused on the task at hand: getting Arlo to the rift. The others would know what to do from there.

The group followed Ceres's lead. He had scouted the woods a few times with his troops—always in search of people who went missing.

"How are you doing?" Nova glanced at Arlo, his forehead glinting with sweat in the bioluminescent light. Eris, just ahead of them, turned his head, as if listening to their conversation.

"Having the time of my life."

"Really?"

He cocked his head at her. "*Please* tell me sarcasm is a thing here."

"Never heard of it," she said, voice dry. Nova touched his arm, and he offered her a sad smile. It was still odd seeing him in her world. "But really. How are you doing?"

"There's a lot to take in."

"Alright," she said. "What's *one* thing?"

He sighed low and long. "This might sound weird. But . . . I feel so lost, and also like I've found something I've always been looking for. Both feelings are tugging at me." He massaged his chest.

Nova's face heated and she glanced at the back of Eris's head. She wished he couldn't hear their conversation. But her curiosity got the better of her.

"What have you been looking for?"

Arlo smiled, then motioned around them. "This place, I think. Another world."

Nova's heart sank. "Right. Yes."

She felt Arlo turn his gaze on her, but she kept her eyes on the forest. The spindle tree branches and caps were decorated with glowing orange fungi and tentacled plants. A multi-colored lampyris worm skittered across a rubbery flower as large as Nova's head. The petals snapped shut a moment too late, missing the lampyris. The plants around it swayed, caught in the wave. The Void hadn't touched this pocket of the forest yet.

"*You* are in this world, Nova," Arlo said softly. He looked around at the bioluminescent wood before squeezing her hand. She looked at him, hope filling her lungs. "And as far as I'm concerned," he said, "that's the best part."

Chapter Nineteen

Moths decorate the night
With wings of powder white.
A forest alive with color and sound.
Mushrooms the size of oaks,
With liquid fire in their veins.
Plants like coral reefs
Swaying, glowing, hungry.
A moon much too large
Somehow alive with power,
And the girl in my dreams
Of my dreams,
Beside me, hand in mine.
Her silver eyes more warm
In reality—*her* reality.

But I am unwanted here.
All I've caused is chaos.
A simple boy. A human.
But *they* are human too.
With hearts that beat like mine,
Hopes and sorrows that bleed
From every conversation and glance.

I am meant to return—*go back!*
But with each breath I become stronger,
More alive.
A new song of *what if?*
Plucks in my chest
Even though my world,
My home,
My life is a flare—*come back!*

So I carry the smoke
In the fibers of my clothes.

And I carry a secret too.
It has followed me through the stars.
A secret not even night, I fear,
Will continue to conceal.

CHAPTER TWENTY

As the group trudged further into the forest, Nova noticed subtle changes in the plant life and creatures. The bioluminescence in veins and roots was dimmer and the flora grew larger—giant rubber leaves blocked Selene's light from above. The air grew colder, damper.

Nova felt as if they were plunging into deep waters.

After talking with Arlo for a while, pointing out the plants she knew, and encouraging him that they would find the rift in time for him to get home, she left him with Ceres. She caught up to Eris and Cally, who led the way.

Cally's eyes scanned the forest floor for danger, her brain, no doubt, ticking through next steps—ways to keep them all safe.

"Where are we going, Cally?" Nova asked.

"Polaris."

"I know that, but we won't reach it by moonfall."

"There's a cave ahead where we can take shelter."

Nova glanced at the sky. Selene was already descending toward Darknight. "I doubt a cave will protect us during Darknight, against"—she looked around the forest and shuddered—"all the creatures out here."

"We have some protection," Eris said. He pulled a moon blade from the bag Cally had handed him. Ceres's sword clanked at his side behind them.

"That won't be enough."

"It will have to be," Cally said, wearily. "These are all the weapons we could gather and carry on our own." She felt around in the satchel across her shoulder. "And this." She pulled out the blue-orb necklace that had been their father's and handed it to Nova. A lump formed in Nova's throat. It was a pitiful light compared to the engulfing dark, but it somehow still buoyed her spirits. She slipped it over her head.

"What comes out at *Darknight*?" Arlo asked quietly in a voice full of dread. Nova felt the air grow colder, as if it was feeding on their fear.

"Things that thrive in the dark," Ceres said.

"The miedo beastias?" Arlo asked.

Ceres hesitated. "The miedo *belong* to the Void—they are its hands and feet. But there are other creatures who hunt under the cover of Darknight."

Arlo made a strangled sound and Nova peered over her shoulder at him.

"Good," he finally said, face clearing. "I was worried there was just one type of beast that wanted to eat me. Glad to hear we won't be bored."

Ceres chuckled. "Do not fear. There is safety in numbers."

Nova smiled at Arlo who returned it with a wince.

A distant shout echoed somewhere behind them. Everyone stilled, except Arlo who plowed into Nova. He steadied her before she could topple over. "It sounded far off," Cally said, "but I want to make sure." A spark and gust of wind brushed past Nova and the others as Cally sped off to investigate.

Another shout caught Nova's ear and she stopped breathing, straining to listen. Ceres's jaw was tight and his hand was on the pommel of his sword. If Cally didn't return soon—

Another gust announced Cally's return.

"Sentries. But they were heading North. We should be safe for a while," she said.

Ceres cursed as they picked up the pace again. "Someone must've spotted us entering the forest. But it's strange they're giving chase."

"Uh," Eris said. "That might be because my Thread explosion took out part of a building."

Cally and Ceres cursed at the same time. Cally said. "No wonder they're hunting us. They think we attacked the city!"

"Sorry!" Eris exhaled. "I wasn't in my right mind after we fled."

"Well, we can't go back now." Ceres motioned forward. "Hopefully we'll find enough dirt on the Ancients that it won't matter in the end."

Nova felt the increasing threat like a cornered animal. Moving forward was leading them into the darker parts of the forest where more wild things lived. Going back would lead them straight to the Ancients for questioning.

As if Arlo was dwelling on the same thing, he said, "What would happen to me, if we were caught?"

Silence spread around the group for a moment.

"We don't really know," Ceres said.

"But they wouldn't try to send me back." Arlo's voice was stiff.

Nova slowed and walked beside him to slip an arm through his. "We won't give them a chance to consider what to do."

Arlo swallowed hard and squeezed Nova's linked arm more tightly.

"They definitely won't let him return," Eris said from up ahead. There was a coldness in her friend's tone she'd never heard before.

"But *why* do they hate humans so much?" Arlo asked.

Nova shifted. She'd told Arlo quick snippets of their Genesis, but she didn't like talking about how Lyra began, especially with someone from Earth.

Ceres shared a wary look with Cally before answering. "Because our world was found by scientists and soldiers who came through a rift from Earth. When some people began developing powers, and some didn't, well . . . fighting broke out. Fear overtook the humans.

Self-preservation overtook the newly formed Lyrans. The bloodshed summoned the Void and the parasite took over our skies. That is what destroyed our sun so long ago." Ceres's shoulders lifted with a labored breath. "Many perished, but the Lyrans who survived closed the rift so no other humans could find us. If they did . . ."

"More violence," Arlo whispered.

Ceres shrugged. "So the Ancients believe."

"That's why we're careful not to leave a trace of our existence. Whether in their world or in their dreams." Eris glanced back at Nova and she dropped her arm from Arlo, frowning at him.

"We were careful, Eris."

He shook his head. "Not careful enough." He flitted his gaze to Arlo. "Clearly."

Nova's heart broke at his words. She wanted to have it out with him, to question his coldness, or even remind him that his Thread's explosion had been just as careless, but there were too many ears. So instead, they fell into a quiet rhythm. No one disagreed with Eris's comment—and why would they? He was right. But the longer the silence stretched the more suffocating it felt.

Cally led them around a blue pulse plant glade and then suddenly stopped. Ceres came up beside her. "We will have to go around."

Cally moaned. "But this is our path!"

"What is it?" Nova pushed through to see what had made them stop.

It took her eyes a moment to adjust to the darkness, and when they did, her stomach squirmed. Wet, black vines crawled over a huge section of the forest. They covered caps, trees, the moss—everything. Nova gagged as the scent of decay rolled over her. And something else. Something malignant pressed into her chest and raised the hair on the back of her neck.

"The Void?" Arlo asked, eyes wide.

Nova nodded. This was so much *more* than when she'd seen it eating away the moon bear.

Eeeeee!

The sound jolted Nova and they whirled around. A miroir hare squirmed at the edge of the Void. Its long back legs and curled tail were in the clutches of the Void's tendrils. The rest of the hare's silver fur, so shiny you could see your own reflection in its coat, was scrambling in the green moss, trying to pull itself to safety.

Nova bolted to the creature. Its eyes were wild and it screeched again when she dropped to her knees before it.

"Don't touch it!" Cally said.

"What?" Arlo said. "We have to help it! It's being eaten alive." He kneeled beside Nova.

Nova's gaze landed on the hare and she stifled a sob. The Void's touch was already consuming its fur, its flesh. Boils and pus formed up its rear legs. She scrambled back, away from the horrible sight. Away from the screams. The suffering. The hare's inevitable death.

"Th-there's nothing w-we can do," she said.

"*What*?" Arlo gestured wildly. "It's right here. Don't you guys have magic? Or Healers?"

"None of us are Healers," Eris said. "And even if we were, our power is no match for the Void's disease." His lip curled in disgust.

The hare screamed again and Nova's eyes grew wide as panic crowded her chest.

"He's right, Arlo," Ceres said. "There's nothing we can do for it."

Tears swarmed Arlo's green eyes as he looked between the Lyrans. "Seriously? It's . . . it's suffering." He reached out a hand to the hare as if to stroke its head.

"Arlo, don't!" Nova lunged forward.

The sound of metal sliced the air, then there was a flash, as a sword struck the miroir hare down its middle, a scream dying on its tongue. Arlo fell back, breathing heavy as he glared up at the sword-thrower.

Ceres stepped forward. His eyes were hard as he wrenched the sword from the dead creature and wiped its blood on a patch of moss. He sheathed his weapon and extended a hand to Arlo who had grown rigid.

Arlo pushed his hand away and stood on his own.

"There had to be another way." A vein on the side of Arlo's neck stood out. He took a deep breath, anger ebbing into something softer as his eyes fell back on the creature, on the spreading parasite. "I thought this world would have answers," he said bitterly, kicking a clod of moss with his boot. "But suffering. Death. It's everywhere. No matter where we go."

"Arlo —" Nova said, but her words tangled in her throat. She tightened her lips to keep them from quivering.

Arlo shrugged. "Do you feel it too? Your parents, my mom. This —" He turned back to the decaying wood. "What if nothing works? What if we get to the rift and . . . you can't get rid of the Void? I can't get home? What's the point?"

Nova's throat ached. She'd been so sure her father's research would lead them to answers, but at the moment their task seemed impossible.

Her shawl shifted and she glanced down. A pink Thread had unwound itself and was clinging to her arm. Nova could feel it trying to infuse her with courage. At her touch, the strand transformed into an Earthen flower — a dahlia struggling to grow through a patch of weeds. The flower lifted its petals upward. Nova had kept the Thread, not for its usefulness, but for its reminder. But in that moment, its perseverance felt weak in the face of the Void's cruelty.

She tucked the Thread back into her shawl, hope dimming again. No one else had noticed the Thread — all their gazes were fixed on Arlo and the dead creature at his feet.

"We have to keep going," Ceres's voice broke into the muddled dark. His tone was grim but not without the same strength she'd felt in the dahlia. "We have to find the answers others refuse to acknowledge — that there's a force stronger than what we see here." He swept his hands at the dead forest, at the hare. "Something we can use to rid Lyra of this darkness for good."

Arlo bowed his head, hands on his hips as he drew in a deep breath.

Ceres gripped Arlo's shoulder. "You can trust us."

Arlo nodded.

Eris, who had been standing with his arms crossed, jerked his head to the side. "Let's go. If the miedos catch us, we'll manage no better than that hare."

Nova tried to keep her focus straight ahead as they edged around the glade, but her eyes wandered to the dark parasite every few steps. The chill bumps never receded from her arms.

"Do you hear something?" Arlo asked, his voice so low and close it tickled her ear. "Voices?"

Nova held her breath and listened, but all she heard were their footfalls and the occasional creature crying in the trees. "No." She glanced at him. "Do you think it was Sentries?" She cursed and glanced over her shoulder. "We stopped too long back there. They could've found our trail."

"No. No, it wasn't Sentries." He scratched his jaw. "It sounded like whispers. But this place is weird. It's probably the wind or something."

Nova nodded. "Probably. But tell me if you hear it again."

"I'm sorry about back there." His hand dropped to his side, brushing her knuckles every few steps. She tried not to think about reaching out to hold his hand. "I saw that rabbit and something came over me."

"Me too." She shook her head, a sliver of hair falling over her shoulder. "It was horrible. And you've never seen the Void before — I can't imagine how you're feeling."

"For once." He laughed lightly.

"Right." Nova flushed. "I miss the safety of your dreams. But it's nice to be with you in real life." She sighed. "If only the timing was better."

"Agreed."

After a break to rest and eat provisions, they finally came to the edge of the decay and found their path again. Besides an entanglement with a pustal plant's petals that tried to pull Cally into its poisonous mouth and Arlo exclaiming, *do all Lyran plants try to eat you?*—and a moon moth landing on Arlo, leaving behind glittering dust on his neck—they didn't run into any other creatures.

Nova grew tired and footsore, and she strained to see the faint blue glow of Selene through the trees. The foxfire in the caps was dipping into the roots. The flames in their globes grew manic. Her lungs felt too small.

"Moonfall," Nova said, voice tight.

"It's alright," Cally said. "Because we're here."

Nova squinted into the murky landscape and spotted a mound of moss between two spindle trees. There was a dark spot just in the center of the little hill. "The cave?"

Cally nodded, and Ceres and Eris left to investigate with their globes and blades. The entry was small and Nova didn't think her friend's broad shoulders would fit, but after a bit of wriggling, he disappeared.

"How did you know there was a cave here?" Nova asked her sister.

"It was our contingency plan. In case we needed a place to hide." She glanced at Nova, her braided hair slipping over a shoulder. Even after all this walking her curls were still perfectly tamed. Nova's hair felt wild and unkempt in comparison. "I Walked all over this area, trying to find somewhere far enough from prying eyes, but close enough we could run to together."

"You and Ceres?"

Cally frowned. "You too, Nova. I would never leave you behind. We're family."

Nova's eyes stung. "Right. Of course." For once, she was thankful for her sister's preparedness. Nova wasn't sure what would've become of her if Cally hadn't been willing to become her guardian when their parents died. Or what she'd sacrificed since.

A scuffling sound caught Nova's attention and Eris emerged from the cave. "All clear."

Arlo and Cally squeezed through the opening, but Nova caught Eris's arm.

"Can we talk?"

He clenched his teeth. "It's getting darker."

"Eris. *Please.*"

He turned to her, eyes flashing. "I don't know what there is to say, Nova."

"We haven't had a chance to discuss anything since Arlo came through. Since learning about the rebellion." *Since the Void spoke to me.* She hesitated when he seemed to withdraw at Arlo's name. "I-It's a lot, Eris."

"Yes. It has been."

"I'm sorry I didn't ask sooner. Arlo has needed me to—"

"He needs quite a lot from you, it seems."

Nova flinched. "What does that mean?"

"Ever since you've met with him in his dreams, he's all you can talk about." Eris looked away, squeezing his lips together.

"That's not true!"

"And I thought whatever, that's fine, he isn't really *here.* She can't form a relationship with a vision. But then, surprise, he *is* here! And then *bam* our lives are turned upside down. For what? A boy—a *human*—you're obviously falling for."

"That's not—I don't—" Nova stammered, trying to force her angry words into a coherent sentence. "Cally and Ceres's mission to find the rift would've happened whether or not Arlo was in Lyra."

"But it could've been planned better. I could have had more time to think."

Nova folded her arms, glaring up at him. "Do you *regret* joining?"

"No." Eris softened as all the fight left him. "I don't think so. I just don't like . . . *him.*"

"Because he's human?"

"Because he's *your* human. Or you are his, or something." Eris scratched his head in agitation, his Callisto mark stretching on his arm. He exhaled and met Nova's gaze. True hurt lay behind his hardened façade. "I'm losing my best friend and I don't know what to do about it."

Nova shook her head and took a step forward. She gripped both of his arms, just above his elbows. "Eris. You will never lose me. Not to anyone."

"I wish that were true." Eris gave Nova a sorrowful smile, then reached up and playfully tugged a strand of her hair. His hand hovered near her shoulder, and she stiffened as his gaze searched hers. He cleared his throat and dropped her hair as if it were on fire.

Before she could ask him anything further, Eris squeezed into the cave's entrance, leaving her mind spiraling like the galaxies in the Inbetween. She stared at the cave and the soft glow now coming from inside. Sleep. They all just needed sleep.

But how would sleep ever find her after the night she'd had? And if it did find her, she feared what new and complicated visions would flood her dreams.

Chapter Twenty-One

I wear this shame like a tie,
Strangling me, but
If I don't fidget with it,
No one will notice it's tight.

This voice in my head
Is my dad's. Is mine
Reminding me of my failures
And laughing at the mess I've landed
Myself in once again.

But it's more than an echo of past.
One voice is forceful, alive,
Present.
Speaking to me from elsewhere.
A deep pressure spreads through my chest,
My head
Like I'm in the space between worlds again.
I'm imploding.
Who are you? I scream.
I am a friend, the voice responds.

But there are more whispers.
Prattle that rattles my brain
Like a busted fan, over and over
And I can't catch the words, only sounds.

I look at the girl whose world is falling apart,
Who needs me to be strong,
Though I feel paper-thin.
If I told her of these voices, my secret,

Would that glint in her eye fade?
Would she wish she'd never dreamt of me at all?

So, I hold this shame close
Tight, around my neck
Like I always have
And hope no one notices the choking.

CHAPTER TWENTY-TWO

Nova sat beside Arlo in the cave watching his breathing grow deep with sleep. Her body began to relax until she thought about the insurmountable obstacles they faced. Not just the Void, but the Ancients too. The leaders who guarded a secret so tightly they would kill innocents just to keep it safe. It made Nova's head pound with the injustice. If they had spared her parents, she would still have a full family.

Nova stared up at the ceiling. Unfamiliar lichen glittered on the surface like starlight, even though Darknight was at hand. She blinked back the tears brimming her lashes. Would the rebellion really accomplish anything? Would it shed light on what had happened to her parents? And even if Nova and Eris somehow sensed a rift, could Arlo go through it without any obstacles?

Nova's breathing tightened.

Father would know what to do.

"He'll be okay."

Nova squinted at Eris across the cave. He nodded toward Arlo.

"How do you know?"

He shrugged and studied his hands. "Because he has you, and you don't give up on people. Even if they're *sporing* jerks." He offered her a half smile—an apology—and she let out a relieved laugh, though she felt as if *she* should apologize.

"Thank you," Nova said.

"We need sleep," Ceres said from the opposite wall. Cally was tucked under his arm, head on his shoulder. "I'll take the first watch. You two—rest."

Nova slid down the wall and used a mossy stone as a pillow. A few shrieks and caws echoed from outside and she shivered, imagining what horrible things crept in Darknight. Things hardly documented. Legends exaggerated by childhood playmates and tamed by cautious parents.

Arlo shuffled around behind her, mumbling in his sleep. After a few more flops, he stilled. His hand was close enough she could feel it touching the strands of her hair. The tightness in her shoulders relaxed as she leaned into Arlo's familiarity.

A flicker at her chest made Nova close her hand around her father's necklace. The orb warmed her palm, and she felt the slightest movement, as if the flames were tickling her skin. So different than how unharnessed foxfire behaved in the wild: Dangerous. *Brilliant.*

Unlike the Void, foxfire was honest, warm. Their protector.

Nova brought the necklace up to study it. The liquid blue flame was intense, almost proud, as if it owned the world. And maybe it did. Foxfire had existed in the veins of Lyra since the Genesis— when humans first came through a rift from Earth. It was part of Lyra, unlike the Void, which their ancestors claimed had been drawn to Lyra by the scent of bloodshed.

Nova's eyes grew heavy even as her mind spun with more questions than answers. *Why?* was the last thing lingering in her brain before she found her way into a . . .

Dream? *Nightmare.* Nova shivered and spun in a circle.

"Fancy meeting you here."

Arlo?

They stood inside a cave, but a much larger one than they'd fallen asleep in. The lichen dotting the walls were larger, glittering like jewels. And it was just the two of them. Nova moved toward him, hesitating. "How can you be here? You're not a moon mage—you can't Harvest, you—"

Arlo took her hand, and she stilled. "Feels real," he said.

"It shouldn't be possible." Nova pulled away from him and walked to the glittering lichen, touching them lightly. They felt like rainwater. "I had a nightmare last Darknight. About the moon splitting and our world dying."

"That must've been terrifying," Arlo said.

"Very."

"But I thought Lyrans don't remember their dreams."

"They don't." She smiled lightly, even as her stomach clenched. "I have no idea why I remember it."

"Well . . . I hope this is a good dream," Arlo said, with a lopsided grin. "Maybe that's why *I'm* here."

Nova glanced at the cave floor where she and Arlo were now, where they were *asleep*. Where Arlo's fingers were entwined in her hair. She touched her own black strands.

Arlo's eyes followed Nova's movement and a flush crawled up her neck.

The cave dissolved into a million crystals. Nova squinted through the glaring light. They stood at the edge of a brine, stars littering the sky and waters alike, trailing off in a vestibule of space.

"Whoa," Arlo whispered. "Is this a real place?"

Nova dipped her hand into the wave that traveled up the white shore and over her toes. It washed the sand away and then rolled forward to spit it out again in a quiet dance between tide and land. "It's the Black Sea." She cut her eyes to him. "Do you remember me telling you about the Black Sea?"

Arlo ignored her question and shot her a tight smile. "It's okay if you're feeling confused, Nova."

"Wait," Nova said, horrified. "Can you . . . read *my* emotions?"

Arlo laughed and Nova grimaced, covering her face.

"Do you feel vulnerable, Nova?"

Arlo tugged down her hands, holding her wrists firmly, his thumb brushing along her thudding pulse. "It's all right. Your feelings are safe with me." There was something feverish in his gaze and it scared her. "*You* are safe with me."

Her heart danced a beat she didn't quite recognize, as if she'd plucked a Thread and was using its heady power.

"Arlo," she said. "Let me go. Please."

"If we find this rift," Arlo said. "Would you come back to Earth with me?" He ran his eyes over her face. "We could be together there. No more hiding. Or running."

"What?" She tried to step back but his nails cut into her wrists. "Arlo, what are you doing?" Never had he acted like this. Not in dreams *or* reality. "You're hurting me—stop!"

Arlo's eyes gleamed silver and something cruel swept over his expression, like a cloud passing over the moon. "You haven't even begun to understand pain, Nova Celeste." Her name rolled off his tongue in a low growl.

Nova tugged herself free and fell back, her hands sinking into sand. A wave crashed behind her, its water grasping at her arms, tugging her backward. She fought the tide and scrambled back to her feet, glaring at *Arlo*. No, not Arlo. A nightmare.

"You're not him."

The thing stood taller as if her words made it proud. "I'm afraid I cannot disguise myself so easily in lesser beings. Their idiocy makes it impossible."

Nova's salt-coated throat constricted. "*Lesser* beings? Who— what are you?"

The thing chuckled. But then she saw the ancient gaze behind Arlo's once youthful eyes. She noticed how it stood; somehow confident while also holding its body awkwardly, as if it had pulled on skin and bones without a care for how they fit.

"The Void," she said.

Its eyes were now fully black, and they slitted at her. "I have many names, but yours is the most amusing. A void? No, no, my speck. There is no lack in me—I am more than you could ever imagine." It cocked its head and smiled, but the skin of Arlo's mouth stretched too wide. The Void didn't blink or even seem to breathe. "I am Eijlek. A name given to me at the beginning of time."

"And—and what does it mean?" Nova wasn't sure why she provoked the thing. But if it kept talking, maybe it wouldn't do anything to her. She was no longer sure it couldn't harm her in her dreams.

"It is from a tongue that no longer exists. From the first planet I consumed." His smile remained, even as he spoke. But the words no longer came from Arlo. He looked like an empty shell. "It means *hunger*. Because I can never be satiated."

Another wave rushed over Nova's ankles and she grounded herself in its cool touch.

Wake up. Wake up.

"There's no waking until I allow it." Eijlek turned Arlo's head to the side. "Where do you think your nightmares come from, little speck? Did your kind imagine they *forgot* how to dream?" Its laughter was as deep and dark as loam.

Nova turned and sprinted down the beach, sharp shells slicing at her bare feet.

The scene shifted and Nova tumbled forward.

She was no longer near the brine, but in the mountains, or rather, in a narrow valley between two mountains that jutted up like flat teeth. It was the same mountain range from her previous nightmare. Between the two ridges was a cave.

Nova felt very small. Air rushed past her, as if the mountains themselves were sucking in and blowing out a chilly breath, buffeting her back and forth. Arlo—or Eijlek—stood like a malevolent force beside her.

There was a vileness here, weakening her knees and pulling her in at the same time. It took her a moment to realize there was no wind at all. It was her own body, leaning in, drawing back.

But the nightmare was fading—she could feel reality folding in. Something warm and safe tugged at her consciousness, in her gut, like how she felt in the Inbetween before she was ushered home. A presence even older than Eijlek.

Then, she felt the press of stone on her back, the slightest touch of Arlo's fingers tangled in her hair. The smell of damp mildew. The sound of whispers. Her name.

"Nova?"

Nova jerked awake, her eyes falling on her sleeping sister.

"Nova," Eris repeated. He was leaning over her, having shaken her awake. He stood and began packing his bag. "It's moonrise."

Nova nodded, glancing at Arlo who was rubbing the sleep from his eyes. She skittered away. "Did you —?" she asked, suddenly not sure what was real and what were remnants of nightmare.

"Huh?" he said. "Sorry, still waking up."

"You — you *weren't* with me just now . . . in a dream."

"Nova" — he gave her a bemused smile — "we're on Lyra. You told me it doesn't work like that."

"Right," Nova said, quickly, hoping no one else had heard. "Um, right." She fiddled with her shawl, magic throbbing with life in each Thread. Her hands still shook.

"Hey, are you okay?"

Nova rested her head back against the rock. "I don't know what to think anymore." She sighed. "Maybe I'm just worried about the Void, and you, and Cally . . . Do dreams work like that?"

"Yep. I dream about my teeth falling out when I'm stressed."

"Oh." Nova laughed, eyeing his teeth and thanking the stars they were all intact. He really did have a nice smile. So much better than Eijlek's. She silenced her thoughts. *It wasn't really the Void, it's just stress.* Arlo's cheeks reddened under her gaze.

"Are you feeling any better after resting?" Nova asked. She studied Arlo's expression — he wouldn't meet her eyes.

"I mean, not really." His shoulders slumped. "Not about coming to Lyra, that is."

"But that was an accident."

Arlo shifted, scowling at the ground. "I . . . don't know if it was, actually."

Nova leaned closer. "What do you mean?"

"We need to head out," Cally said. Her bag was on her shoulder and Eris and Ceres had already left the cave.

Nova held up a hand. "Just give us a moment. Please."

"Make it a quick moment."

Cally left and Nova looked back at Arlo. His remorse painted his pale skin crimson. "The last time you visited my dream, when we were in my father's office . . . as you were leaving, something like a tear or a rip appeared. It was glowing at the edges—just like your tattoos."

"And?"

He threw up his hands. "And I stepped through."

Nova's stomach soured. A tear? Had they *made* . . . a rift?

"What would you have done?" Arlo said, clearly agitated. "Besides, I wasn't totally convinced it wasn't part of my dream."

"It's not that," Nova said. "I would've gone through too."

"I hate that I left her." He mussed up his hair in agitation.

"But you didn't know—"

"But I did!" He shot up, nearly cracking his head on the cave's ceiling. "Part of me knew exactly what I was doing—where that tear in reality would go." His gaze was all pleading, as if he were begging Nova to put him out of his misery. "I wanted it to lead to *you*—to this world that I've been dreaming about since I was a kid. And . . . and to leave behind all my responsibilities. Even for a moment." He ran a hand over his face. "I can't live with myself if she dies and I'm not there for her. She's sacrificed so much for me." He shuddered. "Nova, I—" His eyes shone with unspent tears. "I'm still there." He touched his chest. "Stuck between two worlds."

Nova stood and placed a gentle hand on his shoulder. He stepped forward, wrapping her into a hug. It was nothing like the nightmare. There was comfort between them. "We will get you home in time, Arlo," she said, hoping it was not a lie. She closed her eyes and willed it to be true.

"I'll get you home," she repeated.

He pulled away and she reached up, sweeping his freckled cheek with her thumb and collecting his tears. "Arlo James."

He stilled at her stern tone.

"You are not your father."

His green eyes glowed with emotion, and before he could blink and cause more tears to fall, Nova thought she saw silver specks shining around his pupils.

CHAPTER TWENTY-THREE

Selene rose as the group waded through the forest's depths. The deeper they went, the older the forest became. Quieter too. Nova's skin tingled with uncertainty.

"Are you sure this is the right way?" Eris asked, his voice strained—from nerves, maybe, or exhaustion. Nova couldn't tell.

Ceres stopped. "I think so. I've never been to Polaris, but we're traveling adjacent to the road that leads there."

The group cut around a small, clear pond and Arlo paused to stare at a school of fish, each the size of a child. Their multi-colored fins undulated like long, glowing ribbons. Large plants lined the pond and Arlo knelt by the edge of the water.

"Wait, Arlo—" Nova went to pull him back but the fish were too quick. A yellow ribbon-tail caught his wrist and yanked his arm under water.

Arlo yelped. The ribbon fish swarmed.

Nova and Eris dove to Arlo's side and tugged him back to land. Bubbly, popping noises emanated from the creature as it tried swimming deeper. Its bulbous eyes rolled into the back of its head.

Ceres unsheathed his sword but Nova said, "We've got it."

After a few moments of tugging, the fish seemed to realize they wouldn't give up and relinquished its grip. With more popping noises, it disappeared in the murky water. Nova rolled away and jumped to her feet.

Arlo stumbled back rubbing his soaked sleeve. "What in the world?"

"You'll be fine," Nova said. "Their tails are harmless. It's the venomous teeth you have to watch out for."

"Venomous teeth?" He stepped further from the pond's edge.

"Oh yeah. But you would've drowned before the pain set in," Cally said with the hint of a smile.

"How comforting."

"How about you just don't touch anything," Nova said. "Lyran forests aren't like forests on Earth."

"Um, what makes you think forests on Earth are safe?" Arlo said with a laugh as they started walking again. "You do know we have bears, and snakes that can eat you whole. Tigers. And tiny frogs tha—"

"*Tiny frogs?*" Eris said, putting a hand dramatically to his chest. "How have humans *survived* for so long?"

"I didn't finish! If you touch them, they poison you."

"So don't touch them."

Arlo pinched his lips together. "Never mind."

Nova elbowed him. "We're just teasing you, Arlo."

"Oh." He flushed and a slow smile crept back over his face. "Good. All the frogs of Earth would have been offended otherwise."

As the forest swallowed them further, Nova became more agitated, and she noticed Arlo's distress as well. He kept glancing over his shoulder as if he'd heard something, but when she asked about it, he only said it was the wind. But this part of the wood was thick with humidity and swarming bulb bugs that were drawn to sweat and blood. There hadn't been a breeze for hours.

When the moon rose just overhead, they stopped at the edge of a ravine. The rubber tree leaves blocked out Selene completely and not a single plant lit up with bioluminescence. A chilled wind trickled through the gorge just below them that seemed to go on for miles either way.

"Give me a moment," Cally said, rushing away with a spark. She reappeared, out of breath, hair coming out of her braid. "I can't find the end of the ravine that way. The other way hits the road—with a guarded bridge." She looked at Nova and Eris. "Do either of you have a Thread to help here? We have to go over or through."

Nova shook her head. She didn't have anything bridge or rope-like.

"No," Eris said. "But I don't like the looks of that place."

"Me neither," Nova said. The ravine was deep and wide, and the shadows in its bed reminded her of the Void, though she didn't sense its oppressive decay.

"What do you think?" Cally asked Ceres.

"I see no other option. We go in and hope whatever lives inside stays asleep."

Nova gripped the foxfire pendant and followed Ceres and Cally down the side of the rocky edge. The stones were slick and the air turned colder as they descended. Chills skittered up Nova's back and she listed off the Threads in her head, thinking of any weapons that might help them—depending on what they came up against. Nova had collected very few weapons from dreams, and using her shadow Thread was her last resort.

Her fingers and calves cramped as she clung to mossy rocks and clay that crumbled under her grip. When they finally reached the bottom, her limbs trembled.

"Alright," Ceres said. "Move swiftly to the other side."

Nova squinted across the dark pit. It was so much larger than it had seemed from above. She felt as if she were standing in an open maw, its lips pointing to the stars. She gripped her shawl, feeling for the shield Thread. Cally touched her wrist. "Only if absolutely necessary."

Nova dropped her hand and fell in step beside Arlo. He twitched a few times and she glanced at him. His eyes were closed and his face contorted in a grimace. "Arlo?"

He took a deep breath and opened his eyes. "I-I'm fine. Just a headache."

"Are you hearing voices again?" she asked.

Ceres turned. "Voices?"

"It's nothing," Arlo said, frowning at Nova. "I'm still adjusting to this place."

"Keep moving," Cally said.

"We'll talk about this later," Ceres said, eyeing Arlo warily. For a reason Nova couldn't comprehend, Arlo seemed ashamed. He looked away, ears turning a deep purple in the globe light. She was about to ask him more when something snapped and Cally cried out. Her globe clattered over the dirt as the ground devoured her.

"Cally!" Nova screamed. They raced to the edge of the sunken area. Cally gripped the ledge, eyes wide in terror. Nova couldn't see how far down the hole went.

Ceres hauled her up and she fell, shaking, into his arms.

Nova touched her sister's back. "You're okay. It's okay."

"I don't think we're okay," Eris said.

His moon blade was drawn and he studied the ground. Nova noticed the shaking then. She'd assumed it was her body trembling. But she saw now that the dirt bounced like boiling water. Muffled clicking and scratching echoed around the ravine.

"What is it?" Arlo asked. He squeezed Nova's hand and she squeezed back.

Before anyone could answer, soil exploded. Nova and Arlo toppled back. Another hole opened at their feet. A glowing head with antennae emerged, clacking its pincers. Nova screamed and Arlo cursed. The creature scrambled up the rest of the way; its glowing segmented body was longer than Nova.

Arlo tugged Nova to her feet, but the giant insects were bursting out everywhere.

"Centipedes? Giant *freaking* centipedes?" Arlo swung around as another beast emerged behind them. She and Arlo stood back-to-back, his strong grip the only thing steadying her.

"Scuttlurias," Nova said.

"Let me guess." Arlo's voice was breathy. "They eat people."

Nova answered with a squeak.

She pressed back into Arlo and touched her shawl. Would a storm do anything? Or a sunrise? Doubtful. Eris and Ceres were battling a few of the scuttles, and the other creatures turned their way. Eris was using a whip Thread, while Ceres was hacking at heads. Though he was barely making a dent against their armored bodies.

Where was Cally?

She looked around for her sister but couldn't see past the wriggling bodies of light. They were all drawing nearer to Eris and Ceres as if enraged by the clanking sounds of their weaponry.

"No eyes!" she yelled, then bit her tongue. The scuttles nearest turned their antennae on her. *Spores.*

"What?" Arlo said.

"Shh! They can't see. Only hear."

Nova had read about many bioluminescent creatures of the forest over the years, and her knowledge was coming back to her. She didn't need a sharp weapon, she needed noise. Something even louder than the ruckus Ceres and Eris were making.

"Arlo," she breathed in his ear. "If I act *strange*, make sure I don't die."

"Uh . . . *what*?"

Nova tugged out an orange-yellow Thread and tossed it as far from them as possible. As it flew it transformed into a loud . . . radio. Music blared through the ravine, louder than she remembered it being in the dream. But Nova's Threads were intelligent things and knew she needed help.

The scuttles instantly changed course, their spindly legs flying over the pits to get to the noise. Nova willed her Thread to rise from the ground. The radio floated up, and the insects climbed up one another to get to it. Some began fighting, their hisses and screeches grating in her head.

"*The Beatles*?" Arlo snorted in disbelief. "You went to war on giant bugs with *The Beatles*?"

"Fitting, huh?" Nova laughed, and then kept laughing. She didn't think she would ever *stop* laughing. And she didn't want to.

Arlo's smile turned to a frown. "What's going on? We need to get to the others."

"Look at them! They look like a wiggly ladder. I want to climb them!" Nova started walking toward the mound of scuttles. *I wonder what it's like to ride one?*

"Nope, not that way." Arlo took her hand, tugging her toward Ceres and Eris.

"Arlo, stop! I want to go over there." She pointed to the radio. "The music is *that* way!"

"So are the flesh-eating bugs."

"Oh, Arlo." She giggled. "They eat *more* than flesh."

But when she broke from his grip and began skipping toward the writhing mass, Arlo grabbed her around the middle. "Sorry, Nova." He dragged her further from the music.

"Let. Me. Go!" Nova squirmed and she imagined she looked just like a scuttle which made her erupt into giggles all over again.

"For crying out loud," Arlo said. "Eris, help me here!"

A pair of strong hands grabbed Nova and shook her gently. She looked up into her best friend's bright eyes. "Nova. Get your Thread back."

"You just don't know how to have fun! None of you!"

Ceres was pulling a limping Cally along beside him. Her shin had a gash in it. Though Nova wanted to find something funny about the situation, she couldn't. Seeing her sister injured gave her a moment of clarity. She shook her head trying to rid herself of the Thread's emotion. "Agh."

"Call back the Thread," Eris said.

"Not until you get Cally up there." Another giggle slipped from Nova and she slapped a hand over her mouth. "*Hurry.*"

Ceres nodded then scooped up Cally, and they all jogged to the other side of the ravine. When they reached the edge and looked up, it seemed nearly impossible to climb. So impossible it was funny.

"She can't stop laughing," Arlo said, looking at Nova with concern. Why was he being such a spore? "She can't climb like this."

"Nova, release the Thread. We will take our chances," Ceres said. He looked at Eris. "We'll start climbing, but make sure she comes back to reality."

Ceres set down Cally and the two of them made their way slowly up the side. Cally slipped a few times which was enough to give Nova a brief moment of urgency. She called the Thread back with a snap of her finger. The radio unwound, the music ended, and the scuttles stopped their clambering. When the Thread was safely back in her shawl, any fun she'd been feeling left her completely, dread sliding into its place.

The scuttlurias turned their antennae on Ceres and Cally. They were making too much noise. But how could they *silently* escape?

Eris pushed Nova and Arlo toward the wall. "Climb. I'll hold them off."

"Like spores you will!" Nova said, though she was shaking both from the wall of scuttles racing toward them, and her magic's drain on her system. "We do this together."

Arlo picked up a rock and cocked his arm back.

"Another Thread?" Nova glanced at Eris.

He shook his head. He looked as exhausted as she felt. "It would wipe me out."

Eris and Arlo pressed close on either side of her, but it offered little comfort. She was numb with shock at the horrible wave of creatures bearing down on them. Nova had no weapon, and what use would it be anyway? A shield would delay the inevitable for seconds at most. She could only hope that Ceres and Cally could get to the rift. "Arlo! You have to go with them!" Nova said. "The rift."

He shook his head, as stubborn as she was.

"I'm with you," he said.

She breathed out. "Then let's make some noise."

CHAPTER TWENTY-FOUR

Nova yelled. The scutlluria that had been charging toward Ceres and Cally changed direction. Nova closed her eyes when the pincers were nearly upon them. She gripped her friends' hands. The sound of clattering and skittering and the sticky, damp air filled her senses then —

Nothing.

Nova peeled open her eyelids.

Lights, everywhere, illuminating the pit. She blinked and stepped back. The air looked as if it had caught fire. Creatures floated above them, tentacles dangling.

"Okay, but those are *definitely* jelly fish," Arlo said in amazement.

Nova gaped. The drawings in her books were nothing compared to the vibrant orbs of the jelly-like creatures swimming through the air. Each was large enough for their entire group to stand on. Purple light shone from their orbed bodies and trickled down through tentacles as thick as Nova's thigh.

"Aurelia jellies," she whispered. The centipedes were confused, swiveling their antennae at the low humming sound of the jellies.

"Also called whisps."

"Should we be running?" Arlo said from the corner of his mouth.

"As far as we know, they don't harm people."

"Okay, so, what *do* they harm?"

As if in response, the whisps struck, their tentacles lashing out with ferocity against the scuttles. The bugs' shrieks cut off as they were curled up in the underside of the jellies—into their mouths, huge and gaping.

"Agh!" Arlo stumbled back. Nova choked on a scream.

The remaining scuttluria dove back into their holes, scrambling deep into the soil and away from their attackers. It was over in a few breaths.

The ravine was bathed in deep purple, and though there was still a chill in the air, the whisps made Nova feel warm. Safe. One hovered a few feet away and she stepped toward it.

"Nova," Eris said.

But they did not appear threatening, and if the stories were true, their intelligence was unmatched among the animals of Lyra. Some even called them a gift from Selene; floating moon-like jellies that bathed the wilderness in light. Standing in their presence, Nova believed they *were* a gift.

The aurelia unfurled one of its tentacles and drifted toward Nova. The gesture reminded her of the Void as she'd seen it in Arlo's dream, and she hesitated. But she sensed no malice, no hunger, in this creature. It was simply curious.

The tentacle slipped onto Nova's palm then drifted along her fingers, as if memorizing her. It slid up her arm, past her Harvester mark, and touched the shawl, then gingerly caressed the foxfire pendant. The whisp's color burned brighter, as if excited. Drawing back its appendage, the creature floated down until it was eye-level with Nova. Its eyes were small and embedded into translucent flesh and its bioluminescence seemed to flow from its heart, highlighting all the organs inside.

"You're incredible," Nova said.

It dipped to its side, tentacles dragging on the ground.

"What is it doing?" Eris asked.

Nova smiled. "I think it wants to get us out of here."

"How?" Arlo said. "It's not going to grab us with its tentacles like it did those scuttle things, is it?" He shivered and looked over his shoulder toward where the scuttluria had disappeared.

"No, I . . . I think it wants us to ride it," Nova said.

Eris's mouth hung open. "I don't think so."

Nova felt her own trepidation returning, but when she stared into the creature's golden eyes, she calmed. Tentatively, she touched the aurelia's back. It was rubbery—solid. With a deep breath, she climbed up and kneeled on the giant beast. The jelly hummed, and Nova nodded at the other two. Arlo eased forward and lifted himself up. He let out a heavy breath and rubbed the jelly's back.

"Eris?" Nova said. "Let's go."

"I would rather climb the ravine."

"There's no need to be *scared*."

Eris tensed. "I'm not scared."

Nova huffed. "You're being ridiculous. Arlo did it and he's not even Lyran. Now come on."

Eris glowered and darted his eyes at Arlo. "Move over," he said. Being less lithe, it took Eris a few tries to scramble onto the whisp's back.

The creature floated upward and Nova's stomach dipped as they left the ground. The rim of the ravine rushed up to meet them, and they arrived to find Cally and Ceres on their backs in the underbrush, panting.

"I see you made a friend," Cally said, wary. "When we saw your idiotic attempt to kill yourselves, we tried turning back, but these things swooped in out of nowhere. One wrapped itself around us so we couldn't get to you. Thought we were all done for." Ceres helped Cally scramble to her feet, and she leaned into him, fixing Nova with a hard look. Her lip quivered when she spoke again. "Never do that again. Do you hear me? I—" She looked away, hands on her hips. "I can't lose you, Nova."

"I'm sorry, Cally. We didn't have a choice."

Cally looked as if she were about to argue when Ceres placed a hand on her back. "We're just glad you're safe." He cocked his head to the creature. "Now, what are you thinking, Nova?"

"There are stories . . ." Nova fiddled with a loose Thread, eyes shifting between her sister and Ceres.

Cally's eyes grew. "*Oh no*. No way." She folded her arms then winced when she put her weight on her injured leg.

"The Sentries are still looking for us," Nova said. "And we need to get to Polaris quickly. What if they figure out our plans? They could have an entire troop guarding the rift by the time we arrive." Nova placed a palm on the aurelia's back. "We need speed, Cally."

"Hold on. What are we talking about?" Arlo asked.

"She wants to *ride* these things to Polaris." Cally shook her head. "How would you even communicate with it? It might take us deeper into the wood and turn us to . . . to jelly!"

"Actually, we have someone here who can communicate with intelligent beings. Right?"

Ceres shifted uncomfortably. "I've never tried to message with animals. But Messengers have done it before. It's less speaking with them, and more like *impressions*."

"Works for me." Nova raised her brows expectantly.

"But the plan was to take this path. Follow the road and—"

"Plans change, Cally," Nova said.

"We don't know anything about these things!" She pointed at the aurelia jelly and its humming turned a bit deeper. "What if it attacks us? You saw what it did to those scuttles! *Spores*, Nova. It isn't safe!"

"You told me the secrets about our parents' deaths. About the Movement. You trusted me then! Why can't you trust me now?"

"You're just a kid! Sometimes you don't think through things—and look where that gets us!" She gestured at Arlo. "You're just like Father," Cally said, then clamped her mouth closed as if she knew she'd said too much.

"You're right." Nova swallowed, her throat scratchy and tight. "I *am* like Father. Mother was too scared to act, and I don't want to be like her." She took a shaky breath. "But I *do* think through things and sometimes the risk is worth it. Our father knew that. I think you do too." Nova wrinkled her brow. "You joined a revolution, Cally!"

Her sister scoffed. "That's different. It's organized and we've been moving toward this moment for years."

"Until I ruined it."

Cally hesitated, glancing at the others before closing her eyes for a beat. "No. You just . . . changed things."

Nova felt the sting of her sister's lie. She didn't need to be in her dream to sense it. She looked away and screwed up her face to keep the emotions at bay.

"Nova's right," Ceres said quietly. Everyone looked at him in surprise—especially Cally. There was sweat on his brow as if he were in painful concentration.

"While you two have been arguing, I've been listening to the whisp. I showed it an image of the lake near Polaris."

"I thought you haven't been there," Arlo said.

"There are plenty of drawn images, and I've memorized the map."

"Does it know where it is?" Nova asked.

Ceres nodded. "*She* knows the area well." He smiled at the creature and his forehead, always so concerned, smoothed. "The aurelia come from the Eridanus mountains, and at their foothills is the lake and Polaris."

He turned to Cally and cupped her cheek. "You're injured. We can treat you as the whisp takes us north. Being off the ground will keep us safe from predators. Please, Calypso."

Her sister softened at the way he said her name so tenderly. Nova flushed and looked down.

"Fine." Cally growled under her breath.

Relief fluttered in Nova's chest. After the scuttle attack, she didn't think she had enough courage, or energy, to continue on foot. She yearned to be up in the sky, closer to Selene. Though she'd agreed with Cally that she was like their father, she knew how deeply her fears ran. She wondered if—in her core—she was actually more like their mother. Scared and resistant.

Cally climbed up the aurelia and her arm grazed Nova's, causing Nova to flinch. She felt raw, like a rotting spindle tree ready to topple over. She and her sister usually didn't talk about their feelings—let alone yell them in front of people—and now that their emotions were exposed, it was hard to stuff them away again.

She scooted to the front of the jelly and her stomach dropped again as the animal glided upward. In moments, they burst through the tree line. She could breathe easier up here, overlooking the expansive glowing forest.

"It's like Christmas lights," Arlo said, scooting to sit beside Nova. He lost his balance when the whisp shifted, and Nova grabbed his arm. Seeming to understand their distress—or perhaps Ceres's distress—some of its long tendrils floated up to them.

"Er," Arlo said, looking hesitantly at the tentacle wagging in his face. "I feel uncomfortable."

"She wants us to hold on so we don't fall," Ceres said.

They grabbed onto the makeshift reins and the whisp began to move toward a shadow on the horizon. The Eridanus Mountains. With a chill, Nova noted how far away they still were. They wouldn't have made it before another Darknight fell. Fighting the scuttluria had put them behind.

The rest of the aurelia rose to join them, and soon it looked as if they were swimming in a brine of stars. She turned to Arlo who was gawking at the landscape. "Tell me about Christmas," she said.

"Oh, you'd love it, Nova. I'm sure you've seen parts of it in dreams."

"I have, but I want to hear about it from you."

Arlo smiled and closed his eyes. "When I was little, I'd help Dad decorate the outside of the house with lights that made halos against the snow. It was always freezing and my hands would go numb, but the lights made me feel warm, too, you know?" His grin widened as his gaze softened. "When I was older, before mom got too sick, she and I would drive real slow around the neighborhoods, windows down, drinking cinnamon hot chocolate. Mom was in love with Bing Crosby, so we'd listen to his Christmas album on repeat."

Nova didn't know who Bing Crosby was, but she was very interested in *drinking* chocolate.

"I've always wanted to taste chocolate." She had seen and smelled it in plenty of dreams. Humans were obsessed with the food.

"I wish you could. I wish—" His shoulders fell. "I wish so many things." He opened his eyes, rubbed them. "I'd take a nap on this thing if I didn't think I'd roll right off."

Nova stiffened at the idea of going to sleep. After the past two Darknights, she didn't think she ever wanted to sleep again. Even if the Void wasn't really appearing in her nightmares, her brain was projecting it. Either way, it made her stomach tighten with anxiety.

Cally hissed in pain and Nova turned. Her sister was fumbling with a bottle of healing cream and a bandage. Ceres was trying to help but she kept swatting his hand away.

Holding her breath, Nova scooted to her sister. "Let me help. I know how to do it."

Cally hesitated but then finally relented.

"You'll let her do it and not me?" Ceres said.

"We were trained by our mother." Cally's voice was softer than before. Nova wondered if her sister felt just as raw as she did. "You can keep watch." Cally smirked playfully at Ceres. "That's what you're good at." He chuckled but turned his conversation to Eris who sat on the other side of him. Nova noted how rigid Eris looked, and she remembered how terribly afraid of heights he was. It should have come to her sooner—no wonder he hadn't wanted to get on the jelly—but more pressing things had been on her mind.

There were beads of sweat sparkling on his brow and he gripped a tentacle so tightly she wondered if he was causing the creature pain. He shot her a miserable smile which looked more like a wince. Nova furrowed her brow at his expression, then focused again on her sister. She took Cally's white starrow tincture and poured some on the gash to disinfect the wound. Cally barely flinched.

Why had Eris said those things about her and Arlo—*now*? Arlo was going back to Earth, and then everything would go back to normal. Unless they were caught. Which seemed more likely now that the Sentries were after them.

Nova capped the bottle and glanced at Arlo. His head was thrown back, staring up at the multitude of twinkling stars caught in the sky. She already missed him, and he hadn't even left.

"You look conflicted," Cally said.

Nova's eyes snapped back to her sister's leg. She pulled out a roll of bandage spun from moon moth silk. It glowed in Selene's light and had healing properties of its own. Nova clenched her teeth but nodded.

Cally touched Nova's wrist, causing her to glance up. "I'm sorry about what I said back there. This" —she patted the aurelia—"was a good idea."

Nova finished wrapping the wound. After tying it off she sighed. "I miss them. Father and mother."

"Me too."

"But more than what we *had*. I miss . . . what we *could* have had."

Cally fidgeted with the bandage, no doubt checking Nova's work. "I know I couldn't replace them, Nova. But I did—I *do*—try to make sure your life is good." Cally snorted, eyes darkening as she took in the horizon. "Well, a good life despite our world trying to kill us."

Nova's eyes flicked to the owl wings that decorated Cally's collar bones, and then she awkwardly took her sister's hand, fumbling a bit before gripping it tightly. "You've been amazing, Cally. *Really*. You went from being my sister to my guardian overnight. And I'm now just realizing how much of a burden that must've been." Nova laughed lightly. "I wasn't the easiest kid."

Cally placed her other hand on Nova's shoulder and squeezed. "You weren't easy. Too curious for your own *sporing* good. Still are. But you were *never* a burden, Nova. Not ever. Do you hear me?" Cally's expression shone with more emotion than Nova thought her sister possessed. Nova was pulled in by the gravity of her sister's words, at the *love* blazing through her gaze. "I thank Selene every night that I still have you." Cally's voice wavered. "That we have each other."

Nova bit her lip and swiped a tear from her trembling cheek. "Me too."

Cally gingerly pulled her pant leg over her wound. "You did well. Mother would be proud."

Nova stiffened, thinking of their mother and her Healer powers.

"She would think it sufficient. Nothing more."

Cally shook her head. "She loved you, Nova. But you know how Lyrans are. Too much affection is weakness. Is *human*." She rolled her eyes. "The Ancients would've been *appalled* at my blubbering just now."

Nova grimaced. "As much as I despise the Ancients for what they did, they might have a point. Sometimes . . ." She scratched at her arm, suddenly hesitant to share. "I feel so much, and it can paralyze me. And my . . . my nightmares keep getting worse." She touched her forehead. "I think something is wrong with me."

"You remembered another nightmare?" Cally said, so loudly Eris and Ceres glanced at her. Nova dipped her head.

"Only bits and pieces." *Lie.* Nova remembered every detail — from Eijlek-Arlo's eerie smile to the way the white sand felt between her toes. She turned toward their destination.

"You need to stop using your Threads," Cally said. "They don't help. They only heap on more strain."

Nova bit her tongue. She disagreed. She would use her Threads whenever they were needed. But there was no use fighting Cally about it, especially after their unexpected and heartfelt chat. Their truce felt nice.

"Arlo," Ceres said after a time. "I was actually meaning to talk to you."

"Uh. Sure." Arlo turned toward them, his outline silhouetted against the mountain range.

"Earlier, Nova said you'd been hearing whispers."

Arlo's entire body tensed like an animal caught in a trap. "It's nothing."

"Well, it *might* be nothing. Or it might be something."

"No," Arlo said. "It's just this place. It's messing with my mind. I'm fine."

"Arlo." Nova nodded at him. "It's alright." Why was he acting this way? His jaw was tense, as if biting back a slew of angry words.

"I agree," Ceres said to Arlo. "I think Lyra *is* messing with your mind. More specifically, your DNA."

"Wait. What?" His taut muscles relaxed. "What do you mean?"

"I'm not certain, but Selene's magic could be changing you."

Nova sat up taller. "What makes you think that?"

"The voices. That's how it started when I was a child—when my powers first manifested. Before I learned to control it, I would hear snippets of people's thoughts. Whispers."

"You—you think I'm getting magic?" Arlo leaned forward, his entire body vibrating. Nova remembered seeing the flecks of silver in his eyes. Was it possible moon magic worked so quickly? Lyran children acquired their power gradually.

"How long did it take our ancestors to change?" Nova asked.

Ceres lifted his hands. "The timeline is muddy, but it was quick enough to spook the ones who *hadn't* changed. Violence broke out between those Selene had touched and those who were left unchanged."

"He's only been here for three nights," Eris said. "He's probably just going mad."

"I thought I was going mad too," Ceres said. "But I wasn't."

Arlo stared at Ceres. "And if you're right, what do I do? How do I control the voices?"

"Focus on one. The most prevalent voice. If you concentrate on only one, the others will fall away."

Arlo squinted at Ceres. "Can you hear *our* thoughts so easily?"

"Not anymore. Once a Messenger's power grows stronger, it's impossible to catch thoughts unawares. The magic becomes as discreet as someone hammering on a door."

Cally snorted. "I always know when he's trying to read my mind."

Ceres held up his hands. "Accidentally. I promise." He wrapped his arm around her waist and winked. "Though it *would* be easier to communicate that way."

"Not a chance." She leaned away and gave his shoulder a playful punch.

Ceres laughed and turned back to Arlo, studying him. "I'm here if you need to talk through any of this. Don't keep it to yourself."

Arlo blinked at Ceres in surprise. Ceres's offer to help seemed to confuse Arlo more than it did to gain magical powers. He cleared his throat and nodded. "Um, how long did it take you to have complete control?"

"A few years, with a lot of training."

Arlo's jaw came unhinged. "A few *years?*"

"I was also eight. My mind wasn't necessarily *disciplined*. I was more concerned with fighting my brothers." He smiled, eyes twinkling. "But you will catch on quicker. You'll be a master in no time."

The aurelia jelly dipped and Nova clung to the tentacle. They all glanced toward the mountains. They were getting close. Nova noticed large black areas dotting the forest now. Decay.

"The problem is," Arlo said, his gaze still locked on the mountain range. "I'm not sure I have time to master anything."

Chapter Twenty-Five

What if I really belong here?
A mind reader, a Messenger,
Lyran.
Here, with Nova, in a vibrant, weird world—
Skimming mushrooms and rubbery trees?
What if?

I've been looking, searching
Pleading to belong,
And then I found *her.*
From two different worlds,
From too different worlds
But hearts that beat in rhythm.

What if you stayed? the voice says.

What if? I ponder.
But the thought floats away.
As unbelievable as the neon
Jellyfish we ride.

The feelings tying me here
Cut off the blood flow to my brain.
Of course I can't stay
Though my bones beg me to.

I can't be like Dad
Even though the voice
Tells me I am.

I'm running *to*

Not from.

Hold on, Mom.

CHAPTER TWENTY-SIX

As the mountains loomed nearer, the aurelia descended into the trees. It deposited them near the mouth of a village curving around a lake so large it could have wrapped Callisto in its shores. Its dark waters and reflected starlight made Nova feel dizzy, it was like looking at a sky carved into the belly of land.

Sliding from the whisp, Nova placed a palm where she imagined the creature's forehead was. "Thank you," she said, though only Ceres could truly express their gratitude. Night would be taken over by Darknight in a few short hours, and they would be safely within Polaris's boundaries by then. The jelly flared a bit brighter, hummed a gurgling noise, then ascended with the rest of its swarm. Nova wondered where they were headed next.

"Do you two sense anything?" Ceres asked. He was looking between Nova and Eris, expectant. Nova wrinkled her brow until understanding settled over her. Eris still looked confused.

"You mean, do we feel a rift nearby?" Nova said.

"Yes."

Nova glanced at Eris who seemed small under the gargantuan

tree that loomed behind him. It was a species Nova did not recognize, but instead of rubber leaves, like the trees around Callisto, this tree's leaves were feathery and long, nearly draping the ground.

"How is a rift supposed to *feel*?" Eris asked. He adjusted his bag and glanced past the road to Polaris. A low wall surrounded the city—a large wooden gate at its entrance.

"Our father never described how they were sensed," Cally said. "He just said that the key to finding them were Harvesters. But we still might be too far away." She glanced at Nova.

"I don't feel anything." *Besides fear of getting caught.*

"It's alright," Ceres said. But he looked disappointed. "We'll find our contact and lay low until we figure out a path forward. We can stay with her tonight." He took in a deep breath and held it as he surveyed the village walls. "I hope."

"Do you want me to use my shadow Thread to sneak us in?" Nova said. "I'll have to make a couple trips, but they won't see us."

"*No*," Eris said sharply. He eyed her shawl with disdain. "I saw what that magic did to you in the Harvesting Center. It isn't worth it." He nodded toward Polaris. "We can scale those walls easily enough."

"Fine," she said, a little relieved. "But if it comes down to using the Thread or getting captured, we use the Thread." They all agreed and crept toward the edge of the woods.

On closer examination, Nova noticed the stone walls crumbling in places. She wondered if this place kept out every beast, or if people huddled in their homes at Darknight.

"Over there." Cally pointed to a broken section of wall further down, curved away from the gate.

Ceres looked around at the group. "Make sure your home marks are covered." He tugged down his left sleeve. "Eris, you help me get Cally across first. Once the coast is clear, Nova and Arlo can follow."

"I should stay with Nova," Cally said.

"I'll be okay."

Cally seemed to be fighting an internal battle before she finally nodded. "See you soon."

The three fled across the road keeping behind scattered bushes and trees as much as possible. Nova glanced at Arlo. His shirt hid his arms, but the collar was low enough to see he had no family crest.

"Here." She reached up and yanked his collar, using the strings to tie it closer to his throat. "That way you don't look *quite* so suspicious."

"Right." He looked down and chuckled, his breath warm on her hands.

She hoped the dark of the woods hid the blush creeping up her neck.

Arlo flinched.

"What?"

"Your hands are cold."

Arlo's face was so close. She studied his green eyes and . . .

"Silver," she whispered. "Your eyes are changing to silver."

Nova glimpsed wonder and sadness, hope and confusion mingling in Arlo's expression. Then it all hardened over and he blinked.

Nova had been mulling over his "belonging here" ever since his conversation with Ceres about gaining magic. She had been fighting so hard to get Arlo home, but another part of her ached for him to stay. Selene's power was changing his DNA. Transforming him. Or so Ceres guessed. And if that were true, it meant he really *did* belong in Lyra. With her.

Nova's hand still hovered over his chest. "All set. We should go." She hated how breathless she sounded.

"Nova." He grabbed her hand, tugging her lightly back to him. "I just wanted to say thank you for everything you've done for me. I've put everyone in danger. And if—" His mouth tightened. "If anyone gets hurt because of me . . ." He looked so young in that moment, eyes round and innocent. "I would never forgive myself."

His words echoed what he'd said about leaving his mother and her chest pinched.

"Arlo, you keep blaming yourself for things out of your control."

"I went through the rift, I—"

"Yes." Nova huffed lightly, gripping his hand tighter as if she could embed the words into his skin. "It was a mistake. But that one mistake doesn't become who you *are*." She shook her head. "You keep heaping guilt on yourself as if you think you deserve it."

Arlo frowned and looked away. "I don't know what I deserve."

She sighed and pulled him to the edge of the forest. "You deserve another chance. And we're going to take it."

~

Unlike Callisto's sleek, glass pods, Polaris's homes were square huts, crumbling in spots and patched together with mud compound. There were no towering buildings. No caps in the streets. Lone foxfire globes dangled off spindle branches curling up between homes and beside wooden doors. The air smelled of fish.

They took as many side streets as possible. Nova knew they should keep their heads down, but she couldn't help looking around.

The villagers wore varying colors and textures of fish-scaled jewelry or armor plates over humble slacks and tunics. The scales in their attire glowed softly in the moonlight.

Ceres led them around a few more dirty streets before they came to the lake they'd seen while riding on the back of the whisp. The Eridanus Mountains looked like sharp-shouldered giants hugging the water. Nova slowed to take in their sight and Eris ran into her.

"Keep moving, Nova."

"But, look!" she said, stopping him from following the others. "They're so . . . *big*."

"You've seen mountains in dreams," Eris said.

"Dreams don't compare." She cocked her head at him. "You know that."

He sighed and pulled her along. "No, they don't. But I'll enjoy them more once we're safe."

They skimmed around the lake's dark shores. Nova knew it

wasn't a true lake, but a sort of brine spring. There was an underground channel that led to the Black Sea and all sorts of creatures could go between the two. Boats bobbed on the glittering waves, fishermen out trapping sea creatures to feed their mountain village. One of the vessels they passed had a clear bottom and the sail looked to be made of hearty moth silk. Two fishermen emptied a large trap of black majidae crabs. A few celestial salt stars clung to the rubber frame.

Nova had only seen a fisherman's catch dead in the marketplace. The crabs' backs swirled like a galaxy, while the salt stars were deep purple, the color of the skies when Selene rose at first night. There was a vividness about them that only living things carried.

In the water were specks of light—bioluminescent algae and fish dancing with the starlight's reflection. Arlo paused, his eyes alight. Nova wondered if someday he would write a poem about what he saw here.

About all of it.

Ceres kept them at a steady pace, always keeping to the edge of the curving lake. Nova's gaze traveled back up the mountains. She had a sudden urge to scale their rocky cliffs, though being a flat-land dweller, she knew she wouldn't make it far.

"Hold up!"

The sharp voice, which was just behind them, echoed off the water. Nova's arms turned to jelly. Ceres spun to face the person who had stopped them, his smile forced as he went through the motions of a greeting.

Nova turned as well, taking in the older man with graying hair at his temples. The robes and sword at his hip confirmed he was a Sentry. But he didn't look familiar. She hoped he was from Polaris.

"Don't let him see your eyes," she whispered to Arlo. There were specks of silver, but the green was still prominent. Arlo nodded, keeping his head down.

"There's been a report from a Callisto Messenger." The man's gaze fell over each of them slowly. Nova tried not to fidget. She couldn't reach her shawl, which was now in her bag since it was so recognizable. The guard hesitated on Arlo before returning to

Ceres. "There was an explosion in Callisto. Some of the citizens saw a group of five fleeing the city."

Cally clicked her tongue. "That's horrible. Was anyone hurt?"

One of the Sentries' eyes ticked. "No. But there was substantial damage to a few of the buildings. The Ancients believe it could have been a threat."

Eris shifted beside Nova, no doubt feeling guilty for his Thread's destruction.

"Well, thanks for letting us know." Ceres smiled and it was far too big. "We will keep an eye out." He turned to leave but the guard stopped him.

"It's just—*you* five seem to fit the description well." He stepped closer and Nova's breath hitched when she saw his gaze on Arlo. "You. Why are you staring at the ground? Something to hide?"

Arlo raised his head.

The Sentry looked dumbstruck. He leaned closer, squinting at Arlo's face. "How . . . *what* . . . are you?"

"He's a Lyran. Same as you and me," Nova said. She lifted her chin, surprised that her voice sounded so strong. She felt quite the opposite.

The Sentry threw back his head and laughed. "Right. And I'm an eau fish." He nodded toward Nova's shoulder. "Show me your identification. All of you."

No one moved. Their shoulders all shared the same emblem, the tattoos that represented Callisto.

The Sentry took a step back and drew his sword. "Thought so. You will all follow me to be questioned further."

"You really should've called for backup," Ceres said. His face contorted, a vein in his forehead popping out.

"What did you—" the guard began, his tan face turning a rich red. But before he could say anything else, his expression went slack. With a smooth motion, he sheathed his sword, turned on his heel, and skirted along the lake.

"Go," Ceres said. "I'll keep leading him away as we move toward the safe house."

Cally took Ceres's hand to lead him. Every few yards, he pointed and Cally directed them. When they reached a row of houses carved into the base of the mountain, Ceres gasped and doubled over.

"I got him outside of Polaris's walls. But now he knows we're here and that I'm a Messenger." He rubbed his forehead. "More will come. I am sorry."

"You got us out of there, Ceres," Nova said. "None of us wanted to fight him."

He nodded, grim. "Let's get inside before we're spotted again."

Nova looked up and found the strangest home she'd ever come across.

Like the other small houses, it was formed from the mossy mountain base. But this one was surrounded by a multitude of carvings. Swirls and lines and etchings of landscape, animals, and Lyran forms. Waves and clouds. And — Nova squinted — was that a *sun*?

Ceres stepped forward and rapped his knuckles on the door in a specific pattern. Nova rubbed her damp palms on her thighs.

Ceres raised his fist again. Each knock felt like a mistake to Nova. More silence.

Nova gritted her teeth. Where would they go if —

The door swung open and Nova nearly jumped out of her skin.

An elderly woman as thin as a whistle reed stared out of the shadowed doorway. Her glasses were so large and thick and her hair so white and wild she gave the impression of an unshorn eweden. Her clothes had an ethereal movement, as if the fish scales sewn into the silk were alive and swimming through water. Her silver tattoos practically made the woman's rich amber skin glow, like the soft clay near creek beds. Nova's eye landed on the woman's family crest. A lucent swan with its wings spread wide. Welcoming.

The old woman peered at Nova's crest, her wary eyes wrinkling in recognition. "So," the woman said, her voice as willowy as her cloak, "another Celeste has found me at last."

CHAPTER TWENTY-SEVEN

The woman waved a wrinkled hand. "Come in. Come in." Her smile was slow but genuine. "I'm Gemini, but everyone calls me Gem. Or mad." She cackled.

Nova shared a worried look with Arlo before they stepped inside.

The dim home had one sliver of a window and was lit with tiny foxfire globes dangling from the ceiling like stars. Considering how small it looked from the outside, the main room was spacious, having been carved into the mountainside. There were two more rooms in the back, their doorways framed with decorative brine shells pressed into the stone. The inside of Gemini's home was just as ornate as the outside. There was so much life, so much *feeling* etched into every square inch.

Eris strode forward, jaw loose and hand outstretched. His palm found the form of carved waves, the foam created with hundreds of tiny white rocks. Nova saw a shift in his eye.

"Eris?"

Eris's hand slid from the carved wall. Nova glanced between him and the artwork, his expression smoothing until it was neutral once more. But he wasn't fooling her. Something in the design had moved him—a stirring emotion they'd been trained to conceal since they were children.

Gemini shuffled to the small stove and grabbed a ladle. "Tuber soup is almost ready, if you're hungry."

"Soup?" Ceres said, obviously expecting something else. Like a map to the rift. He eyed the massive pot. "A Sentry spotted us—he knows we're in Polaris."

She waved a hand, brushing aside his warning. "Bosh! They'd never expect you to visit my house." She nodded toward the soup. "My contact said you were coming, so I made extra."

"Thank the worlds for the rebellion," Ceres said. "I am starving."

The old woman croaked a laugh. "That word sends needles to my toes. I like to call it the Awakening." She spread her arms wide as if she were revealing something grand. When no one responded, she returned to stirring. "Once all those harmony-smoking idiot Ancients open their eyes, it will be so."

Nova lifted a brow at Eris and he shook his head. Had this woman been sniffing moon dust?

"Right," Cally said, leaning against the counter next to Gem. "You recognized our family crest. You've met Atlas and Ascella Celeste, right?"

"Met them!" Her spoon flew up, splattering the ceiling with chunks of tuber. "I *knew* them." Her eyes sparkled, as if fond memories swam on their surface. "Yes. I knew them well."

Nova was sure her heart beat loudly enough for the entire room to keep time by it. To hear her and Cally's parents' names roll off Gem's lips with such care nearly sunk Nova to her knees. This woman didn't think their parents were criminals.

"Now. I know what your mission is. But you must stay the Darknight here." Gemini brought out six bowls. "We talk and eat." Arlo looked skeptically at the steaming pot, but Eris pushed a bowl to his chest. Tuber soup tasted better than it smelled.

Once they were crowded around her small table, Ceres asked, "Do you know where the rift is?"

Gemini took a loud sip from her spoon. "Not exactly, no." She turned her gaze on Cally, then Nova. "But it's close. In these very mountains—there is a path that will see you on your way come moonrise. The last night I saw Atlas and Ascella was the night they were killed. Either by the Void or by the Ancients." She scowled into the soup. "Atlas felt pulled to the rift. Uncanny man, that one."

Nova thought Gemini didn't have much room to talk. "But you Harvesters always have a way about you." Her eyes landed on Nova's bag. A handful of Threads had edged out, as if curious, and Nova placed a protective hand over them, their powers giving her a tangle of feelings.

"Did Atlas leave a map or anything?" Ceres leaned forward. His eagerness was a wave. Nova felt herself swept up in it.

Gemini tapped her stomach. "It was all in here." She shrugged and glanced at Nova. "But he was always drawn to humans, just as you are, I see." She winked at Arlo, like his presence wasn't a surprise.

"Why aren't you shocked to see him here?" Nova asked.

"Because he isn't the first human who has come through in my lifetime." She took another long sip of her stew.

"What?" Everyone said in unison.

Gemini set down her spoon and stared at them as if they'd lost *their* minds. "*Scales*! You mean . . . your parents never told you?"

"Told us what?" Cally said.

"You girls are half-human. Born from a parent of Lyra and a parent of Earth."

The room grew smaller. Nova's vision latched onto Gemini's gray eyes and wouldn't let go.

It sounded ridiculous, even more so in her mind. It *wasn't* possible, was it? Arlo was the first to slip through in a thousand years. Nova's brain fizzled between disbelief and wonder.

Atlas.

Her father had always been regarded as much too curious. He didn't give a spore about showing his emotions. Nova laughed lightly and massaged her forehead with the tips of her fingers.

No wonder her father was so odd—always searching for answers to things Lyrans took for granted, always teaching Nova not to hide what she was feeling. And the fights between him and Mother . . .

Nova bristled, her mouth twisting. "Is that why our mother didn't want to go along with Father's plans? She found out he was human?"

Gemini's brow furrowed in confusion. "No, child. It was not your father who was Earth-born." She tipped her chin down. "It was your mother."

Nova gaped, and Cally's incredulous gaze deepened. "Our *mother*?"

Gemini nodded. "Ascella came through when she was a child." She studied Arlo. "Far younger than you. Orphaned and alone."

"That's . . . not possible," Nova stammered. "Ascella was the most Lyran-minded person I knew. And her Healer gift was so strong." She glanced at Arlo who was staring at his bowl. It was easy to see Arlo's humanness, but her mother?

"Humans who slip through *always* procure gifts. It's the reason they are called to this world, beckoned by something deep in their blood to become *more*."

"How did we not know?" Nova said. "Did our father know?"

Gemini nodded. "Oh yes. It's why he was so intrigued by humans and how they ticked. And why he sought rifts."

"But our mother was so . . . *cold*." Nova couldn't correlate the two images of Ascella she held in her mind.

"Because she knew if she was ever found out, they would detain her," Cally said, her eyes brimming with tears. "Not only that, we would be under scrutiny too."

"Because we are part human? What could *we* do?"

Cally laughed and shook her head. "Oh, I don't know. Become part of a rebellion. Drag a human here through their dreams."

Nova slouched. "Right. Well—those things could happen to anyone!"

"Right," Gemini said, pointing a gnarled finger at Nova. "That is right, my dear. But the Ancients think humans are emotion-led and as volatile as their ancestors who attacked our kind thousands of years ago. But the Ancients do not recognize the darkness in their own hard hearts."

"Do *they* know humans come through?" Nova asked.

Gemini shook her head, her gaze turned on Arlo. "The change in a human begins immediately, so they'd barely suspect a thing as long as the human keeps hidden for a short time. There are enough of us who help the younger ones when they're found wandering, confused."

Eris pushed his empty bowl away and leaned his arms on the table. "So these sporadic rifts. Do they close again?"

Gemini was chewing on a tuber and it took her several seconds to respond. "Yes, yes. Rifts are not *meant* to stay open. The Inbetween opens and closes them as it wills. Unless something prevents them from closing, of course."

"Like the Void," Eris said, slowly. The realization settled over all of them like a cold mist.

Gem nodded. "It seems that way. The Void once only existed in the sky. Somehow, it's found its way in. To our world. To our land."

To our minds, Nova thought with a shiver.

She knew the rift and the Void were connected somehow, but she hoped it wasn't because the Void was using the rift as a doorway. How could Arlo get home if that were the case?

"Gem, have . . . you ever heard of a Harvester creating a rift through dreams?" Nova asked in a small voice.

"I haven't, no." She smiled warmly at Arlo. "But that doesn't mean it isn't possible. Connection is powerful when two people belong together. Even if you're worlds apart."

Eris shifted in his chair. Nova's cheeks flamed and Arlo's arm, which touched hers, felt too warm.

"But I don't belong here." Arlo's tone was flat. "I have to get back."

"Ah." Gemini's smile dripped into a frown. "You still have family on Earth."

He nodded stiffly.

"Then I wish you the best. But I dare say the path will not be easy for any of you. Even if you find this rift, it will no doubt be heavily guarded. By what or who, I cannot say."

Ceres nodded and plunked his spoon into the soup. Nova no longer had an appetite.

"Well, you all look more beat than fungus paste." Gemini rose from the table. "I've got mats rolled up over in the corner. Many pass through my home. And here, they find rest."

Nova's brain scrambled with more questions about her parents, but she was exhausted—and she didn't want to overtax Gemini at the end of a long night.

Though half of their night had been on the back of the whisp, tiredness tugged at Nova. Her mind spun with all that needed to be done and now the new revelation that her mother had been born on Earth. A lightness entered her heart. The human dreams she visited, the things they experienced. That was her heritage too.

After the dishes were done, the group bumbled their way into the living room. Gemini waved goodnight and shuffled to her own room.

Ceres peered out the window for several minutes.

"Why aren't they coming around to the homes?" Cally asked. She unrolled a mat next to Nova's.

"Polaris doesn't have many Sentries," Ceres said. "They were probably shaken to encounter a Messenger and an *unknown*." He motioned to Arlo who sat slumped across the room from Nova. "I bet they're guarding the walls and waiting for Callisto to send backup. It's what I would do."

His last comment hung mournfully in the air. What would become of them after all of this? They were on the run from the Sentries, many of whom were Ceres's friends.

He turned away from the window and rubbed his eyes. "I think we can all get some rest. We leave for the mountains at moonrise." He laid down on a mat between Eris and Arlo, leaving Cally and Nova alone to process what they'd learned about their parents.

Nova laid back, staring up at the windowless ceiling filled with tiny blue flames. It helped not seeing the Void's presence. But she felt it anyway, creeping into her bones. A heaviness but also a hollowness—as if her magic was being stripped away bit by bit.

She shivered and rolled to her side, facing her sister. She needed sleep but she was dreading what—or who—would come once her eyes closed.

Cally tapped Nova's forehead. "What's going on up there?"

Where to begin? Nova's thoughts slid from what was haunting her present to her parents' past. A past that was now colored in a different light.

"I wish Mother had told us," Nova said, her voice low so only they could hear.

Cally tucked her arm under her head. "Me too. But you were so young. I could see the softness behind her actions. I just never imagined . . ."

"But it's *such* a big secret."

Cally sighed. "She kept it secret because she loved us."

"No." Nova shook her head into the mat. "She kept it secret because she was *afraid*."

"Afraid of what?" Cally snorted. "Nova, she gave her life, alongside our father, to stop the parasite from destroying our planet! I know two things *for certain*." Cally squeezed Nova's hand almost painfully. "Atlas and Ascella Celeste loved their daughters." Tears glistened in her eyes. "And they died trying to give us a chance to live in a better world." She let go of Nova's hand and dashed the tears from her eyes.

Nova let those words settle like silt in a calm creek. She wished they would sink deep enough that she'd never question their truth. Her father's love made sense. But her emotionally distant mother?

My mother loved me.

She listened to Arlo's breathing across the room as she closed her eyes. She needed sleep no matter if the Void or Eijlek, or whatever, awaited her. As her mind slowly drifted, Nova latched to the truth that was so easily swayed in the dark.

I was loved.

I am loved.

That Darknight, as her mind gave way to sleep, Nova did not slip into a nightmare.

Chapter Twenty-Eight

Sleep hasn't been the same since Earth.
Nova can't find me in the murk.
I am left to my own dark defenses.
The voice oozes in,
Whispering slithery things,
Things that make me wonder
Consider...

But
You are not your father,
You deserve another chance, Nova said.
I want to believe her.
I'm gripping the edges of her words
Holding on tight,
Hoping they're real and
Solid enough to save me.

But Nova can't bear my weight,
Like my mom couldn't bear Dad's.
So I pry my fingers off and truly
Consider...

I might be a coward, but I can fight.
I might be a bad seed, but I can grow.
I might know shame, but I can learn.
I might be the son of my father,
But I'm also the son of my mother.

And Mom stands still—solid
Unshakable even when facing death.
Perhaps that could be me too.

Someone brave.
Giving up an entire world
For the one who needs me.
Learning to see Earth
The way Nova dreams of Lyra.
Oh, the possibilities.

I could be someone with purpose,
Who isn't afraid of what's to come.
Someone who can make amends.
Who is simply Arlo James.

Someone, I might learn to live with.

CHAPTER TWENTY-NINE

G emini's willowy voice dragged Nova from a dream. Or at least she thought it might have been a dream.

Nova remembered the Inbetween and swirling galaxies. An expansive, endless existence. Feeling small and big at the same time. But when she sat up, scrubbing her face, it became a faint impression. Blearily, she looked over at everyone else packing their bags.

"Why didn't you wake me?" Nova combed through her hair with her fingers and tied it in a low bun.

Cally smiled. "You looked like you were enjoying sleep for a change."

"I was." Her lip quirked up. "Cally, I think I had an actual dream. On my own. No human connection."

Cally tied the bag closed and stood. "I would say it can't happen, but the last few days have shifted my perspective on what's possible."

Nova rolled up her mat. "I'll agree with that."

Ceres stared out the narrow window. The moon had not yet risen, but the sky had turned the deep purple she loved so much. The color of promise. Selene was on her way.

Ceres rubbed a hand over his square chin where a shadow of a beard had formed. He looked well rested. Arlo, on the other hand, looked disheveled. Red hair stuck up on one side, his shirt off-kilter.

"Are we ready to go?" Eris asked.

Gemini shuffled in. "Would you like to eat firs—" She was cut off by faint noises.

Shouts. The sound of running.

"*Constellations*," Gemini said under her breath.

Ceres turned from the window. "Backup is here. They must've taken a transport at the tail end of Darknight."

Nova felt the tug of her Threads. Each strand tingled with action, as if they sensed the danger outside the door.

"Do you have another exit?" Cally asked Gem.

"This way."

They threw on their packs and followed Gemini back into her room. There was a small door the same color as her gray walls. It creaked when she wrenched it open, revealing a tight rock tunnel, and beyond, moonlight. "Be quick," she said.

Nova turned to the old woman. "Thank you. For everything." She hoped Gemini understood her meaning—Gemini had *meant something* to her parents. That eccentric house had been the last safe place they'd stayed before they died.

Ceres slipped through the door, but Nova's feet wouldn't move. She went numb. Her parents' faces tumbled through her mind. The thought of Eijleck's all-consuming hunger made her skin prickle. And the Ancients—the leaders who would do anything to keep it all contained.

If they stepped outside, what would happen next?

Nova feared all those she loved would end up like her parents.

"Nova?" Arlo touched her shoulder, his palm's warmth bleeding through her shawl. She looked at his moss eyes and set jaw. At Eris's firm expression behind him. Cally gave her a nod.

Nova took in a shaky breath and imagined her human blood singing to her Lyran blood, slow and soft, pulsing with possibility.

There was a tear in her two homes that needed mending. A boy who needed to fix a wrong.

She followed Ceres into the purple haze.

They tore down a windy path that led them to a small gate at the base of the mountains. Ceres motioned for them to wait. He peered around the open door and exhaled. "There's only a single guard. I've got her."

"Let me." Cally gripped his arm. In a spark and a blast of air, she left then reappeared. There was a soft thud on the other side of the wall, and she nodded grimly. "Let's go."

They raced out of the gate and into a copse of trees. Nova saw the woman lying on the ground, her head lolled to the side. "What did you do to her?"

"She's just unconscious."

But Nova could read Cally's unease. She wasn't a Sentry. None of them were, save for Ceres, and now he was fighting against his own comrades.

The path was easy enough to find through the trees, and when none pursued them, they slowed their sprint to a jog.

Finally, the trees opened to a clearing at a craggy base. Nova didn't notice Ceres stop and plowed into his back. He stumbled forward, but quickly regained his rigid stance.

"What—" Nova said, before realizing they weren't alone in the clearing. Her breath hitched in her throat. Arlo sucked in a wheezy gasp behind her.

Armed Sentries stood in a semi-circle around the clearing. Something snapped behind them and Nova spun. More guards, coming from the trees, hemmed them in.

Ceres cursed. "I knew we got away too easy." His heavy gaze fell on Cally. "I should've been more careful."

The Sentries pulled out their swords and Nova stifled a sob. But then another figure stepped forward, navy blue robes contrasting with her star-white hair. She was slender and tall, and her presence made Nova feel small.

Ancient Belinda. The one who had sent the Sentries after her parents.

Why is a Callisto Ancient here?

She glanced at Cally who looked just as mystified. And nervous.

"You are all being sentenced to five years of containment for your crimes," Belinda said.

Five years? It was far less than she expected, but maybe they didn't know their true mission yet? Nor did they know about Arlo.

"What are the crimes we supposedly committed?" Ceres asked, voice unwavering.

Belinda turned to a Sentry by her side. He cleared his throat and spoke, "For using Threads to cause destruction of Callistian property."

That was it? Surely they knew where they were headed—why they were on this path.

Ancient Belinda walked toward them, and the rest of the Sentries followed, hedging in closer and closer. "That *is* all that has transpired, correct *Captain* Ceres?" Belinda's silver eyes were piercing as they swept the group. She knew what they were doing.

Was she giving them a chance to go home? To forget the attempt to find the rift?

But then Belinda stilled, her gaze catching on Arlo. Her expression grew narrow and sharp.

"And where are you from, boy?"

Arlo stammered, looking down at his shirt gaping wide over his unmarked chest.

"Don't worry, I don't need your voice."

Belinda squeezed her eyes shut and took a deep breath. A vein in her neck throbbed.

Nova's stomach plunged. Belinda was a Messenger. She would see all their secrets in seconds.

"No!" Ceres turned to Arlo. "Resist her voice."

At the same moment, Arlo gripped his hair with a hiss of pain. "She's—too strong!"

There was a spark of light, and in a single blink, Cally had disappeared. But when she reappeared, a man gripped her arms, holding her back to his chest. Another Walker.

"Cally!" Nova yelped.

Cally tugged and sparked but the Sentry's strength held her captive. "Found the Walker, Ancient." And then he said in a lower voice, "If you break free, I'll only catch you again."

Ceres lunged, but Eris held him back. There were too many of them. Nova studied the other soldiers—seven more. And three, she noticed, were not Sentries at all. She recognized them from the Harvesting Center, and they had an extreme dislike of Nova.

Two of the Harvesters wore their Threads around their wrists, and another wore his as a sash. They had brought just enough specific mages for combat.

Arlo groaned and Nova held him up. He slumped into her and blinked open his eyes, glaring at Belinda.

"*Impossible*," she said, taking a step back.

Arlo's chin dropped to his chest. "She saw everything."

"Of course I did! I came because I'm the strongest Messenger in Callisto. And I needed to know who this outsider was." She lifted her chin. "But this boy is not just any outsider raised in the dark wilds. He's a *human*." The other mages shifted, their expressions confused and curious, as they glanced from Arlo to Belinda.

"We just want to get him home," Nova said, stepping in front of Arlo.

"And you will use the rift to accomplish this?" Belinda's eyes glowed cold once more. "You think it will be so simple." A few white strands tumbled from her tight bun. "You know nothing of what we've been trying to preserve."

"Preserve?" Nova said, her indignation rising. "You mean killing our parents to keep the tear in our world a secret? *Why?* The parasite will keep eating away our world until nothing and no one is left!" Her lungs burned and arms trembled, but she kept her gaze locked on Belinda. She could finally get answers. Her parents deserved a better ending. She and Cally *needed* it.

"If we close the rift like your little *rebellion* here wants to, you will doom us much more quickly than the Void will."

Nova's heat died at her words.

"What do you mean?" Ceres said.

"How do you think we remain connected to Earth? That single

176

tear in reality allows us to harvest Threads and to dream Walk into human minds. Into their world." Belinda shook her head. "What do you suppose will happen if it is closed?"

Nova's throat went dry. She gripped Arlo's hand.

Belinda looked down at their joined hands and scoffed. "You would never enter another dream. And what's more. We would no longer be able to process Threads to strengthen our land, to give us energy. And once all the caps are consumed by the parasite, not even our foxfire orbs and walls will hold the darkness at bay."

Cold trickled down Nova's back.

I can never be satiated.

"How can you be so sure?" Cally said, trying to break her arms free. But the man held tighter. "Have you *tried* to close it?"

Belinda's lips puckered as if she had tasted something bitter. "We cannot get close enough to test our theory. The last ones who did, ended up dead."

Nova's ears buzzed with the silence that followed. "Dead? *Who?*"

"Your parents."

"But, it was you," Nova said. "You silenced them. You—"

"Your father was intelligent, but he was also a fool. He believed there was a way to close the rift and kill the Void at the same time. Even though I forbade him." She dipped her head. "He provoked the Void and its decay began to spread faster, consuming your parents along with it." For a moment, Belinda's eyes softened. "You want to blame me—go ahead. But in the end it was your father's naïve hope that got them both killed."

It was Nova's turn to lean into Arlo. "You're lying," she said, her voice no more than a breath. It was easier to punish the Ancients for what they'd done. To get behind a Movement to reveal all the secrets.

But what if the secrets kept them alive longer?

Nova's brain spun. They'd left the door wide open for a monster. And now there might not be a way to rid their world of it.

"He will never stop," Nova said, her voice ringing in the clearing. Selene's light was over the tree line now. "You cannot appease him."

"Him?" Belinda frowned. "Who is *him?*"

Nova glanced nervously at Cally who was watching her with confusion.

"The—the Void. He has appeared in my nightmares and calls himself Eijleck. A name that means hunger. And he will never stop. You can't let him continue to feed." Nova's voice was rising into hysterics. "You can't!" She gripped her shawl but more confusing feelings poured into her from the Threads.

Belinda frowned. "Lyrans do not remember their nightmares. Not even Harvesters."

"But I did."

Belinda sighed and clicked her tongue at the Sentries. "Even if that were true and the Void had a name and intelligence, it would only make me more wary about going against it." Her gaze hardened. "It cannot be stopped. And if you close that rift, it will only doom us sooner."

"But I have to go through it," Arlo said. He winced as if his own voice hurt his head.

"I cannot allow that. Provoking the parasite causes it to spread faster. I won't endanger our people further."

"There has to be another way, Belinda," Ceres said. His hand rested on the hilt of his sword. "Let us pass."

"Do you not believe me?" she said, raising to her full height.

"That's the problem!" he said. "You've kept Callisto in the dark as much as the Void has. How can we trust those who have never earned it?"

"It would have caused a panic!"

"Move." He drew his sword slowly.

Then, Nova felt something niggling at her brain. It grew more insistent. She flinched and then she heard, *Nova?*

Ceres? She tried not to look at him.

I need you to use your Threads—many at once, if necessary. We must distract and immobilize. Then run."

The connection severed but she saw Cally and Eris perk up. Ceres was giving them a plan. A way out.

"Lay down your arms, Captain Ceres," Belinda said, her pale face turning darker. "How d—"

"Now!" Ceres yelled.

The clearing erupted in chaos.

CHAPTER THIRTY

Nova had never used more than one Thread at a time before — she didn't think she could handle the intensity of the emotions. But in that moment, with adrenaline and fear pumping through her, she felt as if she could climb the clouds and skewer the Void itself.

Nova tore off her shawl and flung it in the air. She called on every Thread that could defend them. The shield came first, erupting gray and victorious. Red Thread unraveled, flame exploding like a torrent, filling her with a feral hatred. The ball of Earthen fire barreled toward the other Harvesters, its roar drowning out the cries as they scattered.

Her storm Thread, deep blue and soaked with melancholy, swept the skies, darkening the stars with black clouds that wept electric tears. Lightning struck the ground. More emotions and objects — both natural and human-made — burst into existence.

Eris's Threads joined with hers. But the other Harvesters had gained enough clarity to combat them.

She felt a hundred emotions pour into her as the Threads took form.

She needed to call on more.

Nova gritted her teeth against the shadow Thread's fear and the fun that poured from the radio. She tried to focus on the rage, the thrill of victory, and the frustration that coiled from a large table that nearly squashed a Sentry. But she couldn't help but to take it all on her shoulders. Every single dreamer's emotion coursed through her in a paradoxical mishmash.

She gasped and staggered, her mind a whirlwind.

Every Thread bore down on the enemy and herself.

Rushing blurred shapes told Nova that Cally and the other Walker were trying to overtake one another with speed. Ceres was battling three Sentries with a skilled sword. He also looked strained, as if mentally fighting off Belinda, who hid in the trees. He looked ready to break. And Eris . . . where was Eris?

Sluggishly, Nova turned her head. Eris was in the middle of the battle, wielding three Threads—fireworks, wind, and a large dog. He hadn't used all of his Threads. He'd been smart.

But Nova didn't know how to draw back her magic—it was wild with excitement and her thoughts were being tugged in too many directions.

Nova.

She flinched. The voice had sounded like Arlo's, but distant.

Nova.

A hand took hers and she tore her gaze from the light and noise and fighting. Arlo's eyes burned into hers with what looked like trepidation.

Stop, Nova! He mouthed the words, but they came from somewhere in her mind.

Magic kept pouring from Nova like a waterfall, and she felt herself unraveling.

She fell to her knees, vision blackening around the edges. Darknight?

No, she was losing consciousness.

Sleep sounded good. Far from the horrible noise. The pain and worries and griefs and joys and lethargy and hatred. She could barely recognize herself amidst the chaos.

Let go of them, Nova!

Arlo's voice startled her to lucidity for a moment. A tiny voice in the storm.

Yes. She had to let go of the Threads.

They were killing her.

With a scream she bent into the ground and forced the feelings away from her, like they were a true Thread. She cut it with her mind.

Snap.

The night exploded. Nova crumbled. Pain settled in, and her chest burned as if she were drowning in an icy river.

Nova?

She was too weak to breach the surface.

Her body convulsed, and she felt someone holding her so she wouldn't break apart.

I've got you. Come back to me.

His breath warmed her hair but she was too tired to respond.

Her eyes rolled back and she saw the brilliant stars growing dull. Were they winking out or was it her mind growing dark? Before she could prepare herself for what might be awaiting her, she fell into a deep sleep. And into the shadowy arms of Eijleck.

Chapter Thirty-One

The night is calamity.
Light and storms and
Household objects
Flying from impossible strings.
A girl with the power of the moon
Pouring through her veins.
And I, a simple human
Gripping the tethers of reality
So I'm not swept away.
No—I'm not ready for this world
For this kind of magic.

But is she?

Nova splinters,
Ripping at the seams.
Nova!
She doesn't hear.
Nova!
I scream into the space between.
A space that feels thinner each hour.
Can I break through?

But that other voice is here:
You cannot help her,
You can't even help yourself.
You are weak.
You'll abandon everyone you love.
Fire and swords flash and clash—
Nova sinks to the ground.

This voice in my head
It's not the one I want to hear.
Nova battles.
So do I.
You are not your father, her voice, an echo.
You are free, a warmer voice says.
It's rich — comforting.
Cinnamon hot chocolate
On Christmas Eve nights.

You are nothing, the cold voice says.

But I *am* something.
A son and a friend and more.
And I am needed.

Nova is a dying star,
A supernova ready to burst in a brilliant end.
Stop, Nova! I yell. *Let go of them!*
The Threads — they will kill her.

I can't live in *any* world
Knowing she is gone.

Then — break through!
Her thoughts flutter like moth wings into mine
Her mind is a torrent of feeling.
Arlo?
I grip her shoulders, holding her
As the fight dances violently around us.
I've got you, I whisper,
But I don't know if she hears.

Her magic wains,
Her brow flickers, uncertain.
My head aches but I keep whispering

Into that space between us.
I nearly split.
Yells fill the night.
Sweat and smoke and heat
Sting my nostrils.
But the cold voice has been hushed
It is her I hear —
My Nova.
Crying in the corner of her mind
Where even she can't hear.

I've got you, I repeat.
But I don't have her.

And the night explodes.

CHAPTER THIRTY-TWO

"**I** knew you were weak, but that was pathetic."

Nova blinked at Cally. The world burned around them.

"What?" Nova asked her sister. She coughed on the smoke that poured down her throat and stung her eyes. All she saw was a wall of hazy gray. Cally's red hair swirled around her shoulders. She looked so unkempt. So unbothered. "You aren't Cally." Nova squinted through the smoke. "This is another nightmare."

"It might be, but *I'm* very much real."

Dread crept over Nova and she took a step back.

Cally's smile twisted unnaturally. Nova felt sick.

"What do you want with me?"

Eijleck laughed. "It's not personal, Speck. I am not invading *your* mind—no, you are not important enough for that."

"Am I in your mind?"

Cally's mouth widened in a crash of laughter. Her skin wrinkled and began to shed. Nova gasped as something dark and wet stepped from Cally's shell. It lumbered toward Nova, the smell of decay overpowering her, long arms dragging the ground. It changed again, and it was a smoky wolf panting with husky breath. Its eyes glowed silver then black, and it was a slithering mass, like in Arlo's dream.

"You would not survive in my mind," the mass whispered. "Not with what I have witnessed. Not with what I have done."

"Then . . . how is this possible?"

Eijleck hesitated, a smoky tendril coiling back into itself. Nova sensed something she'd never felt when confronted with the Void before. It seemed . . . *unsure.*

The Void did not control their strange connection.

A spring of courage rushed up in Nova.

"There's something else, isn't there? Something even bigger. Even older than you."

The mass rippled like a mud puddle before shifting back into Cally—but its eyes remained pure black. "Older, but not stronger. Nothing is stronger than my hunger."

Nova took a tentative step forward. If she could understand why the Void did what it did, maybe it could help them destroy it. She took a shaky breath, feeling every bit as frail as Eijleck suspected she was. But she pressed forward. Finding out the Void's weakness was too important.

"And what do you hunger for most?"

Cally's gaze darkened and the gray smoke choked Nova further, clouding her vision and filling her lungs. At the same time, a warm wind rushed through. It did not smell of rot. It tasted like the brines.

Nova's stomach tugged at her, and she was pulled back. Away.

But before Eijleck disappeared completely, he answered her question.

"Fear."

~

The Inbetween cradled Nova and she nearly wept. It had been too long since she'd slipped a circlet over her forehead and felt the comfort of the Inbetween.

She was rushing though the stars. Their heat nipped at her cheeks but did not sear. The stars pulsed a white-blue and almost seemed alive, like they were distant hearts alight in the heavens.

For the first time in many nights, contentment flooded Nova. She was a young girl again—before she worried about the deceits of their world. There was no weight on her shoulders. No striving to finish an impossible job. Not even her parents' deaths grieved her.

Nova suspected she could see the innerworkings of the universe, like her eyes and mind were shaped by the hands of the stars themselves.

Nova was *alive*.

She even imagined she could create her own dreams.

But soon she felt a tug that grew urgent, and her consciousness slipped from the Inbetween.

With a rush of breath she opened her eyes to a sky full of stars.

"Where—?" Nova sat up, head spinning. Reality stormed back with a vengeance and so did the pain. Her skin felt raw. But it was her aching chest and a ringing headache that hurt the most. "Where are we?" Cally, Arlo, and Eris loomed over her. So did craggy cliffs.

She turned her throbbing head and saw they were in a little cavern.

"Eris carried you for about half a mile," Cally said.

"But—" Nova peered behind them. "Where's Ceres?"

Cally looked as if she were trying to control her features.

Nova's eyes widened in horror. "Is he—?"

Eris shook his head. Sweat beaded on his forehead. "He was alive when we escaped. He . . . he sacrificed himself so we could get away." Cally cursed and stood, moving away from them. Eris glanced her way then continued. "When your Threads, sort of, exploded, it knocked out the Harvesters and one of the Sentries, and we took out the rest. But if Ceres lost his focus on Ancient Belinda, she could've used him or one of us to harm each other."

"He stayed behind," Nova said dully.

"To give us a chance."

Nova nodded stiffly. She wanted to believe, now more than ever, that the Ancients hadn't harmed her parents. If that were true and if Ceres was captured, maybe they wouldn't hurt him either. They could find a way to break him out.

"Are you able to walk?" Eris said. "I don't think I can carry you any further."

Nova tried a half-smile. "I thought you were strong."

Eris helped her up, and she glanced at Arlo. He watched her as if she were made of moon glass. "Are you alright?" she asked him. Which was a strange thing to ask when none of them were alright.

He rumpled his hair. "Yeah. Just—I heard your mind when you used all your Threads. It was . . ." He swallowed. "I thought you were going to die, Nova."

"You heard my mind?" She glanced at Eris who shrugged.

"Ceres told me to latch onto the loudest voice," Arlo said. "In that moment, your thoughts were practically screaming for help."

Nova closed her eyes as another wave of pain shot through the back of her head. "Yes," she said. "I heard you. You told me to let go of my Threads." She touched her chest, wanting to see if any had been damaged in the fight. No doubt they would be shaken after such an ordeal.

Her fingers trailed the empty space around her collarbone, above the chain of her father's necklace, then dropped to her exposed arms.

Nova looked down in confusion.

"Where's my shawl?"

No one spoke. Unease dripped down her spine.

"No . . ." Nova grabbed her satchel from the ground and opened it. No shawl.

Cally was staring at Nova again, her mouth and brows pinched. She looked younger, fragile.

"Cally? Tell me where it is."

Her sister cleared her throat. "It was lost, Nova."

"What do you mean?"

Cally hesitated.

"When you cut your ties to the magic," Arlo said. "When you screamed, your Threads unraveled. Some fell to the ground, nothing more than string. But a few others exploded."

"But . . . they re-formed. They came back." She looked at Eris. "Our Threads always come back."

Eris rubbed his forehead. "Not this time. I tried to gather a few of the strands but they crumbled. Their glow and life was gone. I felt nothing."

Nothing?

It couldn't be true. Her Threads always came back. They were a part of her. An extension of her mind. Not only would they have come floating back to her on the wind . . .

She always felt them. Now, she felt nothing.

Nova closed her eyes. "But my magic . . ." All the contentment she'd felt in the Inbetween evaporated. Without Ceres's strategic mind and leadership, without her Threads, their chance of success felt impossible.

Nova was vulnerable without her shawl. Selene's power remained, but now it felt as if it taunted her. What good was it without her Threads? She didn't even have a circlet on hand to harvest more from dreamers.

Cally placed both hands on Nova's shoulders. "I'm sorry, but we need to keep going. The Sentries will wake up soon and likely pursue us . . ."

"But—"

"Your magic can still help us."

Nova frowned in confusion.

"The rift. You and Eris need to find it. We're running out of time."

Right. The rift. Arlo. Stopping Eijleck.

Nova tried to steady herself. Her head had stopped throbbing. But the task at hand seemed insurmountable. Eijleck had called her a speck. And in the moment, she agreed.

Cally smiled with tears in her eyes. "Be strong, little flame."

Father's nickname for her. Nova swallowed a knot tightening her throat.

A warm breeze caught her loose hair, and she smelled the brine of the lake. The reminder of the Inbetween roused her.

The Void had been unsure of their connection. Perhaps something greater than Eijleck was working toward something good. Was it possible?

It was the last, frayed, strand of hope she clung to.

CHAPTER THIRTY-THREE

They walked in silence, luminous emerald lichen dotted the looming cliffs to either side of the narrow ravine, and larger red fungi hung over their heads like layered plates. Small creatures slunk into crevices as they passed, leaving behind streaks of glowing slime in their wake. The air shifted the higher they climbed, the salty scent giving over to thin freshness.

After walking for hours, Nova's legs cramped with fatigue and her lungs worked in overtime with the changing altitude. Jagged rocks and loose pebbles made them lose their footing and everyone's breath became haggard.

"Can you hear any more voices?" Cally called back to Arlo. He walked behind Nova, with Eris taking the lead.

Arlo hesitated. "Uh. The Sentries, you mean?"

"Who else would I be talking about?" Nova winced at Cally's short tone, but she knew her sister's heart ached over Ceres.

"I am only getting snatches of thoughts. But I think they're following us. I've heard 'human' 'the rift.' Belinda's voice is clearest—she's determined."

Cally cursed and increased her stride, though Nova noticed her limp. She would run herself ragged. They were all on the brink of collapse.

"Wait," Arlo said. "If Belinda can press her thoughts out this far, does that mean she can control us?"

Cally's red braid whipped around when she turned her head. "No. Messengers can communicate long-distance with other Messengers, but they can't control other mages unless they are within close range. If you can't see them, you're safe." Cally faced the path again, her voice muffled. "It's a good thing she doesn't know you're developing Messenger abilities, though. She'd try to communicate with you. Fill your head with lies."

Nova chewed on Cally's words. On Belinda's words, too.

"Do you think she was lying about our parents?"

Cally's stride did not slow or falter. "I don't know anymore, Nova. It's something we can deal with later. Either way, our mission right now is the same. We have to get Arlo back to his home and close the rift."

"But the Void . . ."

Cally stopped so suddenly Nova almost bumped into her. She spun around, her heels crunching in the loose rock. There were angry tears in her eyes. "This was the plan. The only plan I have. And though . . . *things* . . . haven't lined up perfectly, it doesn't mean it can't be done." Her breath hitched. "Right?"

It took a moment to realize her sister was *asking* Nova, not telling her.

"Yes," Nova said in a small voice. What else could she say? Her sister needed a reason to keep going, to believe in the Movement. Their only other option was to return and be imprisoned. "If Father believed the rift could be destroyed, then that's what we try to do."

Cally sniffed. "Even though they died trying?"

Nova stood taller. Cally's uncertainty was a strange shock to her system. But there was also something nice about being needed. In that moment Cally didn't feel like Nova's guardian, but her sister. A sister who was as scared as she was.

"Neither one of us will rest until we figure this out."

Cally nodded.

Nova turned to Eris. "It isn't too late for you to go back. *We* have to find this rift for our parents, but your parents are waiting for you back in Callisto."

"I'm doing this for them. And for you. And for our people. Besides"—his voice hitched—"the Sentries, Ancient Belinda, they saw my face. In a way, it is too late for me."

Nova's stomach dropped. He was right. Arlo caught her gaze and immediately looked away, his jaw ticking. Nova was too tired to ask him what he was thinking, and she didn't think he'd admit his feelings in front of the group anyway.

They began walking again, hitting switchbacks that gave them a view of the lake below. The height was staggering. Eris grew shakier with every step, and Nova reminded him not to look down. After another hour they reached a flat trail that skimmed along a ridge. Cally turned to follow the narrow footpath.

"No," Nova blurted. She stopped, staring straight ahead through thick, spindly brush that was littered with more glowing lichen. "I think we should go this way."

"But . . . the path." Cally motioned ahead of her.

"Nova's right," Eris said. "I feel it too."

Relief softened Cally's frown. "You feel a pull?"

Nova and Eris nodded.

Nova stepped closer to the bush. Spindle trees and glowing knee-height caps dotted the path. "It feels *wrong* not to go this way."

Eris followed her. "Exactly."

"We can't!" Arlo gripped his hair, chin burying into his chest as if he were in pain. "We can't go that way." He gasped and gritted his teeth. "His voice is too loud. It—it *hurts*."

Nova ran to Arlo and tugged down his arms. "Who's voice?"

He shook his head, eyes clenched shut. Mouth screwed up in pain.

"Arlo!" She took his face in her hands. "Look at me. Who's voice?"

He fell back from her touch and gripped his stomach as if he were going to be sick. Nova looked at Eris and Cally helplessly. Then,

Arlo stood up straight, blinking rapidly. "He's gone." A single tear traced his freckles but the agony from whatever he'd heard still lingered.

"Who?" Nova moved closer.

Arlo swallowed hard, his face flushing a deep red. "The voice I heard in the dream. Before I came through the rift. It's his voice. It . . . *he* still whispers to me."

"The Void?"

Arlo blew out a breath and wiped his face. "I think it must be. Ceres told me to focus on the loudest voice and his is the loudest. Or it was, until the fight back there." His gaze sharpened on Nova. "Until I needed to help you. To reach your mind, your voice, I had to fight *him* off."

"How?" Nova breathed.

"I finally believed in something else—something *more* than what he was filling my brain with."

Nova gripped his trembling arm. "Thank you, Arlo. Your power, your voice, it woke me up. But never listen to him again." She shivered. "I'm so sorry. I thought I was the only one connected to him." Her shoulders dropped. "I wish I'd known."

"What do you mean, connected to him?" he asked.

Cally was beside them in a moment. "What are you saying, Nova?"

"The nightmares," Nova said. "I told you I saw the Void. He takes different forms. Sometimes a miedo, sometimes people I know, or other horrible things. But it is always him. *Eijleck.* He makes me remember my nightmares, somehow. Somehow we are connected." Nova rubbed her forehead. "I'm terrified to go to sleep because I know he'll be there. Waiting."

"Oh, Nova." Arlo's brows pinched together.

"It seems all three of us are tied together." Nova's eyes flicked up to Arlo's. "In your dream, before you came through to Lyra—the rift we opened in your mind. He was there. I think that's when he in-infected us." Cold dread coiled in her gut like a snake.

"No." Cally shook her head. "You haven't been Void poisoned. We would have seen the effects."

"But we're still bound to him somehow."

"Then we find a way to break the bind," Eris said. He placed a hand on Nova's back but looked between her and Arlo. "It *has* a weakness. All living things do. And we'll find it."

"He's right." Cally hitched up her pack. "Can you lead us to the rift, Nova?"

Nova hesitated, glancing at Eris who was a better leader than her in almost every respect. His eyes twinkled with amusement as if he had read her mind. "You made a rift with your brain, Nova. I think you'll have a better chance at finding it than me."

Nova wanted to argue, but his point was made. With trembling legs and a pounding heart, Nova stepped off the path.

~

They hiked through the wilderness, resting occasionally to replenish themselves by drinking the water squeezed from sponge plants. The woods were not as thick on the mountain, and the plants were more scraggly than rubbery and tubular—though they still had to watch out for the tentacled variety on occasion. At one point they startled a small herd of eweden sheep, their wool as fluffy as a cloud and glowing blue like Selene.

Without caps and rubber leaves above their heads the moon and her stars shone down fiercely. Nova felt as if she could reach up and touch them. Her magic hummed powerfully in her, and she pressed her hand to her chest, feeling a renewed pang of grief for her shawl. Even if she gathered more Threads, they wouldn't be the same. She'd been collecting her Threads since she was a child— each one a beloved friend.

Her palm fell on the foxfire pendant, and she lifted it, gazing at its light. She had a sudden urge to let the foxfire free. There were enough things being held captive on Lyra. But it was dangerous when unconfined. Sighing, she set it back on her chest, its warmth tickling her skin.

Though she was exhausted, the pull toward the rift was becoming irresistible. It almost made her giddy, though she dreaded what lay at the end. The Void had been pouring forth from the rift for hundreds of years.

"Wish those whisps would swoop down and carry us to the rift right about now," Eris said from behind her.

Nova snorted. *She* hoped they wouldn't come anywhere near it. The aurelia jellies were beautiful, pure. It would break her heart to see any of them ensnared by the Void.

After another hour, Nova could feel the magic in her blood slow to a trickle. She glanced up and saw the edges of Darknight creeping across the sky. But the rift did not seem far now. It could be beyond that ridge ahead. Or on the other side of those trees.

"Nova."

Nova turned to her sister. The group stopped.

"We need sleep. And we don't want to face the Void when it's strongest."

It took everything in Nova to drag herself back. She groaned. "It feels wrong stopping when we're so close."

Eris rubbed his chest and wrinkled his forehead. "It's a weird resistance."

Nova settled down near a mossy clump of stones and Arlo plopped down next to her. He massaged his calves, his shoulder leaning into hers.

"I would've exercised more—or at all—if I'd known we'd be hiking mountains."

Nova smiled, her body warred with the pull to keep moving, needing rest, and fear of sleep. Eris found a tree to lean against a few yards away, and Cally curled up under a spindle tree, its branches dripping over her like a cage. They should find a better place, but there were no caves. Nothing to stop the miedo beastias or any other creature if they came.

Nova was almost too tired to care.

She laid her head on Arlo's shoulder and he tensed for a moment, then relaxed. Tentatively, he took her hand in his lap, his thumb brushing over her knuckles.

If their plan worked, Arlo would be gone soon.

She entwined her fingers in his.

And if they managed to shut the rift . . . she couldn't even visit his dreams any longer.

She gripped his hand harder.

"Nova?" His breath was warm on her hair.

"Hmmm?"

"What if you left with me? You and your sister. Even Eris if he wanted to."

This made Nova sit up. "What do you mean?"

Arlo looked nervous and he fiddled with her fingers, not meeting her eye. "I just mean, if you guys are going to be locked up, why not come with me? You could start over again on Earth."

Nova laughed lightly, incredulous.

Arlo frowned. "It isn't such a far-fetched idea. I came *here* didn't I?"

"I know." Her smile slid away. "It isn't a bad idea. It's just . . . Cally would never leave Ceres. Nor Eris his parents."

Arlo sighed, mouth tightening. He glanced at Eris's silhouette, barely visible in the darkness. "And you would have to leave them both."

She twisted her mouth. "But I don't want to lose you either."

"We always seem to be in a pickle, don't we?"

"A *what*?"

He laughed. "Never mind. It doesn't matter." He turned his head to peer at her. They were so close she could count the silver specks in his eyes. Everything around her faded, her fears and worries, her exhaustion, even the tug toward the rift. For a moment it was only her and Arlo. Like it had been when they were thirteen. Or fourteen. Or fifteen. Or any time before things were heavy.

"What I mean," he said quietly, "is that our destiny is to *almost* belong together." He glanced up at the twinkling sky that Darknight had yet to extinguish. "Like two planets going around the same star but in different orbits."

"Arlo —"

He shook his head. "It's alright. I know what I'm asking of you is too much." When he looked at Nova again his eyes seemed to burn like fire. "Even though these last few days — er, nights — have been terrifying and hard, meeting you has been the best thing that's ever happened to me." He smiled. "I'd be an idiot not to be thankful, even if our time is short." He looked down at their woven fingers. "My mom's suffering has felt like it would last forever, but now I realize how much time I've lost. How much I want to get it back. Coming here has shown me that." His thumb stilled. "I just hope my disappearance hasn't made her worse. What if—?"

"She'll be there."

He arched a brow at her. "How do you know?"

"Claire might be weak in body, but her mind is strong. She loves you so much, Arlo. She'll fight even harder against her sickness so she can see you again."

Arlo took a deep breath, chest heaving. "I hope you're right. But part of me feels selfish for wanting her to hold on too. I wish she could be free from the pain."

Nova didn't know what to say, so she squeezed his hand.

"You need sleep," said Arlo.

She tucked her loose hair behind an ear. "I know." She sighed. "I'm scared to sleep."

Arlo was silent for a moment. "Maybe, try to act like a Messenger. You need to focus on a voice—but a different one. Not Age-lick or whatever you called him, but on something else that will keep your mind from slipping into a nightmare."

"But Lyrans only have nightmares."

"Nope. I don't believe that. The alien-girl who gave me such comfort in my own dreams? Who lives in a world that glows? A world with magic and flying jellyfish?" Arlo shook his head. "I don't believe it one bit that you guys can't dream."

"You don't have to believe it. It's true."

Except that she had dreamt. Could she do it again?

"Pah." He waved his free hand. "Maybe it's true since the Void has been here. But he hasn't always been here, right? So maybe your ancestors dreamt. Heck, humans are your ancestors, Nova! Of course your people used to dream."

Nova's heart raced. "I mean, technically, yes."

"And your mom definitely dreamt on Earth, before coming here."

Nova nodded. "Probably."

"If I can get superpowers, you can find a way to dream."

"Actually, I have had a dream."

"What? You let me go on a rant about this for nothing?"

Nova looked down. "I don't remember what it was about. But I know I didn't have a nightmare. It was after speaking to Cally in Polaris about our parents. I went to sleep feeling so hopeful, lost in thoughts about my mother and how . . . how she loved me."

"There it is." Arlo said. "Think on that as you drift to sleep. That's the 'voice'—the truth—you listen to."

Arlo sat up enough to curl his arm around Nova's shoulders. "You can lean on me. In case you're having any nightmares, I'll wake you up. But I doubt I'll need to."

Tension unraveled from Nova's shoulders and back. "Thank you, Arlo. I wish—" she hesitated.

His face fell. "I know. You wish so many things." His voice grew quieter, deeper.

Her eyes roamed his face, wanting to memorize every fleck and freckle, every quirk of his mouth. The length of his dark eyelashes. The scar over his left eye. The waves of his hair.

"It wasn't just your mom who loved you." He nodded toward Cally and Eris. "You're surrounded by people who love you." His gaze met hers again, full of vulnerability. "And I . . . well . . ." Color bloomed on his cheeks, but he didn't look away. "I love you too, Nova."

"You do?" she said breathlessly.

He laughed dipping his head so close she felt the warmth of his face. "*Yes.* I love you, alien-girl."

Nova closed her eyes. His lips brushed hers lightly. It felt as if Selene's magic hummed wildly in her veins, in her brain, though she knew it wasn't the cause.

It was Arlo. This funny, sweet, broken boy who she may never see again. She touched his cheek. His russet hair. And she found that she loved him too.

The moment was like a meteor carving a path across the heavens—blazing but ephemeral.

Beautiful.
Gone in a single breath.

CHAPTER THIRTY-FOUR

When Nova finally slept, she found herself back in the cap forest outside of Callisto—just off the path to the Harvesting Center. She took in the glowing setting, wondering if it was a nightmare or dream.

A black form lay a few yards away. Decay on a chilled breeze wafted toward her.

A nightmare, then. That awful memory.

Curling her fingers into shaking fists, she approached the mound. Her stomach tightened. It was the dead moon bear she'd seen as a child, half its ink fur speckled with glowing white, the other half mutilated with black vines. Except this time, its side rose and fell slowly. Too slowly. Alive, but barely.

"Wake up," she muttered to herself.

"You aren't enjoying the scenery?" The voice was familiar but with a cruel lilt. Eris leaned against a tree to her left. But he was too rigid, even for her best friend.

She willed her voice not to shake. "Get out of my head."

He scoffed and walked in a jerking manner toward her. He was more menacing in Eris's form, given her friend's height and strength. "I told you, Speck, this is not my doing. But I shall enjoy it anyway."

The forest is a dangerous place, little flame.

Her father's voice rippled through the air and she looked around, half expecting him to walk from the trees.

Eijleck seemed not to have heard. Instead, he stared hungrily down at the bear. "I wonder," he said. His head twitched her way, eyes like liquid smoke. Lurching closer, his arm snaked out, transforming into a tendril to latch onto her wrist. Nova cried out and tried prying out of his grip.

Dread bloomed as her hand turned pale. Her flesh sprouted black veins and she could *feel* the poison slicing like knives into her blood. Rot climbed over her, and she tried to hold her breath, so as not to breathe him in.

"This isn't real," she said, hysteria rising. *Wake up!*

Echoes of Arlo's words from moments before tried to break through.

But he hasn't always been here . . . Of course you guys used to dream.

It was a guess, but one Nova desperately wanted to be true. Especially now. But how did one force a nightmare to end?

Eijleck pulled her in closer and Eris's skin crumbled away like moon rock. Inside was the wriggling Void mass—it shifted into a miedo beastia, its fur matted with something slick. Skeletal teeth opened and its throat was so wide she imagined herself falling in. Endless scraping and gnashing and rotting just like everything else Eijleck touched.

She screamed as smoke curled around her.

But her scream was cut short when something glowed blue, startling them both, and highlighting the monster before her in vivid light. She looked down. The foxfire flickered wildly in the pendant. She and the flame were both trapped.

But they didn't have to be.

Nova closed her eyes, silencing her mind and listening. Find one voice in the multitudes. She lingered on voices that she loved: her father, Cally, Arlo, Eris, even her mother. But they were still fleeting. She needed something louder, something bigger than flesh and blood. More ancient than the Void.

Further in.

She felt herself tunneling though her feet were still on the mossy forest floor. Eijleck's tendril still tugged at her wrist. But she was there, too, in the Inbetween.

The one place she felt fully seen and unafraid.

Dream again, little flame. Do not fear.

The voice had sounded like her father's but richer as if it would resonate for eternity in her bones. With her free hand, Nova grasped the necklace and let the heat lick her palm. Calm floated over her like moon dust, numbing her fears entirely.

"I want to dream again."

As if she entered a vacuum in space, silence sucked at her hearing. There was no pressure on her wrist. No choking scent in the air. She opened her eyes.

She was alone in the forest.

The Void's presence oozed from the half-dead moon bear, but she did not sense him lurking in bodily form. She did not hear his voice. Had she broken their connection, or had the Inbetween? Either way, she was free.

Nova still grasped the pendant and opened her hand to release it. But the glass and the chain were gone. Only the blue flame remained. It did not burn but hovered just above her palm. She should be afraid—the powerful voice still mingled in her thoughts—but she found she was only curious.

She brought her other hand up to cup the strange fire and it shifted. Her skin caught, pain lacing up the wrist Eijleck had gripped. She tried to fling the pendant from her, but it remained on her palm. She was burning, not her flesh, but inside. Deeper than she thought possible.

"Stop!"

The flame lifted from her skin and hovered once more. She stared at the back of her hand. The black veins were gone. So was the sludge from the miedo. The parasite had been burned away, leaving her sore, but otherwise unharmed. Already, the pain was dulling to memory.

Her eyes flicked to the moon bear. An idea struck her and she fell to her knees, tipping the flame. It poured from her hand like water, engulfing the bear's fur. There was a confined shrieking, like the whistling howls of the miedo beastias, and the low moan of the animal.

Again, the foxfire only touched that which had been taken by rot and infection. When it was done, it shrunk back to a single flame.

The moon bear lifted its head. Its fur was still missing on one side, but its flesh had healed. It stared at her curiously, and she was thankful this was still a dream.

Yes, a dream. Not a nightmare.

She stared in wonder at the foxfire.

This was something good.

"You did well, little flame."

Nova jumped at the voice and spun to see her father—he looked just as he had when she was seven. The same blue-black hair as hers. Same tan skin. There was nothing cruel or unnatural in his warm, silver gaze. It was truly him. She smiled and stood, then hesitated, heart squeezing. It wasn't possible. Her father was dead.

"You aren't him. You're not real." Just another dream.

His lips turned down. "It is true I am not your father. I didn't want to frighten you, so I appeared as someone you love and trust. But that does not mean *I* am not real."

She chanced a step closer.

His skin shimmered and the man changed from Nova's father into something . . . *Other.* There was an aliveness to him that made the plants around them look withered. Nova's breath caught. She felt shy in his presence, but also safe. Comforted. Like swimming in the Inbetween.

"You searched for help," the man—the Other—said. "But help was always with you." He nodded toward the flame dancing over the bear's head. The animal swatted playfully at it, as if it were a bug.

"Foxfire," Nova whispered.

"A gift."

A gift? Had the Ancients ever dared use it against the parasite? Their fear had kept them from trying anything so dangerous. She wondered if her father had discovered its power in the end.

"How did my father die?" she asked, knowing innately the Other would know. Was he the voice that freed her from the Void's connection?

"He tried to harness the fire while his mind was still held captive by Eijleck. Its beasts consumed your parents in the end."

Nova's head dropped; a whooshing noise pulsed through her head. *Consumed them.*

"But all is well now. They do not suffer."

"But—where are they?" Nova thought of the Inbetween and the secrets held in its expanse.

"There are rifts that can only be opened in life, and some, only in death." The longer he spoke the less like her father he sounded. His voice filled out, as if it were made up of the trees and caps and moss and stones and air surrounding her. "But you can finish what he began."

"But . . . how? If he couldn't harness the fire, why would I succeed?" She shook her head. The thought was almost laughable. "I'm not strong. My magic is gone. My Threads have been destroyed."

"There are different types of strength, and some are cloaked in weakness." He cocked his head. "And your Threads, your magic, was only borrowed. Harvested—we could even say stolen—from humans. That was never the intention of my magic."

His magic?

"What do you mean?"

"Lyrans were meant to dream up a world capable of beauty and wonder. And now that you have learned to dream again, perhaps you can help them remember." His eyes fell on the bear that was chasing the foxfire in a circle. "Look closely, little flame."

With a warm breeze, the Other was gone.

"Wait! Who are you?" Though she suspected he would have only answered in riddles anyway. Or perhaps the meaning would have been too much for her mind to handle. But he *had* been familiar. In the same way the Inbetween was both familiar and otherworldly. Were they one and the same?

She stepped closer to the bear. "Look closely at what?"

Fear coated her for only a moment as the moon bear sniffed at her hand. She reminded herself it couldn't really hurt her. It dipped its head, and she ran her fingers through its silky fur.

The moon slipped around a cap overhead and something shivered at the end of the bear's black ear. Something like a loose string. Her breath caught.

A Thread.

With a shaking hand, Nova pinched the edge of the ear, then tugged. "Sorry," she said as the bear unwound. But it wasn't real. It was all from her mind.

Nova's breath caught as a shining black Thread pooled into her hand. It wasn't anything like Harvesting in the minds of humans. Chills sparked through her nerves. But the Thread didn't remain curled in her palm. It spiraled up her forearm then sank into her skin.

"*That* was unexpected," she said, slightly horrified.

Nova touched her arm and she could feel the magic humming, as if the Thread was eager to be used.

She unraveled a cap, then a purple crocus. The Threads came to her with ease and seeped into her skin, as if they had found their home. From her mind to her soul.

Watching the foxfire flame dance, she found the bright blue Thread at its edge and unwound it. Heat and danger curled into her fist and sank into her veins.

The skies skewed strangely and she felt a tug in her stomach. She was waking up. Tunneling through the Inbetween was dizzying, but soon she opened her eyes to Darknight once more. Now, though, she did not cower from its opaque fullness. She had dreamt during its oppressive gloom. Slipping from under Arlo's arm, Nova scooted a few feet away and sat back on her knees.

A mountain breeze skimmed over her bare neck and shoulders, but the sting of missing her shawl had faded to a soft ache.

Something else had filled its place.

Nova looked down, clenching her hands and opening them. The dreams had become part of her.

The magic didn't hum in her veins anymore, it *sang*. Even during Darknight. She closed her eyes, imagining that she could hear the words and feel the rhythm. It moved through her in perfect harmony.

She held up her palm.

Calling on the magic was not like before. This felt less like a push or a command, and more like a thought—a breath. A crocus bloomed in her palm, purple light cutting through the darkness. Nova's eyes widened.

"You have a Thread?"

Nova turned to find Arlo staring at the flower, a broad grin plastered on his face.

Nova nodded, speechless. How could her magic be so strong without Selene's power?

"How? Did you find a dreamer?"

"I found a dreamer." She smiled. "Me."

Arlo's brows shot up and he leaned forward, studying the crocus with renewed interest.

"I also met someone. Someone older and wiser—kinder—than the Void. He said . . ." Her throat burned, but she felt an urgency to tell Arlo. To encourage him one last time before they were separated. "He said my parents were well. That there were some rifts only those who leave us for good can enter through." Her voice caught, and she hoped he understood her meaning. "They are *well*, Arlo. Death wasn't the end for them."

His eyes glistened. "Just another rift," he whispered.

Nova nodded and then looked at the crocus.

"Also, I think I know how to defeat the Void." The foxfire flickered warmly in her mind and veins and she smiled grimly. "I know its weakness."

Chapter Thirty-Five

How many doors does the universe hold?
Are we all just waiting to step through?
Possibility flits in my chest.
Hope props up my chin.

They are well, Arlo.
Will Mom be well, too?

There is something different
About the girl before me.
She was a playful spark
But now, she radiates.
She helps me believe —
To believe there is more
Than we can see or hear.
Rifts where those who leave us
Can find rest,
Comfort.

I smile.
My lips tingle with her kiss.
An impossible alien-girl,
No longer a supernova
But a newborn star
Bright and sure.
When I close my eyes
Her outline burns in my vision.

I hold her hand, and
She smiles.
What's left unsaid —

The things we've seen and felt—
Could fill the brines and seas.
And we, the continents severed.

Will we ever bridge that gap?
Cursed to be *almost* together.
Can I hold her kiss
In the palm of my hand?
Clench it so tight it bursts in light,
So she never stops illuminating
No matter the distance?

All we have left now
Are almosts and dreams.
Memories.
Haunted by what could
Have been.

CHAPTER THIRTY-SIX

When Selene rose an hour later, Nova explained to Cally and Eris what had happened in her dream and how she believed foxfire was the answer.

"So . . . fire? That's it?" Cally asked, staring at her skeptically. "I'm guessing Processors have tried that before."

Eris nodded.

Nova sighed, fidgeting. It did sound more unlikely now that her dream was fading. But the magic singing in her blood was real. She couldn't have imagined it. Even after she'd demonstrated the crocus Thread to Eris and Cally, they still hadn't totally bought in to the idea.

"I'm not sure, exactly. I think it has to do with the Void not being in control. Or something." She scratched her head, wishing the Other was there, speaking for her. "It made sense in my dream."

"But dreams aren't real, Nova," Cally said gently.

"I was real," Arlo interjected. "Nova spoke to me. What we saw in my dreams might have been projections, but *I* was real." He shrugged. "I believe who she saw was real too."

Nova nodded, grateful.

"It's the only lead we have." Eris looked at Nova. "And you can summon a foxfire Thread?"

Nova nodded, flipping her hand over, palm up. "I can."

"Let's wait—" Cally said quickly. "Until we are facing actual danger." She eyed Nova's hand with a twinge of fear. "Who knows what it will do."

"It will listen to me."

"Nova, this new power is untested. Possibly dangerous." Cally touched her arm. "Let's wait until it's absolutely necessary."

Nova clamped her teeth together. She could wait. She had a feeling it would be *absolutely necessary* very soon. She slung her pack over her shoulder and began walking toward the pull of the rift. "This way."

But after an hour, they met a wall of rock on all three sides. It went up as high as the Harvesting Center. "We can't climb that," Eris said, craning his neck. "It's too steep."

"*Spores,*" Nova said. "But this *is* the way. Right?"

Eris nodded.

"We'll just have to go back," Cally said. "There has to be a way around."

Cally and Arlo began making their way back down the scree-laden path, but Nova didn't move. She squinted at the rock wall before her. The longing to continue this way grew stronger. More *right*. Ignoring their fading footsteps, she marched up to the wall and ran her hands along the stone. There was a thin shape, maybe two feet wide and six feet tall, that looked slightly discolored. She touched the spot, and something flaked under her fingers. "Moon dust," she said, staring at the blue and gray powder. It had been mixed with other soft stone and filled into the gap.

Stepping back, she looked around for something to slam in the spot. But her skin tingled and she thought it would be nice to stretch her new-found powers.

Closing her eyes, she thought of the moon bear. A black Thread unspooled from her palm and raveled around until the gleaming black creature stood before her. The bear nudged Nova's arm with her wet nose and hot breath. Stars sparkled in the creature's coat. A crescent moon shone on her forehead.

"Nova! Watch out!" Cally said, running back. Nova held up her hand to keep her sister from using a blade on the bear.

"Ready to do some digging?" Nova said.

The moon bear lumbered to the discolored crack. It raised up on hind legs and began tearing at the wall. Stone crumbled in heaps at its feet.

"What is going on?" Cally asked.

"She's my Thread." Nova nodded toward the bear. "Beautiful, huh?"

"I'm not sure beautiful is the word," Eris said, coming up on the other side of her. "But useful. You found a way through?"

"I'm guessing the Ancients filled this in long ago so no one would stumble across it."

Eris chuckled. "They hadn't considered the stubborn Celeste daughters then."

The bear's front half was now inside the crack, squeezing into the tight space to keep digging. After a few more minutes, all they could see was dust behind it.

Eris studied Nova. "You don't look effected by using this magic."

"I'm not, at least mentally. Maybe because it's from my own mind, so I have a better grasp on it? A clear head. I do feel a physical strain though."

"That's incredible," Cally said.

A muffled moaning caught Nova's ear. The bear was stuck.

"It's okay, girl, I've got you." Nova pictured the bear unraveling back into a Thread, and when she opened her eyes, the Thread slipped from the crevice and into her wrist once more.

"That doesn't . . . hurt?" Arlo said, touching her wrist.

"No. It feels like part of me."

"The bear did it," Eris said, staring into the tight fissure. "I see moonlight down the tunnel." He coughed, swatting away the dust. "Just don't breathe in. We'll go mad before we get through."

"Can *you* fit in there?" Arlo asked.

Eris glared. "What are you insinuating?"

Nova patted her friend's arm with a smile. "We don't want your biceps getting stuck."

Eris laughed, cleared his throat, and nodded toward the crevice, as if he were embarrassed. "Want me to go first?"

"If you get stuck we'll never get through," Arlo said.

"I'll go first," Cally said. "I'll Walk and make sure the coast is clear."

"Just make sure to"—Nova began as her sister burst away—"hold your breath."

"I'm through! It's a bit . . . *different* . . . on this side. But I don't see any immediate danger."

Moving as quickly as possible, Nova, Arlo, and then Eris, scuttled through the tight space. When they emerged, Nova's pulse picked up pace.

Different was an understatement.

They stepped out of the mountain onto a ledge that overlooked a dark valley filled with spindle trees. But nothing was alive. Everything was smothered with coiling black tendrils. The air was heavy with putrefaction, as if the smell couldn't rise past the looming rocks hemming in the entire ridge. Nova felt as if she were in an arena.

The presence of death coated her tongue.

A stream ran through the valley, but Nova imagined its currents bled with diseased spores, spreading into the veins of the land through some underground route. Though she didn't trust the water, her gut told her it was a pen writing their way to the Void's source. To the rift.

The foot path around the inside of the rock wall was narrow, leading down to the valley in winding switchbacks.

"Why did this rift have to be on a sporing mountain," Eris said, gritting his teeth. His back was plastered to the rock face.

They kept close to the wall, and Nova was grateful the parasite had not climbed it yet. A few times her foot slipped off the edge, and Eris grabbed her before she toppled over.

"How are we going to get through the parasite once we get down there?" Cally asked. "I don't see a safe path."

"It might be absolutely necessary to use my magic," Nova said, breathlessly. She felt dizzy whenever she glanced down. Her back was sweaty, and her fingers ached from clinging to the rock face. She couldn't imagine how Eris felt with his fear of heights.

They were so close.

That thought sent a new wave of nervousness through her.

She shivered as her nightmare of Selene cracking open assaulted her—the entire world dying. Arlo had assured her it was how her subconscious showcased worry. But it had felt so visceral; so real. Eijleck had been real. So had the Other.

And Ancient Belinda—someone so much older and wiser than her—believed closing the rift would kill their world faster.

What if their actions *did* make everything worse?

If anything, maybe they could distract the Void long enough for Arlo to slip through the rift. It wouldn't help their world, but at least he'd return safely to his mom.

After another fifteen minutes of perilous scrambling down the trail, they hit the belly of the valley. Feet away, the decay began.

Eris gasped, leaning over his knees, arms and legs quaking from overexertion and nerves. Nova patted his shoulder. After a few moments, he wiped his brow and straightened. "I hope there's another way out of here."

Nova tried to smile but their surroundings made it impossible.

The smell had worsened. Skeletons of beasts littered the bleak, slick-black landscape. It all throbbed with malignance. With hunger.

She wondered how it would like the taste of fire.

Opening her hand, she summoned the blue flame. Thinking of Cally's worry from earlier, she kept the foxfire tethered close.

Burn us a path.

The fire dripped through her fingers to the ground, flowing over the tendrils. Nova held her breath. If this didn't work, they couldn't cross without becoming infected.

The flame kept rolling, and behind it—

"Yes!" Eris cried, surprising them all with his exuberance. "It's eating the parasite away!"

Nova laughed, relief nearly knocking her over. The tentacular vines closest to the clean path curled away at the taste of the heat.

"It's really working." Cally gaped. "The answer was *foxfire*. All this time."

"I think that's why it burned me when I touched the cap in Callisto," Arlo said. "That *thing* was in my head, whispering to me, and the fire didn't like it."

Nova hoped they found a way to get rid of it in its entirety, otherwise, it might always be stuck in Arlo's mind. Whispering.

"Ready?" Nova asked.

As they walked down the newly burned path, Nova's elation returned to gut-churning worry. Each breath felt like her last.

Was this where her parents had died?

Were their bones still in this valley?

All she felt was the tug of the rift and a horrible pang of nausea.

We can do this, Arlo's voice seeped into her mind, but it was as if his words were slogging through a swamp. She rubbed her forehead with the heel of her hand.

The pull became inescapable.

A streak of recklessness coursed through Nova, and she picked up speed. She needed to get to the rift. Had to. The path curved. Rounding a bend in the high cavern wall, Nova came to an abrupt stop.

Her chest was ice.

The teeth-shaped cliffs loomed before her.

Her eyes drifted to their base. Black vines crept from a cave entrance like inky tentacles emerging from the deepest seabed. She shuffled forward even as her heels dug into moss and black soil. Push and pull. It was just like her nightmare.

"Nova. Wait." A hand wrapped around her arm, tugging her to a stop. The tug slackened momentarily, and she turned. Arlo's hand slipped into hers. They were no longer alone in the valley.

She hadn't heard or sensed the miedo beastias' approach.

But now they were surrounded.

"But Selene—how can they be under her glow?"

Nova knew the answer even as she asked the question. The Void's presence oozed from the rift not fifteen yards from them. They were stronger here. Did that make a mage's power weaker?

"What do we do?" Cally said.

"We fight," Eris said. He drew his moon blade and unraveled his wind Thread. Cally drew her blade as well. Nova handed hers to Arlo and then called her flame back to her.

The beasts kept shifting, as if they were trying to terrify everyone at once and couldn't settle on a body. "We're confusing them," Nova said.

"I don't think it matters," Cally shouted over the wind. "They'll kill us either way."

One of the beastias, its body thin and crooked like a skeletal bipedal, lunged for Eris. It shrieked, slashing its long claws through the air where Eris had been standing a moment before. Numbing horror rolled over Nova.

Cally Walked around the other four Void monsters, slicing at their smoky skins. Nothing seemed to affect them. One of the beastias turned its lurching neck and found Nova and Arlo. The flame in her hand flickered.

The beastia shifted as it moved toward them, fur giving way to something scalier.

"N-Nova," Arlo said. "Your fire."

The beastia slithered toward them. It was a giant snake with a Lyran face. Its eyes completely white. Fangs as long as blades.

Her fire grew dimmer.

Nova. Arlo's voice was quiet but it cut through her mounting panic. It reminded her of being in his dreams—of safety. Her flame burned brighter, and she felt it tugging at the invisible Thread she still held tightly. It wanted to be untethered. To be let free.

Cally wouldn't like it, but her sister was currently fighting for her life. She didn't have much of a say.

Nova knew a single flame couldn't defeat the beastias if she constrained it.

Arlo had shifted so his body was partially in front of hers, the blade raised, shaking in his hand—willing to risk his life for her.

Go, she said to the foxfire Thread.

Something snapped in her wrist, in her blood, and then the flame burst from her hold. It had become a real, tangible thing. The fire grew until it formed a wall between her and the oily serpent. She thought she saw something person-shaped within the flames, but then it rolled like a wave, consuming the beastia. The creature hissed and then disappeared.

Nova gasped, breathing in heat. The foxfire picked up speed and began consuming the other beasts. A scream rang out and Nova turned to see the remaining beastia sinking its teeth into Cally's side. It looked like a wild cat with spikes down its back.

"Cally!" Nova raced toward her sister, unraveling her moon bear Thread in the same breath. But the fire was already on the move. It poured over the miedo until it was nothing, its yowling cry dying on the wind.

The fire kept moving through the valley, taking no heed that the miedos were dead. It was burning up everything. Trees, bones, parasite, stones.

Cally gripped her side in pain. Nova moved her shirt and saw black veins spreading.

"Come back!" she shouted at the foxfire, but it was a wall of blue flame, roaring with vengeance on the parasite. It couldn't hear her. She no longer controlled it.

"The—the rift," Cally said. "Go. Get him through."

"But your wound!"

Cally squeezed Nova's arm. "If what you say about this fire is true, then it will heal me eventually. But it might also defeat the Void and cause the rift to close before Arlo gets home."

Nova's breath caught and her head whipped to the cave. The inky tendrils were already curling inward into the opening, away from the scorching decay.

"I'll stay with her," Eris said, blade still drawn. "I'll jump into the fire myself to get its attention if she gets worse. Now go." His eyes darted to Arlo. "I hope you get home in time."

Nova stood. "Take care of her. We'll—*I'll*—be back."

Cally gasped. "Don't take any chances."

Nova grimaced. "We're here to take chances, Cally. I love you."

Nova and Arlo turned and sprinted toward the cave. She thought she heard her sister shout *Nova* over the roaring fire, but she didn't slow. Though the flame was beating back the Void around them, Nova knew it wasn't the entire parasite. She'd seen his mind. His vastness.

Eijleck was too large to be contained in a single valley.

CHAPTER THIRTY-SEVEN

The tendrils along the tunnel walls hissed and writhed, but none seemed to take notice of the human and Lyran running in their midst. The stench grew stronger, along with the pull to Earth. Nova felt battered between the two.

Arlo's breaths and footfalls steadied her. They had to get him home.

They rounded a corner and entered a tall cave. Dim light filled the space. But what drew Nova's eye first was a gouge in the wall, running from the stalactite-filled ceiling to the stone floor. It was easily twenty feet high.

It reminded her of a tear in cloth, frayed and billowing at the edges from an alien wind. And on the other side of the tear was infinity. The Inbetween with its mysteries and secrets. Its comfort and belonging. She sensed the spark of a presence in that space— the same presence that had made up the Other—but she also sensed other roaming things. Things and creatures that sought worlds just like the Void had.

The tendrils on either side of the rift swirled into a form. A single smoky form, not quite a person, not quite the mass she'd seen in Arlo's nightmare. It was something mixed between the two, but it still held all the animosity from before.

"Do you believe," it said, its voice quiet and dangerous, "that a single Speck can damage something so all-consuming?"

Nova's throat was dry, but Arlo held her hand and the foxfire pendant thrummed warmly against her skin.

"We already have," Nova said.

The shadowy shape smiled, white, sharp teeth forming like the stalactites above them. "You've thrown sand at a mountain. You've tossed a spoon of water into the sea. Nothing you do affects me."

"But foxfire can."

His laugh sounded like a crashing wave. "The names you people invent. If only you knew what it truly was." He waved her away as if she were a crumb to be flicked from his billowing cloak. "But I am hungrier than normal, and I smell plenty of despair on you." Eyes formed, gleaming white in its stormy silhouette. "I think I would like to taste it."

Nova and Arlo took a step back.

Even as she felt her smallness keenly, the memory of her father rose up in her. Her mind hummed with his voice.

"W-what is it?" she whispered.

"The Void," Atlas said. "In the flesh."

"But I thought the Void lived in the sky!" Nova shivered and looked up.

"The Void lives everywhere now," her father said. "There"—he pointed up—"here"—he gestured around the forest. "And that means sometimes, also, here." He tapped his chest, then hers, right above her thundering heart.

She blinked at Eijleck's form, studying her as if it had all the time in the worlds.

Was that what the Other had been trying to tell her? Did Eijleck have his cold tendrils in all Lyran minds and hearts, reaping their world?

He was hungry. He had told her himself that he fed on fear. And what was the simplest way to embed fear? He buried himself in their subconsciouses. Their nightmares.

But dreams could be just as potent.

Arlo's hand had grown sweaty in hers, but when she looked back up at Eijleck, she felt brave. Her fear hadn't left. She still trembled. But there was something bigger she could cling to, and it gave her wings.

She remembered the good and true things. The warmth of home. Blooming crocuses. Laughter. Cally's fierce protection. Eris's loyal friendship. Her parents' faint memories. Moon glow dousing magic over her. And Arlo.

There were things more powerful than despair.

There was love. It could stretch to all hearts, all worlds, and never be at its end.

And there were dreams. Dreams to banish nightmares.

Eyes streaming tears, Nova filled her mind with sweet memories until they burned within her. Magic flitted in her chest like an untethered flag. Then she opened her palms and held the crocus flower Thread in one, moon bear Thread in the other.

When she looked up at the Void and his cocked head, she saw him falter. Uncertain. Magic and light seemed to pool off of her.

"We do not want you here," Nova said. "Leave."

Eijleck stumbled back when the bear lunged. More miedo beastias formed to ward off the attacks, but Nova no longer felt like a Speck. It wasn't just her fighting the Void, it was also something far grander than herself. The Void could be resisted. The moon bear grew larger, fiercer. Her hope rose along with its height and strength.

"This is *our* home," she said, her voice magnified in the large space.

The moon bear's roar vibrated the stone floors, and in swift movements, the bear began to swallow the beastias whole. Eijleck slunk back, then vanished. But he was not gone. The parasite was a hive mind. The source had to be destroyed, or it would keep coming.

"It's out there," Nova said, pointing to the black mass writhing in space, covering stars with its treacherous teeth. "In the Inbetween. We can't get to it there." Nova felt a dip in her strength. She would need to unravel her moon bear, or she, herself, would unravel.

With a pull at her power the Thread returned, and she fell to her knees. The miedos reformed as she knew they would. They slunk closer.

"Go while I distract them!" Nova shouted at Arlo.

But he didn't budge. "I won't leave you like thi—"

His words were cut off by something that sounded like Eris's winds. But stronger.

And hotter.

Nova and Arlo rolled out of the way as a funnel of blue flame rushed through the cave then tore out of the rift. Her Thread! Or what was once her Thread. It was true fire now.

The foxfire headed straight toward the Void, its light streaking across space like a shooting star. The beastias in the cave and the tendrils melted like wax.

Nova and Arlo ran to the mouth of the rift, peering through to a celestial battle. Blue light rolled over black smoke, twisting and curling into one another. The soundlessness made it even more eerie.

"I can hear them," Arlo said, touching his forehead. "It's awful. And . . ." his gaze met hers. "It's . . ." He shook his head, wordlessly. But there was a gleam in his eye. "I think it's over."

A moment later, the black mass diminished. It was being burned up as the fire grew brighter. And then, a great, silent explosion. Nova covered her eyes against the brightness. When she dropped them again, no inky blackness covered the heavens. And the foxfire had separated into—

"*Stars*?"

Arlo huffed a laugh. "You guys had starlight *inside* your giant mushrooms? Now I've seen everything."

"He said it was a gift," she said, remembering the dream with the Other. "That we'd had help all along."

Arlo nudged Nova's shoulder with his in their familiar way. "It just took a true dreamer to see it."

Nova smiled at him, but it fell away when she glanced at the rift. It wasn't closing. She wondered if it had become too ripped and torn over hundreds of years of being forced to remain open.

"I think I have to shut it from this side," Nova said.

"*You're* going to close it?" Arlo said.

She shrugged. "See anyone else?"

"Right." He mussed up his already messy hair.

Nova stepped forward, wrapping her arms around Arlo. He tucked his head into her hair, holding her so tight she heard his heartbeat. She collected the sound, storing each note of his heart in her own. "I'm sorry I can't be there for you, when . . ." Her voice was muffled in his shoulder.

He pulled back and wiped her eyes.

"It's okay. I think . . ." He glanced at the Inbetween and the bright blue starlight. "I think it will be okay now." He looked back at her. "*Gah*. I'm going to miss you like crazy. But maybe Belinda was wrong. Maybe we'll find each other again."

"You do belong here, Arlo. A rift opened for you."

He smiled. "Yeah. Maybe another will open someday."

"Maybe."

It didn't feel true, but Nova appreciated the lie. It would give them enough strength to do what had to be done.

Arlo swallowed hard, tears shining in his eyes. "Thanks for everything, alien-girl." He chuckled. "You know, I came here for the worst, most selfish reasons, but I'm leaving changed. Maybe I'll be the son my mom needs now, to help her get through . . . everything." His gaze twitched to the rift, expression torn.

"You will be," she said.

He smiled and kissed her forehead. "Dream of better things?"

"Only if you do."

He stepped back and his hands slipped from hers. With a confidence that she thrilled to see in Arlo, he strolled up to the ledge of the rift and its gaping boundlessness. Fear tingled over her skin. What if he stepped out and just . . . fell? Surely the Inbetween wouldn't let that happen.

This was a doorway for the living.

He glanced back and the intensity of his stare, the heartbreak pressing his brows together, stooping his shoulders, nearly caused her to leap into the rift beside him. To slip through and meet Claire.

To see Earth's wonders.

But her life was here. And Arlo's was there.

If she left her world, she might never return.

With a trembling smile, Arlo lifted his hand in a Lyran farewell, and stepped into the Inbetween.

Gone.

Nova's heart split.

All she saw through the tear in reality was a vast forever—and it did not involve Arlo James.

Chapter Thirty-Eight

I am lost—
Lost in starlight,
Lost in the shards of my cracking heart.
But the pull is urgent.
My weeping is hushed
In the vacuum of space.
But I am heard—this I know
That warm voice cradles me
As if I am a child again.

I am going home
Or at least, the home I was born to.
Down, squeezing and
Unable to breathe.
But only for a moment
Then, I'm stepping through
A door in my bedroom
That wasn't there before.

It smells like Pine Sol and vanilla.
Rumpled clothes fill a chair.
My desk, full of half-written poems
About an impossible girl.
A girl I love.
And a sunless world
That is not without its own light.

A voice—
But this time, not in my head.
No trace of that cold voice remains.

This voice echoes down the hall
Quiet and trembling.
I feel the pull and I do not run away.
Heart pounding with gratefulness even
Though it shatters like moonlight
On choppy waves.

I'm not too late.
This is where I need to be.
Mom, it's me!
Wiping my face,
I run through the door
As the one behind me —
The door that leads to Nova —
Closes.

And I can no longer hear her mind.

CHAPTER THIRTY-NINE

Nova stared into the abyss, lost in the trance of light and celestial clouds and swirling clusters. She chewed her lip, knowing what she should do, but . . . what if she *didn't* close it? Could her people still connect to dreamers? Could she still connect with Arlo's mind?

Would the Inbetween still beckon to her?

But then her vision sharpened, and she saw shapes lurking in the dark space. There would always be something sinister wanting to invade their world. And this was a wide-open invitation. This door was meant to be shut.

Throat constricting, Nova called her moon bear and crocus back, but before they disappeared into her wrist, she latched onto them.

She felt as if she were in a trance as she began stitching the space between their worlds back together. Though she'd felt physically weak moments ago, the action replenished her. It seemed as though the Inbetween was closing the rift from its side, and she was a child imitating the parent.

When the black and purple Threads zigzagged across the edges, she pulled them taut. The fissure grew closer and closer until the two sides kissed. Nova unraveled the Threads back to herself. A moment later, something brilliantly blue shone in the crack, the foxfire—no, *starlight*—was welding it.

A moment later, the wall was perfectly smooth. Nova placed a shaking palm on the stone. No cracks. No blemish. No rift.

Earth and Lyra were cut off from one another.

Arlo.

Nova fell to her knees and let out a sob. Her weeping hit the cold cavern walls and it echoed back to her. A chorus of sorrow. She squeezed her arms around her stomach, letting her tears coat the stone. No one could hear her. She let herself come undone. Her sister would—

Nova sat up. *Cally.*

Wiping her face, she stood and raced out of the cavern and back into the tunnels. She pressed away her broken heart and focused her thoughts solely on Cally and Eris. Had the fire healed her, or had it merely swept them up in its scourge? Her steps quickened, and then she emerged under Selene's glow, the smell of smoke and burning filling her nostrils.

"Nova!"

Cally raced across the ash and slammed into Nova, nearly sending them to the ground. Nova gasped and laughed. "You're alright!" She pried herself from Cally's arms to look her sister over. "The fire?"

"I don't know what foxfire is, but it definitely isn't what we thought."

Nova smiled, though she felt the sides of her mouth waver. "No, it isn't." She scanned the valley and saw Eris grinning brightly. She and Cally walked toward him, arms around one another.

"Wait—the rift. Arlo. What happened?" Cally turned toward the cave.

Nova didn't glance back. Her throat threatened to close. "I have a lot to explain, but it will be alright." She squeezed her sister's middle. "Everything is how it should be."

Eris greeted Nova with a tight hug.

"Eris. Can't. Breathe."

"Sorry!" He dropped his arms and stood back, awkward. "I just—I thought I lost you. When the fire rushed into the cave . . ."

"I told you. You will never lose me."

He swallowed hard and nodded to the path leading up and out of the valley. "Should we go home? We'll either be greeted with blades or honors. The odds are about even."

"Yes," Cally said, fire in her gaze. "Belinda has something of mine, and I want him back."

The walk up out of the valley was easier than going down, though Nova's legs and lungs screamed for relief. It felt good. There was no oppressive force or decay smothering them. Even the burning loam and dirt was a welcome smell. It reminded her of all that had been accomplished.

They reached the top of the path and shimmied through the crack in the wall. Selene was falling now. Darknight would be upon them and—

"Wait!"

Without the Void, there should *be* no Darknight.

"Nova, where are you going?" Cally said. But Nova didn't slow. She ran through the spindle trees and caps and all the lichen bleeding with bioluminescence. Eris and Cally's footfalls told her they were following.

Nova burst through a cluster of spiral brush and nearly toppled over a cliff. She scrambled back. Eris and Cally came to a stop beside her.

"What is going on?" Cally said.

"I had to see if I was right."

"About what?"

Selene was setting, the stars were fading, but the sky did not grow darker.

It grew lighter. In a different spot, more to the east, something bright was peering over the horizon. It was not timid. It was brilliant.

"*That*," Nova said.

"No way . . ." Eris said. He squinted and raised a hand to shield his eyes against the rising glow. "But how?"

"The Void. It didn't destroy the sun like we thought. It was concealing it."

All these years.

Chill bumps pricked over her flesh as warmth filled her body. She had seen a similar scene play out countless times in dreamers' minds—in Arlo's.

Never in living memory had it happened on their world.

"I don't understand what I'm seeing." Cally rubbed her eyes.

She grabbed her sister's hand and squeezed.

"We're seeing our first Lyran sunrise, Cally."

Nova placed her palm over their family crest. It almost felt as if the soleil owl's wings were beating. She smiled. This was what their parents had died for. What they were fighting so hard for, even if they didn't know it exactly.

Atlas and Ascella had dreamt up a better world.

Now, it was on full display.

~

"Thought I'd find you out here."

Nova jumped at Eris's voice. It had been a month since the Void—Eijleck—had been destroyed. A month since returning to a city in chaos.

After weeks of adjustment, the people of Callisto and the Ancients had worked out a new way of living. Though their world—and manner of life—had drastically changed with the vivid days of sunlight, everyone saw the good in what had been done. Even the Ancients. Quick to cover their own dark deeds, the Ancients treated Cally, Ceres, Eris, and Nova as heroes rather than rebels. Ceres was certain the leaders would never admit their wrongs, but he was determined to join their meetings and help with decisions moving forward.

Now that all the infected farmlands and forests had been released from the parasite's hold, the world was made new. The rest of the foxfire in the caps had been called back to the heavens, and in the process, every miedo beastia had been burned up. The minds of Lyrans were their own again, and dreams became more common than nightmares.

"I like coming here at night," Nova said to Eris, looking at the Dream Glade's pulse plants. The Harvesting Center stood empty. It was no longer needed now that they could harvest their own dream Threads to rebuild Lyra. She mourned the loss of human connection, but rejoiced in her new connection to Lyrans—how much her feelings had changed and grown in a few short weeks.

"It's weird to say night and *day*," Eris said, his fingers trailing over the purple glow of the rubbery tubes. Nova was glad the pulse plants could withstand the sunlight. And that everything still glowed at night. Except for the now-withered caps. When the foxfire had shed its skin and returned to the stars, those who saw the phenomenon had said it looked like a backwards meteor shower.

"I don't think I'll ever get used to it." Nova laughed. Her skin and eyes were just now adjusting to the sun as well, with the help of Processors who had developed creams to stop the harsh rays from burning their skin.

"Nova," Eris said. "How have you been with Arlo gone?"

Nova tensed, hugging herself and turning to face her friend. No longer a boy, but a man. Maybe she looked older too. They'd been through so much, seen and *felt* so much. Enough for a lifetime. "It's hard some days. Easier others. We cared a lot about each other."

Eris nodded. "I know."

"And you? How are your parents?"

"Better now that they're getting more rest. And me . . . ?" A smile crept over his face—it was the same expression Nova had seen him wear when he'd studied the brine art on Gemini's walls. "Did you hear about the expeditions?"

Nova's brows lifted in surprise.

Now that the beastias of the brines had been destroyed, there was talk of sailing a few ships over the Black Sea—to explore what lay beyond its shores.

"I'm thinking of going," Eris said. He shuffled his feet. "Well, not just *thinking* about it. I *am* going. Once the ships have been fitted for long travel."

"What?" The breath knocked from Nova's gut. "You're *leaving*?"

Their eyes met. "Would you ask me to stay?"

Nova sensed deeper feelings in his gaze than she knew what to do with. She loved Eris, but as a friend, a brother. Nothing more.

Her fragmented heart belonged to someone a world away.

Eris's shoulders dropped, as if he were reading her very thoughts. "It's alright, Nova." He tugged her into a hug. "It's better I go." He pulled back and squeezed her shoulders. "Who knows what wonders this world really holds." His hands fell away, gaze skimming past her, past the warm yellow pulse plants, and far beyond. Nova recognized that look of longing—adventure beckoned him.

A lump formed in her throat.

Nova had assumed she might lose Arlo, but Eris? She wanted to be mad at him for leaving, but she knew this was his chance to find something beautiful, just as she had. "You've become quite the dreamer, my friend."

Eris grinned. "I've had a good teacher."

"As long as I never lose you." *Not forever*.

"Never."

Swallowing past the lump and blinking away tears, she smiled.

"Should we go back?" he asked. "I admit, Cally sent me to look for you."

Nova shook her head and laughed. "Of course she did."

~

Cally and Ceres were at the table when Nova came through the pod door. It felt strange to be moving out in a week, though Cally had insisted Nova could live with them. Or that they could move out. But Nova had only shook her head. It felt like a clean start. A beginning. And a new pod would help with that.

Cally glanced up. "Did he tell you?"

Nova flopped into a chair at the table. "What do you mean? Wait. You *knew* Eris was leaving?"

"He told us last night," Ceres said.

Nova skewered an enoki puff. "Were there any rifts today?" she said.

Cally shook her head. "None since a week ago." It was the Walker's jobs to scour the land for any momentary doors. They would greet the humans and lead them back to Callisto or the closest town, then begin the transition process. So far, they found all the people who came through were much like their mother had been—orphaned or destitute. They arrived broken and needing help that Earth could not give them. Lyra was their second chance.

A place to dream.

Nova nodded, pulling a piece of bright yellow fungus apart.

"The Inbetween would give him a way through again, if it was right," Cally said.

"Or maybe he won't ever find a way back," Ceres said, offering a dose of reality.

Nova shrugged. It felt like her stomach had been punched.

Cally smacked Ceres.

"*What*?"

She rolled her eyes. "For being able to read minds, you're about as sensitive as a lampyris worm."

He gasped, feigning offense. "If you let me read your mind I wouldn't need to guess."

"You can't handle the full extent of my mind."

He poked her shoulder. "On *that* we can agree."

Nova laughed and played with her food as her sister and her bond bantered. Her thoughts wandered back to the rifts. Cally was right. She was glad Arlo was on Earth with his mother. She couldn't imagine being born on one world and being claimed by another.

Though, she could imagine it a little.

Her thoughts turned to Eris and his excitement—his *purpose*—in exploring their world. Maybe someday she could find such a purpose, or to simply be content. To truly see the good things before her and embrace them.

With a smile, she threw her enoki puff at her sister and got up to leave the table. She was tired, but she no longer feared what would meet her in her subconscious. Dreams happened often, and even when there were nightmares, her magic was strong enough to press them away.

As her head hit the silk pillow, she thought of how much she had lost—her parents, Arlo, her shawl—but how much she had gained as well. She stared up at the winking blue stars and could almost feel their heat. Their life.

When she finally drifted to sleep, she welcomed it with an open heart.

EPILOGUE

One Year Later

Nova felt herself tunneling.

She hadn't felt that in over a year. Neither had she been back in the Inbetween. But suddenly she was there, floating between the blue stars and feeling that familiar comfort and awe.

Perhaps it was simply her mind recalling the sensation, but it felt more real than normal. Like when she used to visit dreamers.

When her feet hit the ground, she was filled with longing and frustration.

These are not my feelings.

She looked around.

I don't recognize this room.

"Nova?"

But she *did* recognize that voice.

She spun and took in Arlo. After a heartbeat of numb disbelief, Nova stumbled forward. The movement seemed to shock Arlo into action and he rushed forward too, gathering her up into his arms. His laughter danced down her spine. She pulled back just enough to study every freckle sprinkling his nose. The scar over his left eyebrow. Every nuanced shade of green in his eyes. The curve of his smile.

"Is it really you?"

"It's me, alien-girl."

Arlo smelled like pine, and she closed her eyes. *Please be real.*

The papers on his desk shuffled around, dancing. Her dream couldn't be cruel enough to conjure such a thing.

"No one visits human minds anymore," Nova said. "Not since the rift closed."

"And no one ever spoke to a human in a dream until you," he said. His hands were still snug around her waist, as if he never wanted to let her go. "You have a history of doing the impossible."

She studied him. He looked older, more worn.

Could this be *real* Arlo?

He finally dropped his hands to give her space. She wanted to jump into his arms again. "How—how is everyone?" he asked.

Nova's eyes were misty. She swiped at them and then said, "Everyone is well. Cally is with child."

"Ceres's I'm guessing," he said with a smirk. "And he's good?"

She laughed. "Yes. Yes."

"Well, congratulations. That's awesome!"

"Is this your room?" Nova looked at the unmade bed and the papers and books scattered on the desk. "Or a war zone?"

"Still as funny as ever." He shuffled his feet. "But yes. I'm still here. After Mom died, and I turned eighteen, I inherited the house."

Nova's shoulders fell. She felt as if she had known Claire too. "She passed."

"A couple months ago."

"I'm so sorry, Arlo."

His jaw ticked. "Me too. Well, I'm sorry she's no longer here. But I'm glad her suffering is over. It was rough in the end."

"What will you do now?"

"I keep wondering about that, actually."

"What do you mean?"

His eyes lit up and Nova thought she saw a silver spark in them.

"I've felt the pull back to Lyra. It's grown strong since Mom passed."

"But—you haven't seen a rift?"

He tousled his hair. "No. I assumed it would happen if it was meant to. You know?"

"Yes."

The walls suddenly expanded and shrunk. Nova felt a tug in her gut.

"No." Panic crested in her chest.

"What is it?"

"I'm waking up. Or you are. I—I don't know."

Arlo took her hand. "We will find each other, Nova. Not even space and time can keep us apart. I believe that."

Nova nodded, eyes hot with tears.

The room melted away and she was tunneling again, gliding through the Inbetween. Were they forever destined to be almost, but not quite?

Nova woke up in her pod with tears staining her pillowcase.

The sun was rising, and she closed her eyes against the bright rays.

"So that's what your sun looks like."

Nova sprang out of bed as if foxfire had caught her sheets in a blaze. She nearly trampled on Arlo, who lay on her floor.

His fingers were laced behind his head, staring up at the glass ceiling. Perfectly calm.

"It's you!"

"Were you expecting someone else?" He grinned and stood, swaying slightly. "I would be okay with *not* going through a rift again in my lifetime, though."

"You're really here. I'm not dreaming?"

"Not this time." He took her hand. "I was right about the pull. Guess I was just waiting on you to find me again and open another door."

"But what about Earth? Your life?"

"There's nothing left for me there." His eyes shone silver again, pain creasing his brow. His mom was gone. And his dad wanted nothing to do with him. And Lyra—it had claimed him.

Nova felt as if her skin might burst with all the joy in her body.

"Then welcome home, Arlo James." She toppled into his arms and they fell together onto the floor, laughing. When they sat up, Nova leaned forward and kissed him. Arlo stilled, then his hand found her cheek.

This time, their kiss was not filled with *maybes* and *goodbyes*. It was slow and beautiful, because now, they had all the time they needed.

Arlo pulled away, blinking at her. "And it's safe for *dreamers* to be here?" Arlo glanced up at the sunlight pouring in from Nova's window.

"Didn't I tell you, Arlo James?" She pulled him to his feet, ready to show him her world. *Their* world. "We're all dreamers now."

Acknowledgements

First off, I want to thank my Savior, Jesus Christ, from whom all good things come. If you glean any truths or revelations through this story, it is because of Him. I am humbled that my words may be used to lift the veil a bit—to see the beauty of now and the wonder of what is to come.

This book would not have been written without the support of my husband, Jonathan. You always make time for my creativity to flourish. Even if you don't read YA fantasy (no one is perfect), you will always be my biggest supporter, and I love you! Thanks for letting me bounce my ridiculous ideas off you.

Hezekiah and Reuel, my sweet boys who see creation as a thing to be enjoyed, to be played in, and to seek the Creator in. You bring your mama such joy while also giving my words more significance.

To my dad, Mark, who instilled in me a love for books at an early age. When you read *The Selfish Giant* to me as a kid, it opened my eyes to lovely prose and analogies. To my mom, Lisa, for always buying stacks of anthologies and telling all your friends about my work. Your support means the world!

Lyndsay, for being the first friend I ever shared a story with. To Amanda, who has been an encouragement in my faith and writing. Lindsey, for being my first mentor and creative-instigator. Brenna, for loving me and my words with so much zeal.

To my first and forever critique partner, Kate. Thank you for the long Marco Polos about plot and characters that always turn into heart-to-hearts. To Bonnie, for sharpening my manuscripts and pushing me to be a better writer. Andrea, my "frond" who understands the beauty of story and inspires me to write deeper and richer things, and silly things too. Rachel, for having more book boyfriends than we can count and being the sweetest fangirl (who changed a certain man's life). To Amber, our sassy chicken, who gives me courage to write the things I believe in. Adelaide, for being the only person who has alpha read all my manuscripts and still puts up with me! To Bri and Abby and our monthly meetings about pop culture, life, and stories.

To the Cottage: thank you for the laughter over ugly pugs, coffins, and wrinkled pants along with the deep conversations on faith and writing. Our little community is a glimpse of Heaven to come.

To Havok Publishing (Teddi, Andrew, and the Fantasy Friday team) for giving me the courage to share my stories with the world. Thank you to Anne J. Hill who published my very first short story. Seeing my name in print was life-changing.

Ellie Tran, for the gorgeous illustration of Nova and Arlo. It is simply breathtaking. Thank you to Amy, for the haunting and beautiful song you wrote for *Thread of Dreams*.

Speaking of music, "Every Star is a Burning Flame" by Andrew Peterson inspired parts of this book. And Thomas Austin's "The Morning" always makes me think of Arlo.

Thank you to the beta readers who helped me make this story stronger through the years! To my Dream Team—I appreciate all you have done to help me with the cover reveal, marketing, and the launch! It takes a village.

To the team at Owl's Nest Publishers (Karin, Katie, Ash, Beth Anne, Lindsey, and all the behind-the-scenes staff members): Thank you for all the hard work on the cover and helping me shape this story into something good and true and beautiful.

And lastly, my thanks go to you, Dear Reader. Someone once said a story isn't truly complete until it is read and experienced by others. I believe this. Your imagination has made *Thread of Dreams* a living, breathing thing. I hope it has encouraged you. I hope it reminds you that you are not alone. I hope it causes you to lift your eyes to the stars.

About the Author

Emily's writing career began at the age of eight with a story about a wizard scribbled in her Lisa Frank notebook. She has upgraded to a laptop, but her wonder has stayed the same.

Emily lives in the misty mountains of Colorado with her husband and two sons, where she embraces the Hobbiton ways of good books and warm drinks, while dreaming up fantastical worlds that feel a bit like home.

Find Emily on her website, www.emilybarnettauthor.com

Thank you for reading this Owl's Nest Publishers book! If you enjoyed *Thread of Dreams*, please share your enthusiasm with others, and be sure to leave a review on Amazon, Goodreads, or StoryGraph—and be sure to tag @owlsnestpublishers on social media.

Find us on the web at

www.owlsnestpublishers.com

For inquiries about our books, authors, submissions, and more, reach out to info@owlsnestpublishers.com

Milton Keynes UK
Ingram Content Group UK Ltd.
UKHW040141210324
439766UK00004B/19/J

9 781957 362212